FUTURE LOST

BOOK THREE IN THE FUTURE SHOCK TRILOGY

ELIZABETH BRIGGS

ALBERT WHITMAN & COMPANY
CHICAGO, ILLINOIS

Library of Congress Cataloging-in-Publication Data

Names: Briggs, Elizabeth (Young adult author), author.
Title: Future lost / Elizabeth Briggs.
Description: Chicago, Illinois: Albert Whitman & Company, 2018. |
Series: Future shock; 3 | Summary: "Elena Martinez must return to
the future one last time to save the person she cares about most and
prevent the end of the world"—Provided by publisher.
Identifiers: LCCN 2017040681 | ISBN 978-0-8075-2687-3 (hardback) |
ISBN 978-0-8075-2689-7 (paperback)
Subjects: | CYAC: Science fiction. | Time travel—Fiction. |
Interpersonal Relations—Fiction.
Classification: LCC PZ7.1.B7545 Ful 2018 | DDC [Fic]—dc23
LC record available at https://lccn.loc.gov/2017040681

Printed in the United States of America
10 9 8 7 6 5 4 3 2 1 LB 22 21 20 19 18

Cover artwork copyright © 2018 by Paul Stinson
Design by Jordan Kost and Ellen Kokontis

For more information about Albert Whitman & Company,
visit our website at www.albertwhitman.com.

For my husband, Gary.
In every future, it's you.

PART I
THE PRESENT

WEDNESDAY

I don't feel safe anymore unless I'm holding a gun in my hand.

Boom. The air smells of gunpowder, but the sound is muffled by my headset.

Boom. Right in the chest. I line up the next shot.

Boom. That one's in the head. A little to the right of where I aimed, but that's why I practice every week.

I've shot two people before. One by accident. One on purpose. I don't regret pulling the trigger either time. I'll do it again if I have to—and I won't miss.

The weapon is a familiar, comforting weight in my hand, yet I also loathe it. I never touched a gun until a year ago. I wish I could live the rest of my life without firing one again. But after what I've lived through, I need to be able to defend myself and the people I care about. Call it paranoia, call it being prepared, but I'm going to be ready for whatever comes next.

Fluorescent lights illuminate the narrow alley as I square my feet and take aim. I fire until the gun is empty and the target is littered with holes. I've been coming to this range for months. The orange paper man never stood a chance.

Out of ammo, I step back and check the aisles on either side of me. To my left, Zahra fires her last couple rounds into a target as tortured as mine. On my right, Paige grins while every single one of her bullets hits the exact center of the target's head. She'd never shot a gun before I invited her to the range a few months ago, but she's already better than me and Zahra.

When the girls are finished, we gather up our equipment, grab our targets, and step out of the range. Once the door shuts, we take off our headsets and shake out our hair.

Zahra eyes Paige's bullet-ridden target. "You sure you weren't on the Olympic shooting team instead of the gymnastics one? There's no way you can be that good already."

"You're just jealous of my mad skills." Paige flips back her blond hair with a grin before skipping over to Rob, the guy behind the counter of the gun shop. Zahra and I roll our eyes, but follow her to hand over our rented gear.

"Stay safe, ladies," Rob says when we're done checking out. He's an older white guy with a big, bushy beard and always wears a flannel shirt, but he has a kind smile and has always made me and Zahra feel welcome here. Since I'm Mexican-American and Zahra is Iranian-American, that's not always the case, especially at places like gun ranges. I've been called a chola or a gangbanger, while Zahra's often labeled a terrorist the second she walks in. We've been told to go back where we came from more times than we can count, even though we were both born here in Los Angeles.

We wave good-bye to Rob and head to the parking lot, where our cars are lined up under a palm tree. A cool ocean breeze ruffles my dark hair. It's one of those perfect LA days when the sky is so clear and blue it doesn't look real, when it's warm enough to go out in a T-shirt and flip-flops, but not hot enough to make you sweat.

The kind of day you take for granted when you live here, except on those rare moments when you can stop, take a breath, and realize how lucky you are to be alive. I'm trying to take more of those moments, to commit them to memory instead of all the bad images crowding my head. I'll never get rid of those memories, but maybe I can shove them aside with better ones.

I lean against my car, gripping my keys. "Have you seen anything strange lately? Cars following you or people hanging outside your apartment?"

Zahra immediately scans the street around us, but I've already checked, and we're alone. No black cars. No strange men listening in. "Nope. Have you?"

"No." Ever since Aether kidnapped me and forced me to time travel into the future for the second time, I've been paranoid they'll try it again. They haven't yet, but I'll be looking out for them for the rest of my life.

Paige shrugs. "Maybe they're keeping their promise to leave us alone."

My mouth twists into a scowl. "Maybe they're being more discreet this time."

"No one is getting near us without me knowing it." Zahra's dark eyes study the street again. "But I can go over our security if you're worried."

A few months ago, Zahra set up special firewalls on all our computers and installed security systems at our apartments with cameras and alarms. I trust her skills and expertise, but Aether has a lot more resources.

I zip up my hoodie. "I'm always worried. If they come after us, I want to be prepared."

Paige rests a hand on my shoulder. "We'll be ready."

3

I nod, but I can't shake the feeling that Aether isn't done with us yet. These past few months have been too calm, too easy, too quiet.

"Will I see you both tonight?" I ask as I unlock my car. It's the one-year anniversary of when I met Adam and Chris, and the six-month anniversary of when I met Zahra, Paige, and Ken. I'm throwing a little get-together at my apartment for all the time travelers—although I'm still not sure if it's to celebrate or to mourn. A little of both, perhaps.

"We'll be there," Zahra says.

"Can't wait," Paige says, then gives me one of her enthusiastic hugs. I should be used to them by now, but it still takes me by surprise.

We break apart, and the two of them get into Paige's car to head to the apartment they share. I watch as the car leaves the lot and turns the corner, making sure they're not followed before starting my own.

Years of moving from one foster home to another prevented me from forming lasting relationships for most of my life, but Zahra and Paige have become true friends over the last six months. Zahra and I didn't get along at first, and I had no clue what to make of Paige and her relentless cheerfulness and energy. Now I can't imagine not having them in my life, especially since they're some of the only people who understand what I've been through.

One year ago, I was recruited by Aether Corporation for their time-travel experiment, Project Chronos. That's where I met my boyfriend, Adam, and our friend Chris, along with two others on our team, Trent and Zoe. The five of us traveled thirty years into the future for twenty-four hours, only to discover four of us would be murdered after we returned to the present. Adam and I were able to change our fate, and I killed the real murderer—Lynne Marshall, an Aether employee who ran Project Chronos—but we weren't able to save Trent and Zoe. I've been haunted by their deaths ever since, although I've gotten better at coping with it. I've learned to focus my anger and control my panic attacks through therapy, kickboxing, and shooting at the gun range with Zahra and Paige.

I met the two of them when Aether kidnapped me, Adam, and Chris six months ago and forced us to return to the future to track down the time travelers they'd replaced us with. Team Echo consisted of Zahra and Paige, along with Ken, a young chemist, and Jeremy, the son of Aether's CEO. Ken and Chris were killed during the mission, so we returned to the future two more times to save their lives. In the process, we saw different visions of what our destinies could be and how much worse things could get for us.

Adam and I discovered that Jeremy was behind all the murders and the changes in the timeline, in an attempt to make himself more powerful in the future and get back at his father. I killed Jeremy to stop him, and then Adam and I destroyed the accelerator, preventing Aether from sending anyone to the future ever again.

In the past six months, Aether has left us alone, and we've all tried to move on, even though it's impossible. At least for me.

No one should know their own fate. A person's future should remain a mystery. Destiny should be a secret. But I've seen my future. Multiple times. Four different timelines, with four different lives I might lead. Sometimes I'm happy. Sometimes I'm in prison. Sometimes I'm dead.

Each time I see the future, things change—usually for the worse. There's no way for me to know which timeline my actions will lead to anymore. I live each day second-guessing every choice, wondering which future I'm bringing about. I boomerang between confident about my fate to frozen with indecision, worried I'll do or say something that will send this timeline into disaster.

No one should live this way, but I don't have a choice. I've seen too much…and I remember it all.

* * *

At 7:02 p.m., I check the table for the tenth time, making sure everything is in its place. Chips and guacamole. Plates. Silverware. I've never hosted a get-together at my apartment before, even an informal one like tonight's, and part of me feels like I'm pretending to be a grown-up, like a kid playing dress-up in Mamá's clothes. I'm almost nineteen, but I'm still figuring out this adulting thing.

The doorbell rings while I'm adjusting the napkins. Adam's little brown mutt of a dog, Max, starts barking and wagging his tail while I open the door. Chris stands on the other side wearing jeans and a gray T-shirt. He's black, with a shaved head, warm brown eyes, and muscular arms that show he's still working out regularly, even with a six-month-old baby.

He grabs me in a quick, loose hug. "Hey, Elena. Am I the first one here?"

"Yep." I step back to let him in. "Where's Shawnda?"

"She wanted to make it, but Michael is sick so she's home with him. She sent these brownies along though."

"Thanks." We head into the kitchen, and I grab him a soda from the fridge. "How's married life these days?"

"It's pretty damn good, actually." He cracks open his soda and takes a chug. "I never thought I'd be a stay-at-home dad, but I'm really digging it, at least while Shawnda's in nursing school."

Chris's son, Michael, is the reason Chris went to the future originally. When he learned his girlfriend (now wife) Shawnda was pregnant, he wanted to provide his kid with a better life than the one he had growing up. In each future we visited, his son's fate depended on whether Chris was around or not. In some timelines

Michael went to Harvard and became a lawyer, while in others he ended up in prison. Chris is determined to make sure his son's life ends up on the right path, whatever it takes.

I can't imagine being a parent at our age, but I'm also oddly jealous. In one of the futures we visited, I met my daughter, Ava, but she won't be born for almost twelve more years. I'm impatient for it, even though I'm not ready to be a mom yet. I only spent a few minutes with her, but she filled me with purpose and a path for my future that I refuse to stray from. Now every decision I make, every action I take, I do with the knowledge it may one day lead to her. But I've seen how fragile the timeline is too. If I take one wrong step, she might be erased from existence forever. I won't let that happen.

Chris bends down to pet Max. "Shawnda's mom is helping out a lot with Michael, so I think I'll be able to take classes again next semester and finish up my engineering degree."

That's another thing we saw in the future. In thirty years, Adam, Chris, and I will start a biotech company called Future Visions that will provide the world with cutting-edge technology, the cure for cancer and other diseases, and make us all rich at the same time. Now the three of us keep that goal in sight. The promise of our shared destiny gives us hope. Together, we're going to change the world for the better.

Zahra and Paige arrive next with a ton of food from the Persian restaurant Zahra's cousin owns. Paige looks at baby photos on Chris's phone, cooing about how big Michael is getting, while Zahra plies Max with dog treats. For a few minutes we chat about our different college classes, before Ken shows up at the door. He's a half-Japanese guy with short black hair, kind eyes, and a blue T-shirt that reads, "All the good chemistry jokes argon."

"Ken!" Paige grabs him in an exuberant hug. "I haven't seen you in forever!"

Their hug lasts a few seconds beyond friendly, like they can't stand to let go of each other. When they finally break apart, his face is flushed and he rubs the back of his neck. "Sorry. I've been working in the lab a lot these days."

"It's so good to see you." She takes his hand and leads him to the couch. "I have to tell you what happened in my class the other day."

Once they're on the couch and lost in conversation, Zahra rolls her eyes. "I need to mash their faces together and make them kiss already."

Chris crosses his arms, leaning back against my kitchen counter. "Didn't Paige dump her loser boyfriend?"

"Yeah, she did. But she's oblivious to how Ken feels about her, and he's too shy to tell her. They're hopeless."

I shake my head. "I thought for sure they'd be dating by now."

After Paige discovered that her boyfriend was going to grow into a shady Congressman and a cheating husband, she dumped him and swore to only date nice guys from then on. Ken, on the other hand, learned he was going to die at age thirty-eight from Huntington's disease, which he inherited from his mother. He didn't want to suffer the same trauma she's enduring now and tried to end his life, knowing Aether would pay his parents a hefty compensation fee. I managed to convince him not to do it and insisted there was still time to change his fate. Now, with Adam's help, he hopes to create a cure for Huntington's disease someday.

Zahra looks over at the two of them with a frown. "Sometimes I think about saying something to Paige, but I don't know if that's overstepping, and I've been so busy with my brother lately..."

"How's he doing?" I ask. Zahra's future revealed that her brother's gambling addiction would lead to him being murdered by the

Russian mafia. In different timelines we saw the Zahra of the future try to help him by paying off his debts, but it never worked out well. She soon realized the only solution was to get him help in the present before he got involved with the Russians.

"He got out of rehab last week, and he seems to be doing okay," Zahra says. "Who knows if it will stick, but at least I tried. I'm keeping an eye on him to make sure he stays out of trouble."

"I'm glad he's doing better." I check my watch. 7:14. Adam should be home by now. Dammit.

Chris's eyes follow my movement. "Where's Adam?"

"I don't know. He must be running late." I pull out my phone but don't have any texts from him. I send one off: Where are you?

Zahra and Chris start talking about computer stuff, and I tune them out while I make sure everyone has drinks and something to snack on. Five minutes later, Adam texts me back. Sorry. Leaving the lab now.

"Adam's on his way," I tell the others, trying to hide the annoyance in my voice. Everyone gives me a long look, so I know I'm not successful.

"Is everything okay?" Zahra asks.

"Yeah." I take a long drink of water, clutching the glass. "He's been working on the cure nonstop, and I guess he lost track of time." The truth is, I barely see Adam these days, even though he lives with me now. I try to give him space because his work is important, but I can't believe he'd forget tonight, of all nights.

"Ken's the same way these days." Paige bumps his side with her shoulder. "Always working in the lab with Adam."

Ken shoves his hands in his jeans and looks down. "Not always. Today I had class and then took my mom to a doctor's appointment."

Paige lightly touches his arm. "I don't want you and Adam to get burned out. That's all."

"We won't. We're so close to a breakthrough. Just a few more days, and we'll have it. And once the cancer cure is done, I might be able to use the research to develop a cure for Huntington's too." Ken's eyes light up when he talks about their work, but then his face drops. "Although Adam, he's…"

When he doesn't go on, Chris asks, "He's what?"

"He's been kind of…off lately."

My throat seems to close up. "What do you mean, *off*?"

Ken's eyes snap to mine, but then he glances at our friends and his mouth opens and closes. He shrugs and forces a laugh. "Eh, it's nothing. He probably needs more sleep."

There's obviously more to it, but he seems uncomfortable talking about it in front of the others. I make myself smile, while inside I'm screaming at him to tell me what he knows. "That must be it. I'll talk to him about it."

Paige seems to sense we need a topic change and starts telling the others about our weekly shooting practice. I slip into the kitchen alone and take a moment to lean against the fridge, closing my eyes and breathing in and out until I'm calm again.

It seems I'm not the only one who's noticed Adam's been acting different lately. For too long I pushed my worries aside and told myself everything would be fine, but I can't ignore it anymore. Over the last six months, Adam has changed. At first I thought it was because of the things we saw in the future or what happened when we got back to the present, but now I'm not sure. All I know is that it always comes back to genicote: the cure for cancer that Adam is destined to develop.

A week after Jeremy's death, I stumbled upon some of his things in Adam's possession—including a sample of genicote from the future. I debated destroying it, worried that if Adam made the cure too early it would change the timeline for the worse, but Adam convinced me that the sample would allow him to create the cure faster. I hoped his desperation to rush genicote's development would subside once he had that sample, but I was wrong. If anything, that only made it worse.

The front door opens, and Max rushes over to greet his favorite human. Adam's voice calls out, "Hey, everyone. Sorry I'm late."

I push those thoughts to the back of my mind and slap a smile on my face as I step out to greet him. A sharp pang strikes my heart at the sight of him, as it always does, even after a year of being together. He's tall and handsome, with a sharp jaw, broad shoulders, and slightly messy dark hair, but the calm, intelligent blue eyes behind his black glasses are what always make my pulse race. He has a way of looking at me like I'm the only thing in the world that matters, and it makes me fall for him over and over again. He's giving me the same look now, except his eyes have dark circles under them and his hair is even messier than normal and a bit longer than he usually likes.

"Elena." He smiles at me and grabs my waist, pulling me in for a quick kiss, but I turn my face away so he gets my cheek instead. His smile falls for an instant, but then he turns to our friends again, and it snaps back into place. If they notice, they choose not to say anything about the tension between us.

For the next few hours, we pretend everything is fine, when it's obviously not. Adam makes a toast to "Good friends—friends we've made, friends we've lost, and friends we'll meet some day," and everyone raises their glasses with a smile. We're six time travelers stuck in the present, trapped between our tragic pasts and our uncertain futures, but at least we have one another.

* * *

After everyone leaves, I stand at the sink and rinse dishes, while Adam finishes cleaning up the living room. He moves behind me, resting his hands on my waist, burying his face in the back of my hair.

"I'm sorry," he says at my ear.

Something snaps in me, like all the emotions I've kept in check all evening can't be held back a second longer. I slide out of his grasp and turn to look at him. "I'm tired of hearing you're sorry. Especially tonight, of all nights."

He runs a hand through his hair, but that only makes it even more unkempt. "I know. I have no excuse, but I'm so close, Elena. I just need a few more weeks and—"

I throw my dish towel on the counter. "I've heard that before too."

He sighs. "What do you want me to say?"

"I don't want you to say anything." I scrub my palms over my eyes, suddenly exhausted. "I hardly see you anymore, and when I do, I barely recognize you. I want the old Adam back."

"I'm still the same person. I'm sorry I haven't been around as much lately, but I can't stand by and let people die of cancer every day, knowing the cure is so close to being ready. All I have to do is figure out how to make it safe. Then things will go back to normal, I promise."

We learned in numerous futures that genicote had one major problem: when used on anyone who didn't have cancer, it killed them. In one timeline, Aether wanted to turn it into a biological weapon for the government, while in another, a rival corporation called Pharmateka was using it in a war with China.

I cross my arms. "Your future self said making it safe wasn't possible."

"He was wrong. I'm so much further along than he was. He took ten years to develop genicote, and it's only taken me months, thanks to the sample Jeremy brought back from the future. But I can't release it into the world until I make sure it won't hurt anyone." He takes a step forward, his eyes pleading with me. "I refuse to let my life's work be used to take lives instead of saving them. I just need a little more time. Why can't you understand that?"

Something in his eyes scares me. That calm intelligence I love has been replaced by a wild look, both determined and manic, and I don't know how I didn't see it before. Genicote has become an obsession for him, and developing it has become his addiction.

I try to keep my voice steady. "I understand. I do. Your work is important, and one day you *will* save lives with it, but right now I'm worried about you. I'm worried about *us*."

His hand comes up and slowly tucks a stray piece of dark hair behind my ear, then trails down to my cheek. "You don't ever need to worry about us."

I lean into his touch ever so slightly. I crave his comfort even when I'm upset with him. I want him to make everything right somehow, but that's impossible. "In every timeline you visited, you took years to develop genicote, and now you're rushing ahead without taking the time to do it right. I'm scared you'll make a mistake in your haste that might cost lives instead of saving them. And I'm terrified you'll lose yourself in the process and change our future to something neither of us can live with."

The madness in his eyes vanishes and he studies my face, his thumb slowly stroking my skin. "You're right," he says softly. "I've become a little obsessed, but I'd never do anything to jeopardize our future together." He pulls me into his arms, wrapping his warmth around me. "I'm sorry."

I lean against him and hold him close, my fingers digging into the fabric of his shirt, my breath against his neck. The relief I always feel in his arms is still there, but so is a knot of anxiety that's become all too common these days. I want to believe him. I really do. I just don't know how.

His hand slides up and down my back. "I love you, Elena. I'm going to make everything right. I promise."

I tilt my head up to him, meeting his eyes. "I love you too."

He cracks a smile. "This isn't how I wanted our one-year anniversary to go. I should have brought you flowers."

"I wasn't sure if we were even going to celebrate it."

His eyebrows shoot up. "Why wouldn't we?"

"We have a lot of bad memories associated with that day." It's not a coincidence I made sure I'd be at the shooting range today, and it wasn't an accident that I spent an extra hour at kickboxing this morning.

I met Adam one year ago when we went to the future together, but I also lost two friends that day and saw things I'll never be able to forget. I couldn't save Trent and Zoe, and I have to live with that for the rest of my life. I'd give anything to be able to redo that day, to make better choices, to be able to save their lives.

"That's true, but meeting you was the best thing that's ever happened to me," Adam says. "I may not have gotten you flowers, but I did get you something else."

"You did?"

He removes a small black box from his jeans and presses it into my palm. I slide the lid open and find a silver origami unicorn, like the one he gave me before, like the one tattooed on my arm, only this one is made of metal and is attached to a thin chain. I lift the necklace from the box and spot an inscription on the bottom.

In every future, it's you.

I rarely cry, but this makes my eyes well up with emotion. "Adam… Thank you. It's beautiful."

"You like it?"

"I love it. But I didn't get you anything. I'm sorry."

"You set up the party tonight with the others. That was the perfect gift." He takes the necklace and sets it around my neck, then I lift my hair so he can clasp it behind me. "I haven't been the best boyfriend lately, but I'll try to do better. Just give me a chance to make things right."

"I'm not going anywhere," I say, spinning around to face him. "You're stuck with me for the next thirty years and beyond, remember?"

He presses his lips to my forehead. "I wouldn't want to live a single one of them without you."

I slide my arms around his neck, pulling him toward me. His mouth trails soft kisses down my face, dusting my eyes, my cheeks, my nose, before brushing against my lips ever so softly. He silently asks my permission and I open for him, inviting him inside, drawing him closer. His hands tighten around my waist, and he captures my mouth with his, while my fingers weave into the back of his hair. He kisses me like a man who's been lost at sea for months and has finally returned home, and I kiss him back like the woman who's been waiting every night at the shore for him.

It's been weeks since he's kissed me like this, and I can't get enough. My earlier anger and annoyance with him are gone, transformed into a desperate need and an urgent hunger. He seems to feel the same because he backs me up against the kitchen counter, his hands sliding under the back of my shirt, our bodies pressed tight against each other. He lifts me up onto the counter, my knees on either side of his hips, while he reminds me with his mouth that I'm his and he's mine. Down my neck. Across my collar. Between my breasts.

Both of our shirts hit the tile floor, but it's not enough. With my legs around his waist, he picks me up, carrying me into the bedroom. His body is rock hard against mine, his chest toned from all the swimming he does to clear his head. I remove his glasses and drop them on the nightstand as we pass by it, and then we sink onto the bed together.

For the next hour we lose ourselves in each other and forget everything but the way it feels to be together. We revel in the promise of our shared destiny together, in the certainty of knowing there's no one else in the world for us. No matter what happens in the future, we'll be together, following the path that leads to our company, our marriage, our daughter. And when we lie in bed afterward and Adam tells me he'll love me forever and that everything will be okay, I believe him.

Even though I shouldn't.

THURSDAY

When I wake the next morning, the other side of the bed is empty.

I shouldn't be surprised, but I am. It's not the first time I've woken to find Adam already gone. I just hoped, after last night, that it wouldn't happen today. I wanted to wake up in his arms, to kiss him good morning, to share those first few moments between sleep and wakefulness. But nothing he said last night has made it into the faded light of dawn, and everything's the same as it was before.

I sit up slowly, blinking sleep from my eyes. Our bedroom is small but tidy, with a queen-size bed, a dresser, and not much more. Adam was living with his mom before he moved in with me, so he didn't bring much with him. The biggest difference is that there's a dog bed in the corner for Max, although he isn't in it.

The clock by my bed reads 9:38 in sharp red numbers. Later than I normally sleep, but we were up pretty late last night. I yawn and head into the kitchen to make some coffee. This morning it's already waiting for me, filling the apartment with its rich, warm smell. I grab my mug and spot a note on the coffeemaker.

I love you. I'm going to make things right. I promise.

I run my fingers across the edges of the note as I sip my coffee. He's trying at least; I'll give him that.

The first time I woke up to find him gone, I freaked out. I used to be a light sleeper, thanks to my years in foster care, but with Adam in my bed every night, I started to feel safe for the first time in my life. When I woke up without him at my side, I was shocked. I couldn't understand how I'd slept through him leaving, or how he could take off without saying good-bye, or where he might have gone. Then I panicked, thinking he had left me for good, that he'd vanished from my life without a trace like everyone else I've cared about. Or worse, that Aether had taken him. After that, he started leaving notes so I'd know he would be back.

A whining noise brings me back to the living room. Max is sitting against the front door, his nose pressed under it, like when he waits for Adam to get home in the evening.

I slip on some flip-flops, pull on a light sweater, and put Max's harness on him. We head down the stairs to the lobby, then step outside into the brisk morning air. It's early enough that the street is empty and quiet, the sun still low and sleepy in the sky. I wait for Max to do his business on the grass and check my phone. I send Adam a text: Thanks for the coffee. Miss you.

Our apartment is in West LA, equal distance from the community college I attend and UCLA, where Adam is getting his PhD. The rent here isn't cheap, but it's not too bad either (by LA standards, at least), especially with the money Aether gave us for participating in their time-travel experiments. When our lease is up in a few months we could get a larger place, but it's been nice not having to worry about moving all the time—a luxury I never had while in foster care.

By the time Max and I get back inside the apartment, Adam still hasn't responded. He must be wrapped up in whatever he's doing at the lab. Sometimes he forgets to check his phone when that happens. Annoying, but not unusual.

I feed Max. I take a shower. I get dressed.

Still nothing from Adam.

I finger the necklace around my neck, tracing the edges of the origami unicorn before letting it fall against my chest again. Did any of his words last night mean anything? Or were they, like his gift, just a way to distract me from my worries?

I've wasted my morning in bed, and now it's time for me to get to class. I get ready quickly and give Max an extra treat on my way out. He sits for the first one, and then I make him catch the next one in his mouth, his tail wagging the entire time. If Adam were here, he'd laugh and tell me I'm spoiling Max, and I'd grin and say he deserves it. I can picture it perfectly: Adam leaning in the doorway with his arms crossed, his shirtsleeves rolled up to reveal his masculine wrists, his hands sliding around my waist to pull me in for a kiss. Those small, tender moments between us were once so common I took them for granted, and I'm filled with a terrible longing to go back to that time.

* * *

By the time I'm done with my two classes for the day—English and psychology—Adam still hasn't responded to my message. It's unlike him not to text me anything all day. Even when he's wrapped up in his research he'll send me a silly emoji or a quick note to let me know he's thinking of me.

I send him another text. Everything okay?

I head home, take Max for another walk, and then get ready for my kickboxing class. Adam's lab is on the way there. Maybe

I'll stop by and make sure he's all right. I'm probably paranoid, but this is the anniversary of Trent and Zoe's deaths, and I'll feel better knowing Adam is safe.

The lab is fifteen minutes away, and I check my mirrors constantly to see if anyone is following me. I don't see anyone, but that does little to ease the worry nagging at me.

Adam's lab is in a small, brown one-story building with a tile roof and round glass lights on either side of the door. The place looks like it hasn't been touched since it was built in the sixties, but Adam says the large space inside more than makes up for that. Plus, it has a parking lot in front, which is a rarity in LA.

My car is the only one in the lot. Adam's car isn't here, but this morning it wasn't in our apartment's garage either. If he's not here, where is he?

At the front door I enter my security code and do the retinal scan, but the system lets out a harsh beep. ACCESS DENIED. I try the code again, just in case I typed it too fast or something, but I get the same message.

What the hell? Did Adam purposefully lock me out of his lab?

Another car pulls into the lot. I spin around quickly, instantly on alert, but it's only Ken's silver Honda Civic. Perfect. Ken must know what's going on with Adam, and he can tell me whatever he wanted to say last night.

He wears a nervous smile as he walks up to the door. "Hey, Elena. I didn't know you were coming by."

"Where's Adam? And why won't my security code work?"

"I don't know. I thought he was with you." He types in a new code and lets the system scan him. "Adam changed the code a week ago. He probably forgot to tell you the new one."

Maybe, but now I'm even more suspicious. The door opens for Ken, and we step inside the entry room. It has plain white walls, an empty receptionist desk, and a long, low couch against the opposite window. I remember when Adam leased the place and I told him it was way too big for what he needed, but he just grinned and said it had room for him to grow.

Ken leads us down a hallway and into the main lab, past another locked door I don't have access to. The lights flicker on, buzzing to life as we step inside. I glance around the large room, at the white work counters, the beakers and other science equipment, and the computers in the corner. Against one wall there are cages with rats in them, and against another a freezer with vials stored inside it. There's no sign that Adam has been here, but I don't know what to look for either. I haven't been in his lab in weeks. Maybe months.

"Adam was gone when I woke up this morning. I haven't heard from him all day. I assumed he was here." I walk over to the rats, whose cages are all labeled with different numbers and words that make no sense to me. "Do you know if he came by?"

"No, I was taking care of my mom." Ken frowns and moves to one of the computers, then types something into it. "I haven't talked to Adam today either."

"Does he have class today?" I should know this. I thought I knew his schedule, but maybe I was wrong.

Ken's frown deepens, and he rubs the back of his neck. "No, uh…" He glances at the rats scurrying in their cages, then at the door, like he wants to escape.

"You know something, don't you?" His eyes widen, but he doesn't answer. My hands tighten into fists, and he takes a step back. My first reaction is to grab him by the shirt, shove him against the wall, and demand answers. But in the last six months I've learned not to rush to violence to solve my problems. I no longer punch first and ask questions later.

I force my hands to unclench. "Please. I'm really worried about Adam. I just want to know he's safe. Last night, it seemed like you wanted to tell me something. What was it?"

Ken's shoulders relax, but he still looks wary. I punched him once before, when we were in the future, when he refused to come with me and was planning to kill himself. He rubs his jaw, as if remembering the same moment.

"Okay." He sighs and sits on one of the stools in front of a microscope. "I'll tell you what I know. But you're not going to like it."

"What is it?"

"First, of all, Adam's not in classes anymore. He dropped out of graduate school."

"*What?*" I practically yell it. "Are you sure?"

"Yeah. He said he didn't need it anymore and that it was taking too much time. Time he wanted to spend developing genicote."

I slump onto a stool beside Ken. How could Adam do this, and without telling me? He knows he has to finish graduate school so that we can then go on to create Future Visions together. We have a plan for our lives, and he's veering way off course already. Not to mention, working on the cure before finishing the relevant classes in school is reckless, maybe even dangerous. What was he thinking? And how could he keep this a secret from me?

"I was surprised too," Ken says. "But Adam's become completely obsessed with developing the cure. That's what I was going to say last night."

"I know. He barely sleeps. He doesn't eat. He's rarely ever home anymore. I assumed he was going to class at least." I rub my hands across my face. "I knew it was bad, but I can't believe he'd go this far."

"There's more." Ken's voice is low.

The air-conditioning blasts cold air on us, but Ken's words are what raise every hair on my arms. *What else is Adam hiding?*

"Tell me."

Ken takes a long breath and meets my eyes. "Last week he had a meeting. With Aether Corporation."

An icy fist grips my heart. "No."

"I couldn't believe it either, but it's true."

It can't be. Adam would never go to our enemy, the source of all our problems, not after everything they've done to us. Not when we worked so hard to keep Aether out of our lives for good. And how could he tell Ken and not me? I shake my head, refusing to accept it. "Why would he do that? Is he out of his mind?"

"I don't know. He told me about the meeting but didn't say what they talked about."

I slam my palm against the counter. "You must have some idea!"

Ken's face is grim as he glances at the freezer on the wall. "All I know is that genicote is pretty much ready to go, but it's not enough for Adam. He's copied the sample we had from the future, and we know it works from the tests we've done on the rats. But genicote will kill anyone who hasn't had cancer by mutating their genes, and neither one of us can figure out how to fix that problem."

"You think he asked Aether for help making it safe?" One of the Future-Adams had done that—gone to Aether for help in developing and distributing the cure, but it hadn't gone well for him. I thought his younger self would have learned his lesson, but apparently not.

"I'm not sure. But if you can't find him, then it wouldn't surprise me if they're the reason why."

I stand up, shoving my stool back, my adrenaline already kicking in. "Where was the meeting?"

"At their headquarters in downtown LA."

"Thanks." I spin on my heel and head for the door.

"Wait. Are you going there?" Ken asks. "Right now?"

I stop at the door and glance at him over my shoulder. "You got a better idea?"

He shakes his head. "No. Just…be careful."

As I walk to the car, I'm so mad at Adam that I can barely see straight, but I'm scared too. If he's in danger, I have to help him. If he's not, he's *going* to be in danger soon—from me.

Adam's betrayal has cut me right to the core. He's the only person I've let get close to me, the person I trusted above all others, but he's been keeping secrets from me again. Big secrets. Dangerous secrets.

I'm going to get answers. And there's only one place to find them.

* * *

I've never been to the Aether Corporation building in downtown LA—at least, not in the present. I visited it twice in the future with Adam and Chris. The first time, we were guests of Future-Adam. The second time, we broke in to steal something.

I walk into the lobby, noticing all the ways it's different from the version I visited before. That's one thing my eidetic memory is good for: remembering tiny details. The floor is different—pale-gray marble floors instead of dark slate. The walls are a different shade of beige, and the potted plants in the corner have white flowers instead of blue. Everything else is the same: wall-to-wall windows, revolving doors, and a row of elevators in the back. I'm not sure where to go, so I walk up to the desk at the front.

"Can I help you?" a security guard asks. Her hair is tied back in a severe bun, making her forehead tight.

"I need to speak to Vincent Sharp."

"Do you have an appointment?"

"No, but he won't be surprised to know I'm here."

Her scowl only deepens. "I'm sorry, but—"

"Tell him Elena Martinez is here to see him, and if I don't get answers, I'm going to the police."

She picks up a phone and speaks quietly to someone on the other line, her eyes never leaving my face. I can't make out her words, but I lean forward on the desk and refuse to look away. If Adam is mixed up with Aether, I'm not leaving here until someone tells me what is going on and where he is.

The woman hangs up the phone. "I need to see your ID."

I dig around in my bag until I find my wallet, then pluck out my driver's license and hand it to her. She scrutinizes it for way longer than is necessary, jots something down on a clipboard, and then hands me a plastic security card with the Aether logo across it. It's attached to a lanyard that I slip around my neck.

"Keep that with you at all times." She gestures toward the elevator. "Fifty-first floor."

"Got it."

I swipe my card and brush past the other security guards, who stand by the elevator with their arms crossed behind them and their eyes always watching. The elevator's empty and silent, except for an instrumental version of some song from the eighties that plays in the background. I lean against the back wall as we travel up, up, up to the very top floor of the building, high enough

I have to pop my ears. The door opens to a large room with a pretty woman sitting behind a glass desk. Plush leather couches line the walls under tasteful but immediately forgettable modern art. I step forward.

The woman stands and smiles at me. Her lipstick's bright red, her blond hair's perfectly styled, and she wears a white blouse and a black skirt. "Elena Martinez? Please follow me."

She knocks softly on the door behind her, then opens it for me. Her smile stays plastered on as I walk into Vincent Sharp's office.

It's huge. Big enough to fit my entire apartment in it. Way larger than any one person would realistically need for an office. Most of it is empty space, but there's also a large seating area with a TV, a long bar with mirrored walls behind it, and a shining silver desk.

Vincent sits behind the desk, facing away from me, looking out the floor-to-ceiling windows at the city below him. Los Angeles stretches out on three sides of the room, the view clear and impressive and never-ending. The ocean on the left, the mountains in the middle, and the endless city reaching for the horizon on the right. It's easy to forget how large the city is until you're standing above it, looking down at all the tiny cars below.

Vincent's chair swivels around. He's a good-looking man in his early fifties, with thick auburn hair, a strong jaw, and intelligent eyes. The kind of person who exudes confidence and power, but also manages to come across as charming, although his eyes have dimmed ever since his own son shot him.

I've only seen Vincent once since I killed Jeremy and blew up the accelerator. Adam and I visited him in the hospital after he'd recovered, and he agreed that the slate between us had been cleared because we saved his life. Vincent swore to leave us alone from then on, and in return, Adam and I would keep Project Chronos a secret.

But Vincent didn't keep that promise.

He leans forward in his black leather chair and takes me in. "Elena. I should have known you'd come by."

"Where's Adam? What have you done with him?"

His eyebrows slowly rise. "You don't know then?"

"Know what?"

A deep frown settles over his face, making him look older. "Oh, Adam."

I slam my hands on his desk, leaning forward. "What is it? Tell me!"

He shakes his head. "It'll be easier if I show you. Come with me."

I start to protest, but he's already walking toward the elevator, his strides long and self-assured. I quickly follow and slide into the elevator after him. We stand beside each other in silence while the elevator plummets, until I finally break down and ask, "Is Adam okay?"

He gives me a long, even look. "I don't know."

The door opens on Level B4. It's darker down here, blocked off from the sun, lit entirely by man-made lighting. There's something large in front of us, something metallic and dome-shaped, with tubes and wires coming out of it. Something I never wanted to see again.

"No," I whisper, taking a step back, pressing against the wall of the elevator. How is this possible? We destroyed the accelerator. We stopped them. Didn't we?

Vincent walks out of the elevator. "Status report!"

"Still nothing, sir," a woman answers.

I stumble after him, each footstep heavier than the last as I approach the machine. Now that the initial shock has faded a bit, I can tell it's not the same accelerator. It's smaller than the one we destroyed. The metal is a slightly different shade of silver. But it's still a time machine.

They made a second one.

"You told us Project Chronos was finished," I say as I get closer. "You swore you'd never interfere in our lives again. We had a deal!"

Vincent leans over a computer, checking something on the screen. "And we kept up our end of the deal. We didn't contact Adam. He came to us."

"Why? Why would he do that?"

"He asked for our help. I told him we'd built another accelerator, but he said he wasn't interested in time traveling again. Until this morning."

This morning. Our fight. His note. He said he was going to fix things. But surely he didn't mean this?

"Where's Adam?" I have to hear them say it out loud before I allow myself to believe it. My heart is racing so fast it feels like it might tear out of me. How could he? What was he thinking? Why would he do something so reckless?

"Sit down," Vincent says. "I'll tell you everything."

"I don't want to sit down. I want to see Adam. Where. Is. He?" My voice is too loud, but I don't care. I'm going to tear down the walls of the accelerator until I find him. And when I do, I'm going to murder him myself.

Vincent gives me a level stare. "You know where he is. He's in the future."

Something snaps in me, and I lunge for him with a roar. I'm not sure if I intend to punch him, choke him, or shove him into the accelerator to make him get Adam back. I'm stopped by a woman with a tight ponytail, who steps between us and raises a gun at me.

I halt, forcing my emotions under control, and glare at Vincent behind her.

"It's okay, Nina," Vincent says, waving her gun away.

She scowls and lowers the gun an inch, although she doesn't put it away. She has dark hair and pale skin, wears little to no makeup, and can't be much older than me. Her clothes are all black and utilitarian, like something the military would wear, along with matching combat boots.

I turn away, dragging my hands across my face, trying to make sense of all this. Adam went to the future again. Without me. How could he do this without even consulting me first? He knew I'd never let him do it; that's why. So he went and did it on his own, keeping it a secret from me. If I thought I was upset at his betrayal before, that doesn't even come close to the rage and hurt I feel now.

"When is he coming back?" I ask, trying to keep my voice steady.

"He was supposed to come back a few hours ago," Vincent says, his voice sympathetic.

Sheer terror pushes aside the rage and hurt and takes control of me. "*What?*"

"Adam had us send him thirty years into the future for five hours, but he missed his scheduled return time. We've opened the aperture numerous times since then, but there's been no sign of him."

"Wait," I say slowly. "He went alone?"

"He did. He refused to let anyone else go with him, and he made us promise not to contact you or any of your friends. I told him it wasn't a good idea and begged him to let me send Nina with him, but he wouldn't listen." He glances at the accelerator with a frown. "I never should have sent him to the future again."

My God. I had no idea Adam's obsession with developing the cure had gone this far. He must have gone to the future to talk to his older self or to figure out if he ever made genicote safe. But in doing so, he brought Aether back into our lives. He kept secrets from me. He went behind my back. And worst of all, he put his life in jeopardy.

That settles it. I'm going to find him. I'm going to bring him home. And then I'm going to demand some answers from him.

A door opens, and two older men in lab coats walk in. The first man, Dr. Walters, has a full head of gray hair and sadness etched into every one of his wrinkles. The other is an Indian man with tufts of gray in his black hair and shrewdness in his eyes.

"Elena?" Dr. Walters asks.

I'm so shocked to see him that everything else momentarily disappears. "What are you doing here?"

Shame clouds his eyes behind his glasses. "I'm so sorry."

"You're a part of this?" I ask. "Seriously?"

"I had no other choice."

"She shouldn't be here," Dr. Kapur says from beside Dr. Walters. Him, I'm not surprised at all to see. He never had a problem doing what Vincent wanted, even if it involved drugging teenagers and locking them in a time machine.

But Dr. Walters, of all people, shouldn't be helping them. He created the original accelerator, but after our first time-travel mission resulted in death, he tried to destroy the machine and was fired by Vincent. Later, we coerced him into fixing the accelerator so we could save Chris and Ken from the future, but after that, he helped us blow it up. Yet now he's here, working for Aether again, sending more people to the future.

"This accelerator was built right after the original one," Vincent explains. "Dr. Walters left before it was finished. We convinced him to return and complete the project."

Dr. Walters looks miserable, and I wonder what they did to him to make him change his mind. At least Dr. Campbell, the other physicist involved in Project Chronos, isn't here. She quit working for Aether after she secretly helped us destroy the accelerator, but I'm not sure what happened to her after that.

I cross my arms. "Fine. It doesn't matter. Turn on the accelerator and send me to the future."

"No, I don't think so," Vincent says.

"You don't think so? You sent my boyfriend to the future *by himself* and now you expect me to just let him stay there?"

"Sending him alone was obviously a mistake, since he hasn't returned. Which is why we won't be repeating the same mistake by sending you after him."

I stab a finger at his chest. "You're going to send me, by myself, right now. I *will* bring Adam back. And if you're lucky, I won't tell the whole world about the shady experiments you're running in the basement of your office building."

"We need to run some tests on you first," Dr. Kapur says.

"Screw your tests. The longer we wait, the more likely the future will change before I get there to save Adam. You need to send me now."

Dr. Kapur gives me a disapproving stare. "You're almost nineteen. The risk of future shock will be higher now. Especially since you've been to the future so many times already."

"I'll take that risk. Just like Adam did." He's older than I am, by about six months. That idiot. When I find him, I'm going to strangle him.

"We're hoping Adam returns safely on his own," Dr. Walters says. "We're opening the aperture every half hour for a few seconds. He might still make it back."

"If he's not back by now, he won't be coming back on his own. You have to send me after him. Our future needs Adam in the present—and I'm not leaving here without him."

Vincent rubs his chin, then looks between his team and the accelerator as he considers. When I'm about to start pleading my case again, he sighs. "Fine, we'll send you. Shall we contact the rest of your team?"

"No. I won't risk anyone else's lives, not after what happened last time. I'm going alone."

"That's what Adam did, and look how well it turned out for him. At least let me send Nina with you."

I glance at the girl with the tight ponytail, who looks like she'd rather knock me flat on my back than help me. "No offense, but I'd rather work alone. I don't trust anyone who works for Aether. It's your fault we're in this mess at all. I'll fix it on my own, thanks."

Vincent's lips flatten into a tight line, but he nods. "Very well. But if you don't return with Adam through the aperture at the scheduled time, I'm sending Nina after you."

"That won't be a problem. How soon will the accelerator be ready?"

"An hour," Dr. Walters says.

Perfect. "I'll need some things before I go."

"Such as?" Vincent asks.

"Weapons. Food. Water. A lantern of some kind. I'll make you a list. I want to be prepared for anything."

He waves a hand dismissively. "We'll get you whatever you need."

* * *

An hour later, I'm standing in front of the accelerator with a backpack on. I don't get déjà vu, but if I did, it'd probably feel a lot like this.

Dr. Walters moves beside me, looking at his creation with resignation. "There's something else you should know. This accelerator isn't fully ready yet. I warned them not to use it. I wanted to do more tests. But Adam didn't listen."

"What are you saying?" I ask.

"The temporal navigation system isn't as precise as I'd like it to be. I've done my best to program you to arrive as close to Adam's arrival as possible, but there's no guarantee."

This keeps getting better and better. "Adam was the first to use it?"

"Yes, he was." Dr. Walters pinches the bridge of his nose. "I'm sorry. I wish neither of you had gotten involved with this."

I want to ask him why he's here, but there's no time. Vincent walks over and clasps both of us on the shoulders. "Ready to get started?"

Dr. Walters drops his head like a submissive dog. "The accelerator is powered up."

Vincent looks me over. "Thirty years in the future for five hours. By yourself. You sure you want to do this?"

I grip the straps of my backpack. "'Want' is the wrong word. But I'll do whatever it takes to get Adam back."

He nods. "Good luck. I hope you both make it back safely."

Dr. Walters opens the accelerator door, and I step inside the small, smooth metal dome. While the other was built for five people and could hold double that if needed, this one is built for maybe half as many. If I stretch my arms out, I can almost touch either side of the walls. When the door slams shut, it's like I'm trapped in a metal coffin.

Every other time I've gone to the future, it was with Adam at my side. Now I'm alone, but I won't be coming back that way.

I will find Adam. I will bring him back. Or I won't come back at all.

There's no other choice. I have no future without Adam.

The countdown starts. The walls and floor begin to tremble. I stand in the center of the dome with a wide stance, ready for what comes next. The shaking grows violent, and the golden light appears, falling on my shoulders like pollen. This part used to excite me and scare me, but this time-travel thing is old news for me at this point. This is my fifth trip to the future. I'm a pro at it now.

But damn, this better be my last trip.

PART II
THE FUTURE

00:00

My first thought when I arrive in the future is: *not this again.*

It's pitch-black and bitterly cold. I can't see a damn thing, just like the first time I went to the future. But this time I'm prepared.

I reach into my backpack and pull out a hand-held camping lantern. No flashlight—electronics get shorted out by the accelerator. This one runs on gasoline and spreads a ring of light around me as soon as I light it.

The illumination reveals the first change to this timeline. I'm still inside the accelerator, which has always been gone in the other futures I visited. The door is open slightly, and it's just as dark and empty outside it. And silent. Utterly, painfully silent.

I raise my lantern and step through the door into the basement of the Aether building downtown. Almost everything from the present is still here, including desks, chairs, and computers, each now coated in a thick layer of dust. I flick a light switch, try to turn one of the computers on, and check the phone line, but nothing works. A calendar on the wall is dated ten years after the present. I can't be sure of the current year, but if they sent me to the right time, then this place has been abandoned for twenty years.

I check each desk and search every room, looking for clues or any signs of life, but there's nothing here. Instead I find a dusty sweater hanging from the back of a chair, a very old, unopened bag of chips on a desk, and forgotten pictures of someone's kids on one wall. As if the people who worked here expected to come back sometime for the rest of their things, but never did.

The elevator doesn't work, so I take the stairs up. The floor above me is a parking garage, with one lone car in the middle of all the empty spaces. I take a moment to study it, circling it with my lantern held high. It's a blue Nissan Sentra and the back left tire is flat. The license plate's registration sticker has the same year on it as the calendar. But the most unusual thing is that it's a normal car, not a driverless car or a flying car like I saw in the other futures I visited.

The other basement floors all lead to other parking levels, each one of them empty. I keep going up until I reach the lobby level.

A few hours ago, I walked through the lobby, and the place was filled with people in suits and security guards. Now it's as empty as the other floors. And this time, all the tall windows have been shattered. Glass and other rubble are scattered everywhere. A warm breeze flows through the open space, sending dead leaves skittering across the marble floor.

But the worst part, the part that makes me stumble forward through the rubble to one of the broken windows with my mouth hanging open, is that the rest of downtown Los Angeles looks just as deserted.

I've never seen downtown empty. Even late at night there are cars driving by, people playing on their cell phones while they wait for a bus, and the smells of exhaust, fried food, and piss in the air.

As the sun beats down from high in the bright-blue sky, making sweat bead on my forehead, I should hear the sound of air conditioners kicking on, of people talking to one another at outdoor cafés, of sirens blaring in the distance. But there are no sounds except for my rapid breathing, my heart pounding in my chest, and the dry wind pulling at my hair.

As I step over the broken glass and into the outside world, I almost believe I'm in a dream. Or that I've wandered onto the set of a horror movie and at any moment something is going to lunge at me from a dark corner. But this isn't a dream, and it isn't a movie. This is the future. A really messed-up future.

The stillness of the city is unnerving, as is the destruction all around me. The Aether building isn't the only one with shattered windows and crumbling walls. Storefronts across from it sit barren, as if they've been ransacked. A broken sign hangs lows over the door of a restaurant, the letters bleached by the sun. The lone car I see has crashed into a streetlight, the fender dented around the pole, the driver's door still hanging open.

I move to the middle of the silent street, then whirl around to take it all in. Other shops and restaurants have collapsed roofs and broken windows, some with scraggly trees growing out of them. A chain link fence is covered in ripped and faded posters, but I can't make out the writing on them. One wall of an office building is decorated with graffiti that says *The end is nigh.*

This future is nothing like the others I've been to. Something must have gone horribly wrong in the last thirty years. I need to find Adam fast and get us the hell out of here.

But I haven't seen any hint that Adam was here. Did Dr. Walters send me to the wrong time? Did I go much further into the future? If Adam did come here, where would he go?

A dirty orange flyer slides toward my feet, and I stop it with my boot. Across the top of it is a biohazard symbol. Below it, evacuation orders to the Palmdale quarantine zone.

What. The. Hell.

Palmdale is over an hour outside Los Angeles, out in the desert with a military base and not much else. I lived in a group home there for a year, and it wasn't pretty. Why would there be a quarantine zone there?

Why would they need one?

I'm starting to get an idea of what happened to the world, but the more I see, the less I want to know—and the more desperate I am to find Adam.

There's nothing for me to do but walk. I head west, toward the scorching sun's descent, because I assume Adam would go that way too. Our apartment and his lab are in that direction, as is our future house, the one we're supposed to live in one day with our daughter.

The desolation continues on every block. The sun beats down on me; the air is dusty and dry, the ground cracked and hard. There's no life, except for the weeds that have grown up between the sidewalk cracks. Trees that were once planted along the side of the road are all dead now, their brittle branches twisting up like skeletal fingers. I spot the familiar arches of a McDonald's, but the golden plastic has fallen off, leaving behind a rusted metal frame. I pass another lone car covered in rust, with broken windows and flat tires. Where the hell is everyone? Are they all...dead?

Something moves near my feet, and I jump back with a shriek. It's just a small lizard, the kind you see out in the desert, but it nearly gave me a heart attack. It's strange to see it here too. The only animals I've ever seen downtown are stray cats and dogs on leashes. The lizard darts under a boarded-up door and vanishes.

I take a moment to gain control of my breathing, then continue down the road more cautiously, taking care not to disturb anything or make a sound. There's something about the empty streets that makes me want to keep quiet. Probably just paranoia, but it's kept me alive so far, and I've learned to trust my instincts.

There's a sound behind me. The brushing of fabric. A quiet step. A quick breath.

I'm not alone.

00:54

The hair stands up on my arms, and I get the feeling I'm being watched. A sharp glance around the area tells me nothing. If someone is there, they're hiding. Waiting.

I duck behind an abandoned city bus on the side of the road, then reach inside my backpack. My hand grasps the cool, hard metal of the gun inside, but I keep it held low as I survey the street. Might be nothing. Could be someone walking by who can tell me what the hell is going on with this future. Best possible scenario: they know where Adam is. Worst: I have to use my gun.

Movement bursts from the shadows. Multiple figures, running toward me, and they don't look friendly. I have only an instant to react, and I swing my gun toward one, but I'm tackled by another. The gun goes flying down the street, just as my body hits the cement.

Dirty hands grab at me. Tangled hair hovers over my face. Teeth snap near my ear. My training kicks in, and I shove the person off me, hard. She stumbles back, but another one reaches for me. With a burst of adrenaline, I jump to my feet and narrowly spin out of the way. As he passes by where I was, I slam his head into the side of the bus. He drops to the ground, but there are two more, still coming at me like rabid animals.

I grab the gun off the ground and aim it at them. "Stop!" I yell. "I'll shoot!"

They don't even slow down. If anything, they get faster at the sound of my voice. Their movements are rigid and jerky, and one of them has a slight limp. They're wearing ripped clothes resembling rags, and underneath them, they're so thin their ribs stand out. Their hair is long and matted, their teeth are yellow, and their nails are caked with dirt.

But the worst part is that their faces look…melted. Their skin sags and droops like a Saint Bernard, giving them big, hollow eyes and hanging jowls.

I hesitate too long. I should shoot them, but it's harder to kill a human being than you might think, even if they look like something out of a horror movie. I keep expecting them to see the gun and stop, but they don't. My hand shakes as they get closer and closer.

The nearest one lunges, and I whip the gun against his face. The woman reaches for me and I duck, then knock her back with a hard kick. But no matter how much I fight back, they keep coming for me. And behind them, two more emerge from a dark building, drawn to us by the sound of the fight.

I spin around and try to run, but one of them grabs my backpack, yanking me back. The others close in. I'm surrounded.

A gunshot rings out from somewhere above me, and the guy holding my backpack drops. I jerk free and stumble forward as more bullets rain down on the attackers. I cover my head as I run past them, ducking under a rusted table outside a former café.

I look up, searching for the source of the gunfire, and spot a woman completely covered in gray cloth, wrapped around her entire body and head except for her eyes and mouth. I can't make out her features, especially with the sun behind her.

There's a guttural sound behind me, and another one of those things—I'm not convinced they're people anymore—comes lunging toward me from inside the café. I raise my gun and pull the trigger before he gets to me, shooting the guy point-blank in the forehead. Blood goes flying. The boom is deafening. But the thing finally stops moving.

The person on the roof is gone, but all the attackers are down. I slowly rise and look around, my hands trembling. Every second in this future makes me more and more worried about Adam, but if I think about what might have happened to him, I'll scream.

Soft footsteps sound behind me and I spin around, raising my gun. It's the woman from the roof. She approaches slowly, holding her hands up in a gesture of surrender. "Sorry I'm late. Got attacked by another group of Infected about two blocks from here."

I recognize that voice. She's completely covered in that gray cloth, but her blue eyes and heart-shaped mouth are familiar, although they have new wrinkles around them. I lower my gun. "Paige?"

"Did they bite you?" she asks.

I glance down at myself, quickly checking myself over, then shake my head. "No. Why?"

She rushes forward, grabbing me in a tight embrace. She smells like the desert, like dust and sun and wilderness. I hug her back, but soon realize this isn't another of Paige's normal exuberant hugs. This one is longer than normal, like she doesn't want to let me go. "It's so good to see you," she says, her voice wavering. "It's been so long."

My stomach twists at her words, but I have so many other questions that are more important than my own fate. "Where's

Adam? What were those things? And what the hell is going on in this future?"

"We have a lot to discuss, but it's not safe here," she says. I can't see much of her face, but her eyes look harder than in the present, and her skin seems more weathered. I can only imagine what kind of horrors she's witnessed in the last thirty years. "The Infected will keep coming for us."

Both of our heads snap to the north, where we hear a sound from a nearby building. She gestures for me to follow her and dashes off down the road, her movements silent and nimble. Before I met her, she was a gymnast and an Olympic hopeful, but she got kicked off the team for stealing. She's always been graceful, but now she moves like a wraith, flitting through the desolate city like she's a part of it.

I try to follow her, but I'm not as quick and my steps aren't as quiet. My hand tightly grips the gun, and I find it impossible not to glance at every darkened doorway, waiting for more of those things to jump out at us. I've been to a lot of futures now, and some of them were pretty bad. But I never expected to walk through the aperture into something like this.

We reach Paige's car, a big, black SUV with solar panels strapped to the top and bars over the windows. A guy on the roof of the car is covered up like Paige is, holding an assault rifle in his hand.

"About time," he calls out.

"This is Jesse," Paige says, nodding at the guy. "My trainee."

I peer at his familiar eyes and mouth, the only thing visible on him. "…Wombat?"

He squints at me. "Huh?"

Seems he only had that nickname in the first timeline where we met him. "Nothing. Sorry. You look like someone I once knew."

43

If Wombat—Jesse—is here, is my daughter, Ava, alive too? The two of them were dating in another future I visited, and she'd be about eighteen in this year. I start to ask but can't get it off my tongue. Maybe because if the answer is no, I'm not sure I want to know.

He eyes my clothes skeptically. "You're really a time traveler?"

"What did I say about questions?" Paige asks, but she grins at him as she says it. "Hurry up and get in the car."

Jesse shrugs but hops off the roof, staring at me the entire time. We climb into the car as more of those deranged people emerge from a building behind us, like dogs following a scent. Paige starts the car, and we tear down the empty roads, darting around fallen pillars, narrowly avoiding abandoned cars and other debris. The whole city has been deserted, looted, and forgotten. There's no power anywhere. And other than those cannibals, there doesn't seem to be anyone else alive.

I sit back in the seat, unable to take my eyes off the once-familiar streets of Los Angeles, which have now become unrecognizable. "Paige. Seriously. What happened here?"

"The Black Friday Virus," she says. My head snaps to her, and she offers me a grim smile. "We have a lot to catch you up on from the last thirty years."

I rub my forehead, where a headache is beginning to grow. "How am I supposed to find Adam in all this?"

She hands me a canteen. "Don't worry. You'll bring him back."

I gulp the water down, even though it's warm and metallic. "How do you know?"

"Because I was at your wedding." She gently pats my knee. "My past is your future, remember? That's how I knew you'd be here today."

A trickle of hope makes my shoulders relax slightly, but I still have so many questions. "If that's the case, why didn't you rescue Adam when he came through the aperture?"

"We tried. But you weren't sure what date Adam arrived here. I've been watching for the last week or so, but I never saw him. I'm sorry."

Dammit. The new accelerator must have put me in the wrong point in time. But did I arrive after Adam…or before him?

Either way, I'm relieved by Paige's words. If I found Adam in her past, I can find him now. We can both make it back alive. And once we do, we have a new mission: preventing this future from ever happening.

01:19

The car slows as we approach a metal wall that must be at least ten feet tall. It stretches between the buildings on either side of the road and is topped with barbed wire. A quick glance up reveals snipers in the windows, ready to take us out.

A gate slowly opens, and two people holding guns stand inside it, surveying the street. They nod at our car and let us drive inside. As we pass by, I notice they're dressed similarly to Paige and Jesse, with dusty clothes that cover most of their bodies and their faces. Their eyes follow me through the slits, though I can't tell if it's with suspicion or simple curiosity. I suspect they don't get too many outsiders here.

"Welcome to Miracle Mile," Paige says. "The last survivor refuge in Los Angeles."

With her words, I realize where we are. Every kid growing up in LA has been here on school field trips to visit the Los Angeles County Museum of Art, the La Brea Tar Pits, or one of the many other museums in this area. We're driving slowly down Wilshire Boulevard, but unlike downtown, this area is full of life and has been completely rebuilt. The buildings are covered in solar panels, and there are big rain barrels to collect water all around them. We pass the old El Rey Theatre, which now reads TOWN HALL MEETING: TUESDAY 6 P.M. below its neon sign, where it once spelled out the names of bands performing there.

People walk down the sidewalk past various shops selling clothes, household goods, books, or weapons. Another store, which used to be a Starbucks, judging by the faded green sign above it, has a sign that says SCAVENGED GOODS: RARE AND UNIQUE – BUY AND SELL. In the windows I see everything from jewelry to a kid's bike to an old PlayStation.

"How long have you lived here?" I ask Paige.

"About fifteen years. Started out with a few survivors who holed up in the museums, partly to preserve the art and fossils in there, and partly because it had the best security around. Now we've reclaimed everything from Olympic to Beverly and La Brea to Fairfax. Our plan is to keep expanding outward until we have control of all of central Los Angeles again. Someday."

"What about the government?" I ask. "Can't they send help?"

Paige's mouth twists. "There's no government anymore. Not like you knew it, anyway."

We continue down the road, past lines of people waiting to get water rations from a building that used to be an Office Depot. The Ralphs supermarket is still there, but it has guidelines posted along the outside about how much food each person or family is allowed per week.

"We've done our best to preserve and rebuild what we can," Paige says. "We've turned the nearby parks into farms, and we make sure everyone has enough food and water. Kids still go to school, but now they learn a useful trade and how to protect themselves. We do what it takes to survive. But there are very few of us left."

Jesse leans forward in the backseat. "There was another refuge in Santa Monica. That's where I lived when I was a kid. But it was attacked by the Militia, and I barely made it out. My parents weren't so lucky. Now this is the only safe place left in the city."

"The Militia?" I ask.

"It'll be easier to explain if we start from the beginning," Paige says.

We drive past the La Brea Tar Pits, with the black lake full of asphalt in the front and the statues of mammoths stuck inside it, and then the large building housing the museum behind it. Except, as we get closer, I see there are people stuck in the tar pits too. Two of them, both men, one in his twenties or so, and the other one probably double that in age. The younger one glares at us as we pass by, while the older one yells, "Please let me out. I didn't mean it!"

"What's that about?" I ask.

Paige doesn't even spare them a glance as she pulls into the parking lot behind the museum. "They're criminals. One of them was caught stealing food; the other beat his girlfriend."

"You leave them to die there?" I shudder. What a horrible way to go.

"Not usually. We'll fish those two out when they've done their time. Might be a bit sick from the methane gas, but they'll survive." She glances at my face and chuckles softly. "I know it sounds barbaric, but we don't have the space for a prison, and trust me, it works. We have very little crime and almost no repeat offenders."

I'm horrified less by their methods than by how much Paige has changed. Gone is the optimistic, perky girl with boundless energy and a kind word for everyone. This future has made her hard. I'm almost scared to ask what happened to the rest of us.

Paige turns off the car, and we all hop out. She moves close to Jesse and speaks quietly to him, while I look around. I can't make out their words, but after a minute, he nods.

"Got it, boss," he says before taking off down the road.

Paige and I head for the museum entrance, which has pictures of ancient animals depicted on the stone above the door. Two armed guards nod at Paige and let us inside. The building is silent, and we seem to be alone. It's warm and stale without any air conditioning, but a few lights are on, highlighting the displays. We pass by a skeleton of a saber-toothed tiger and another of a woolly mammoth, along with a wall of dire-wolf skulls. Each exhibit looks exactly like it did when I was last here as kid, as if this is the one part of the city that's remained untouched since the world fell apart.

"Where are we going?" I ask.

"I'm taking you to speak with our leader," Paige says.

She leads us into a long hallway with doors on either side, the light dim over the dark carpeting. We step inside one of the rooms at the end. As the door shuts behind us, a black woman with braided hair turns toward me. She's wearing a heavy gray coat over cargo pants, but her face isn't covered up like the others.

"Dr. Campbell?" I recognize her immediately, but I'm still surprised to see her here—and leading the survivors.

A weak smile splits her wrinkled face. "Elena. I can't believe you're here." She gives me a loose hug, her movements slower than I remember. She gestures at the conference table and office chairs in front of us. "Please sit down, and we'll try to explain everything."

I take a seat and study the room we're in. The power's on, illuminating the paper maps that cover one of the walls. Most of them seem to be of Los Angeles or California, but there's another one with a map of the United States. Some areas are filled in with different colors, while others have big X marks over them in red tape or pictures tacked onto them.

Dr. Campbell turns to Paige. "Were there any problems?"

Paige sits in a chair next to me and removes the scarf from her face, revealing an older, harder version of the girl I know. Her long hair is more gray than blond, and there's a new scar through her left eyebrow. "Downtown is overrun with Infected again, but otherwise no trouble. We didn't see any Militia. Didn't find anything of value either, unfortunately."

Dr. Campbell nods. "You brought Elena here, and you made it back safely. That's all that matters."

"Do you know where Adam is?" I ask.

"No, but I'll get my best people to look into it. Don't worry; we'll find him."

I'm antsy to get moving, but I can't run out blindly looking for Adam. The world is too dangerous, and I need to know more before I rush into anything. "Can you tell me what happened to this future?"

"Where do I even begin?" Dr. Campbell sits in front of me and folds her hands on the table. Sadness overtakes her features as she watches me for a long moment before sighing. "It started twenty years ago. A bioengineered virus was released on Black Friday at dozens of different shopping centers in all the major cities across America, just in time for it to be spread by people traveling home after Thanksgiving." She stares down at her wrinkled hands as she continues, her voice solemn but steady. "They called it the Black Friday Virus. It quickly became a devastating pandemic that swept through the United States, resulting in basic services being shut down. Hospitals were overrun. Looting and rioting became commonplace. The police couldn't keep up."

"It got so bad that we ran out of room to put the dead," Paige adds. "They just started piling them up on the side of the road."

"My God," I whisper. I guessed some of this from what I glimpsed earlier, but hearing it out loud is even more horrifying.

Dr. Campbell glances at the map on the wall. "The largest cities in the United States, which were hit the hardest, were abandoned except for small, violent gangs of survivors. People were sectioned off into quarantine zones by the military, but the virus kept spreading, no matter what the government did to stop it. It became a global epidemic, and a few months later, the entire world had crumbled. Billions of lives were snuffed out in less than a year—and there was nothing anyone could do but try to survive."

"We lost so many people in those early days," Paige says. "Friends. Family. No one was safe. The only reason we survived was because you and Adam warned us, giving us some time to prepare."

"How did it spread so quickly without anyone stopping it?" I ask.

"After the virus was released, no major symptoms were reported for over twenty-four hours, allowing it to spread unnoticed," Dr. Campbell says. "The first sign of the virus was a light nose bleed about four hours after infection, but then there would be nothing until thirty hours, when the symptoms began to feel like a cold or the flu—fever, headache, muscle pain. Nothing that would make most people visit the hospital. It was only at sixty hours from infection that things started to really go bad. Severe pain in the stomach and chest. Vomiting blood, which soon became blood pouring from the eyes and nose too. This would go on for a few days, during which time doctors tried to treat the symptoms, but inevitably it ended in death. But by then, it had probably already infected someone else."

"Only a few people seemed to be immune." Paige rolls up her sleeve and reveals a large, mangled scar on her arm that almost looks like a bite. "An Infected did this to me a few years ago. Good thing I'm one of the lucky ones."

"So those zombies out there have the virus too?" I ask.

"The virus mutated about five years after the pandemic, when we were just starting to pick ourselves up again," Dr. Campbell says. "But people didn't die this time—they became Infected. Stuck between life and death, their minds so decayed they don't know who they are anymore, their bodies out of their control. It's a miracle they survive at all, but the virus keeps them alive on very little food so that it can spread to others."

"They're not zombies," Paige adds. "They're not dead and they'll eat just about anything, but all their humanity is gone and there's no cure for them. The only thing we can do is kill them and try to wipe the remaining traces of the virus out."

I can't even imagine what it must have been like for them during the early days of the virus or what it's like now, as they try to rebuild a world that's fallen into chaos. So many people dead, and nothing they could do to prevent it. I have to find a way to stop it. "Do you know who released the virus?"

Dr. Campbell's mouth twists, like she's tasted something sour. "A radical neo-Nazi group known as the White Outs claimed credit for it. Their goal was to purge the world of people of color and other minorities, and they thought white people would be immune. Of course it didn't work, or I wouldn't be here right now. The virus spread out of control and affected everyone."

"Ugh." I feel physically sick. How could anyone do such a thing? I will never understand that kind of hatred or intolerance. "Do you know who their leader was? Or where they were located?"

Paige shakes her head. "We know very little, unfortunately. Everything was so chaotic after the epidemic broke out. There were lots of conflicting news reports, and we were all so focused on trying to survive. Then, after the world collapsed, it was tough to find any information about the group."

"You have to know something," I say. "Even something small, like a tiny detail that might seem insignificant to you. Just give me somewhere I can start."

Pity and sadness fill Dr. Campbell's eyes. "Elena, I know this won't stop you, but there's nothing you can do. You spent years trying to track down the White Outs and prevent the pandemic, but you failed."

My fists clench under the table. "Maybe, but I'm not going to give up that easily."

"Of course not." Paige gives me a warm smile. "You never give up. And maybe this time you'll find a way."

01:42

The door opens, and another woman walks in. Her dark brown hair is streaked with gray, and she wears glasses now, but I'd recognize her anywhere. I stand when I see her, relieved to see she's still alive. "Zahra."

She wraps me in a tight hug, tighter than I've ever received from her before. Like me, Zahra isn't normally a hugger. "Elena. It's been too long. Way too long."

"Too long for you maybe," I say, stepping back. "I saw you and Paige yesterday."

"Looking a lot younger, no doubt," Paige says.

Zahra rolls her eyes. "Please. You still look exactly the same."

"Hardly." Paige waves the compliment away, although the two of them do look pretty good considering they're almost fifty.

Zahra pats my arm. "I missed you. Don't tell anyone though."

"It'll be our secret. But how long has it been exactly?" I glance between the three of them. All the sad looks they've been giving me. The tight hugs. I'm scared to ask about my fate, but at the same time, I need to know. "Does that mean I'm…?"

None of them want to answer me first. Their eyes remain down-cast, until finally Dr. Campbell speaks up. "I'm sorry, Elena."

I swallow hard, but I expected that much, and it's not the first time I've learned I'll be dead in the future. I've changed my fate before; I can change it again. "What about Adam? And our daughter, Ava?"

Paige reaches for my hand. "Also gone. I'm so sorry."

Their deaths are harder to stomach than my own. My fingers tighten around Paige's hand. "What happened to us?"

Her voice is quiet, her eyes haunted. "Your daughter was born a few years after the Black Friday Virus, but she got sick when she was only an infant. Adam was so upset he killed himself, and you died not long after that."

I close my eyes for a second, letting the knowledge sink in, fighting back the grief. There's a tightness in my throat that I can't speak through, so I only nod. I start to ask how I died but decide it doesn't matter.

"What about Chris? And Ken?" I finally manage to ask.

"Thanks to your warnings, we all knew the plague was com-ing and were able to prepare for it, as much as we could anyway. None of us got sick right away, but Chris and Shawnda ended up contracting the virus a few months after the outbreak. Their son survived, and for some time, you and Adam raised him as your own. But after you died, he disappeared. I'm not sure what happened to him or if he's still alive. And Ken…" Paige's eyes grow heavy with emotion, and she looks down at our entwined hands.

"Ken died protecting Paige from the Militia," Zahra fills in. "He knew without the cure for Huntington's he wouldn't live past forty anyway. He chose to go out fighting instead."

"What is the Militia?" I ask. Jesse had mentioned them earlier too.

Dr. Campbell stands and moves to one of the maps, pointing to the different-colored zones. "After the government's collapse, small militia groups rose up in rural areas and then proceeded to take over. Now the United States has split into different regions that govern themselves. Here in California, the West America Militia has tried to take control, although we refuse to recognize their authority. We prefer to remain independent."

"Why? Wouldn't joining with others be a good idea?"

"Not with them. The Militia are fanatics who care nothing for personal freedoms or about preserving culture. They demand order and kill anyone who disagrees with their command or steps out of line. Men are pressed into being soldiers, while women are forced to become breeding machines. We refuse to be ruled like that. There's more to survival than just staying alive." Dr. Campbell sits back down in her chair and runs a hand over her braids. "We used to trade with other independent groups, like the one in Santa Monica, but the Militia destroyed their refuge and forced their people to join them. I fear we might be next."

"We won't let that happen," Paige says. Always the optimist, even in a world as dark as this one.

"That's actually what I came to tell you," Zahra says. "Jesse said you were here looking for Adam, so I hacked into the Militia's computers and found a message mentioning a new recruit matching his description."

"You think they took Adam?" I ask. "Why?"

Zahra snorts. "He's a healthy nineteen-year-old male. Even if they didn't know about his science background, they'd force him to join them. But since it's Adam, I have a feeling there's more to it than that."

"You think the president wants him for something?" Paige asks.

"I wouldn't be surprised. The message I intercepted was from the head of the Militia here in LA to the president."

I glance between the two of them. "Why would the president want Adam?"

"Because he knows who Adam is—and when he is from," Dr. Campbell says. "The president of West America is Vincent Sharp."

I blink. "The CEO of Aether Corporation?"

"Yes. My former boss. He started a cultlike survivalist group up in Napa and somehow took over or destroyed the other militia groups and what remaining military the state had left. Now he controls most of the West Coast."

Wow. And I'd thought this future couldn't get any worse. But what would Vincent want with Adam? Why wouldn't he return Adam to the aperture to make sure he went back to the present at the scheduled time?

"The Militia controls an air force base south of the airport," Zahra says. "I believe that's where they're keeping Adam."

I check my watch, counting the hours I have left in the future. "How do we get him out of there?"

Dr. Campbell shakes her head. "We don't. Their base is highly fortified, and they have a lot more weapons and people than we do. Even if we sent everyone in our refuge to fight them, we'd be outnumbered."

"We have to try. And you know I succeed because Adam is there when the Black Friday Virus hits."

"Paige is our scout," Zahra says. "If anyone knows a way in, it's her."

Paige rubs her chin as she considers. "There might be a way, but…"

"What?" I ask.

57

"It's dangerous. A lot of people might die." Paige glances at Zahra. "Including us."

Zahra sits up straighter. "None of our lives matter as long as Elena and Adam make it back. The timeline will change as soon as they return to the present."

"We don't know that for sure," Dr. Campbell says.

Paige slowly nods. "No, she's right. We know it's possible to change the future. We've seen it happen. We have to believe that Elena and Adam can fix all of this too."

"I'll do whatever it takes." I clench my fists, filled with resolve. "I won't let this future happen."

02:55

I'm walking down the street, armed with only a dented baseball bat, in a postapocalyptic future with zombies on the loose. Let's face it. I've had better days.

It's okay though, because I have a plan.

Step one: Find Adam.

Step two: Get back to the present.

Step three: Prevent the end of the world.

Easy, right?

Paige and Zahra dropped me off on an empty road, and now I'm on my own, trying to get the attention of the Militia. And probably a few Infected at the same time.

A rattling sound from a nearby abandoned food truck draws my attention. The truck is faded orange and reads PHO GET ABOUT IT, but the doors have been ripped off and the tires are flat. I grip my bat tighter, wishing I had my gun. Paige has it, since the Militia would only confiscate it from me. If all goes well, I'll get it back soon.

A man with long, wild hair comes shambling out from behind the food truck. His glazed eyes fix on me, and then he darts forward.

A flicker of fear rises in my stomach, but a burst of adrenaline overpowers it. He reaches for me, baring his teeth. I have no choice but to fight back.

I swing the bat at the Infected's head. It connects with a sickening thump, and the guy stumbles but doesn't go down. I hit him again. Blood goes flying onto my clothes, but I'm dressed like Paige, completely covered by coarse gray cloth except for my eyes and mouth. The clothes offer me protection from the unrelenting sun and wind, along with the Infected.

The guy drops to the ground, and I hit him one final time with the bat to make sure he won't get up again. I try not to look too much at his mangled features, at the blood I've spilled on the sidewalk, at his brains leaching out of him. My stomach twists at the gore, but I don't feel guilty. It was him or me, and I'm not dying today.

Besides, this future is only temporary. Once I change it, everyone will still be alive in this timeline. And I'll kill however many people it takes to rescue Adam and get us back safely.

Sweat drips down my neck, but with the cloth wrapped around my head, I can't wipe it away. I pull out the canteen in my backpack and take a long sip before washing the blood off my gloved hands. Then I continue down the road.

"Halt!" a male voice yells.

"Who's there?" I call out, trying to make my voice sound helpless and scared.

"Put your weapon down. We're not going to hurt you."

I slowly drop my bloodstained bat to the ground and raise my hands in surrender. Two men in tan military-esque uniforms emerge from the shadows of a ruined building up ahead. Both of them are holding assault rifles, although they're not pointing them at me.

"Oh, thank God," I say, clutching my chest. "I thought I would never find any other survivors."

"Are you all right?" one of them asks. He's about my age and blond, the kind of guy who looks like he'd be the high school quarterback, if such a thing still existed.

I slowly nod. "I'm okay. Just thirsty. And hungry. I've been wandering around for a long time."

"How did you get out here by yourself?" he asks.

I recite the story Paige gave me, keeping my eyes downcast. "I lived in a refuge in Phoenix, but it got overrun by Infected. We heard there was a group of survivors here so we headed west, but I'm the only one of my group who made it. My food ran out yesterday, and I've been so scared."

"Come with us," the other guy says. He has dark hair and greedy eyes that look me up and down. "We'll take good care of you."

He creeps me out, and my first instinct is to put my kickboxing training to good use on him, but I shove that feeling down. I have to get inside the base however I can, even if it means acting like the helpless victim. "Thank you."

They gesture for me to go ahead of them, but as soon as I take a step forward, my arms are yanked behind me. I let out a yelp and try to struggle, but the gun pointed at my head makes me freeze. "What are you doing?" I ask.

My backpack is yanked off me, and metal handcuffs are snapped onto my wrists behind my back. The dark-haired guy says, "We've been looking for you."

Oh shit. I should have guessed Vincent would be expecting me, especially if the Militia has Adam. Maybe these guys will take me to him or give me a hint where he is, so I can rescue him. Hell, maybe Vincent will help us get back to the present.

"Come along quietly, and you won't get hurt," says the first guy.

There's no point in fighting them, not when they're taking me where I need to go, although the handcuffs biting into my skin make me nervous. If Vincent was going to help me, this seems an odd way of going about it. I'll have to keep my guard up.

The quarterback leads the way down the street, while the other one nudges me with his gun to keep me walking. Both men keep their weapons ready, their eyes peeled for any Infected hiding in the decaying buildings around us.

After a few blocks, we come upon a high brick wall with sentries posted along the top every few feet. We stop at a reinforced metal door along the side of it, which the first guy unlocks with three different keys. The door opens with a screech, and then we pass through a short area before we come to another wall with a second door. This one has two armed guards outside it. Damn, these people are serious about their security. Which makes my task even harder.

The quarterback hands one of the gate guards my backpack. He opens it and goes through it, checking out my supplies, such as my camping lantern and my granola bars. Paige went through it all, making sure there would be nothing they would want or find suspicious. Then Zahra added something extra.

"What's this?" the guard asks. He pulls out an old, beat-up iPhone with a cracked screen.

"It's an old cell phone," the dark-haired soldier says. "Really old. From before the Black Friday Virus."

"A cell phone?" He laughs. "Not much use for those now."

He shrugs and shoves it back in the backpack, then hands it back to the soldier. The door is opened for us. My shoulders slump in relief.

Once we're inside the second wall, the military base looks a lot like a college campus. White rectangular buildings form a square around a courtyard with grass, palm trees, an outdoor eating area filled with people having an early dinner, and even a jungle gym with kids climbing on it. Everything is clean and well-kept, and other than the armed men in tan uniforms patrolling the place, it's hard to believe this is the same nightmare of a future.

I'm taken inside one of the buildings, but instead of going up, we go down. Deep under the ground, to a hidden network of tunnels that seem to stretch under the entire base, judging from the map posted next to the stairwell. I only get a brief glimpse as we pass by, but that's all I need. It's stored in my brain forever now.

I'm hauled into a room with three prison cells, and I'm starting to think I'm in serious trouble. The quarterback removes my handcuffs, and I'm tempted to fight my way out of here, but I can't. Not yet. I have to be smart about this, to see what they want and find out where Adam is before I make my escape. He has to be here somewhere, and I'm not leaving without him. I'll burn this whole base down to rescue him if I have to.

The dark-haired guy gives me a hard push forward, and I stumble into one of the cells. The bars slam shut behind me. "Wait here," he says.

I'm tempted to spit at him, but I don't. The two men leave the room with my backpack, but another guard stands near the door, watching the prison cells with a bored gaze. Iron bars separate me from him, and my fingers wrap around them as I take in my surroundings. The cell next to me is empty, but the far one has an older man in it, though he appears to be asleep. My own cell is sparse, with only a small cot and a dirty toilet.

I sit on the edge of the cot and check my watch, rubbing my thumb over the smooth surface. It was my mother's once, before she was murdered by my father, and it's the only thing I have left of her. This watch has given me comfort in even the darkest of times, and I need that comfort now more than ever, because I only have two hours to rescue Adam and get back to the aperture. Our window to the present will be open for only sixty seconds, and if we miss it, I don't know if Vincent will open another one for us.

Nothing I can do but wait. I lie on my side, away from the iron bars caging me in, to face the wall. There's writing on it, graffiti from people who were stuck here before me, and I trace my fingers along it. Down, down, down, to something drawn in black ink by my elbow. Something small and angular. Something that looks a lot like the tattoo on my arm of an origami unicorn and the necklace Adam gave me. I press my hand against the drawing, then grab the unicorn pendant hanging from my neck, feeling hope for the first time in hours.

Adam was here.

03:38

My eyes snap open at the sound of footsteps approaching. I've been dozing for the last thirty minutes, regaining my strength, but now I sit up quickly. The man outside my cell is handsome, black, and has a shaved head and ripped arms. I've never met him before, but there's something familiar about his intelligent brown eyes, the determined slant of his eyebrows, and the fullness of his lips.

"Elena." He sounds relieved as he unlocks the door and opens it wide. "You're here."

The other guard is gone, I notice. It's just the two of us in here, besides the sleeping man. "Do I know you?"

"Yeah. Sort of." He rubs the back of his neck. "I'm Chris's son. Michael."

Of course he is. I've never met him in any other future, but the resemblance to Chris is strong, though I see some of his mother in him too. He must be about thirty now.

I get to my feet. "Sorry. Last time I saw you, you weren't even crawling yet."

His head tilts as he examines me. "Last time I saw you, you were a lot older."

"Fair enough. What are you doing here?" He's wearing the same uniform as the other men, so he must be part of the Militia. He has a lot more bling on his collar than the other soldiers, so he's probably a higher rank too. I can't imagine why. He should be with Paige and Zahra, not here, working for Vincent.

"Waiting for you." He tosses my backpack to me. "Come on. I'll take you to Adam." He leads me out of the cell, no handcuffs this time. Things are definitely looking up, although I'm not entirely sure I can trust Chris's son. Paige told me I helped raise Michael after his parents died, but a lot must have happened since then. Including my own death.

"Is Adam okay?" I ask.

"He's fine. He'll be happy to see you though."

A long exhale rushes out of me, as if I've been holding it in all day, waiting to hear if Adam was okay. Now I can finally breathe again, knowing he's safe.

Michael leads me through the underground tunnels, past closed doors and other hallways. Other soldiers pass us by and salute him. All men, I notice. Where are the women?

We turn more corners as Michael leads me deeper into the underground maze. I sense we're getting closer to Adam, and I walk a little too fast, trying to race ahead.

He unlocks a door labeled Lab 3, but steps back before opening it. "Go on. I'll get you two some water while you catch up."

When I open the door, all I see is Adam. He's sitting on a stool, his back hunched over the counter in front of him. I rush forward, and he jumps to his feet with a muffled cry, then grabs me in a full embrace. I wrap my arms around him tightly and feel his chest rising and falling, a reminder he's alive and safe and *here*.

"I never thought I'd see you again," he says, his face buried in my hair.

"I'll always find you, no matter where you are in time."

Our mouths seek each other out, and we kiss like it's the first time—or the last. Soft and hesitant at first, a brush of the lips to make sure this is all really happening, and then deeper, devouring each other with desperation and need. I cling to Adam as if he might vanish between my fingertips if I let him go. But then I pull away, just enough to look up at him.

"How could you?" I manage to get out. I'm torn between relief and anger, conflicted between yelling at him or kissing him again.

"I'm so sorry, Elena."

Maybe he is, but sorry isn't enough. I don't know if I'll ever be able to trust him again, and no matter how much I love him, I can't be with him if I don't trust him.

"What were you *thinking*?" I can't hide the rage in my voice, and he visibly flinches. "Coming to the future on your own? Without telling me?"

"I was going to tell you everything when I got back, I swear. I just didn't want you to worry." He drops his head. "I thought I could fix things. It was supposed to be a quick trip, in and out of the future in no time. I'd talk to my older self, figure out the issue with the cure, and be back before you knew it with the answer. But as soon as I got here, I realized I'd made a huge mistake."

I drag my hands across my face. I'm still upset with him, but our time is running out here, and we can't have this argument now. "When we get back to the present, we need to have a serious talk."

He draws in a shaky breath and nods. In the past year, I've learned to read Adam well, and I see regret and exhaustion written

all over his features, although the more I study him, the more con-
cerned I become. He has dark circles under his eyes, and his glasses
are nowhere to be seen. He's wearing a gray work shirt I've never
seen before, and his jeans have a new tear through the knee. His
hair is longer than when I last saw him, and he looks like he hasn't
shaved in days. But most startling of all is the brand-new scar along
his jaw.

I raise a hesitant finger to the scar. "How long have you been in
the future?"

He turns his head away, brushing off my touch. "Seventy-three
days."

"My God," I whisper. I thought the accelerator was only off by
a few hours, possibly even a day or two, but he's been in this future
for *months*. "Have you been in this base the entire time?"

"Yeah. The Militia arrived within minutes of me stepping out
of Aether. It was long enough for me to get attacked by Infected
though." His fingers graze the scar on his chin. "I was relieved to
see the Militia at first. Now I just want to go home."

"Why are they keeping you here?"

"They want me to develop a vaccine or a cure for the Infected.
They won't let me leave until I do." He gestures to the counter beside us, where he was using a microscope when I walked in. For the
first time, I drag my eyes off Adam and examine the room we're in.
It's a lot like his lab in the present, with science equipment scattered around the room, although on a smaller scale. No windows,
and the only door out is reinforced. The room is completely sealed,
probably to prevent contaminants from getting in or out.

"Why you?" I ask.

"Because I'm the one who caused all this. I'm the one who's
responsible for the end of the world."

"What do you mean? I thought a neo-Nazi terrorist group released the virus as some sort of ethnic-cleansing bullshit."

"They did. But I'm the one who made it. The virus that wiped out the world was genicote. They turned my cure for cancer into a biological weapon."

"Like in the other timelines," I say. "First Aether, then Pharmateka, and now this White Outs group."

"Yes, but they did it much faster and made it even worse. Something I did caused that, whether it was making the cure earlier from the sample we got from Jeremy or coming here now. I'm not sure." He gazes across the laboratory with haunted eyes. "It's my fault the world is going to end. And I have to be the one who stops it."

03:50

Michael returns with some water for us, then leans against one of the lab's counters, crossing his arms as he appraises us. It's such a Chris pose that I momentarily see my friend there instead of his son. "You know, until Adam showed up a few months ago, I never really believed you two about time travel. But you look just like you did when I was a kid, and you were here when you said you'd be, so I guess it's all true."

"How much did we tell you?" I ask.

"Not much," he admits. "You two were always pretty secretive." He stares off into the distance as he continues. "My parents died when I was eleven, and you took me in after that, but neither of you was especially open about what you'd been through. But things changed after Ava…"

He stops and glances at me with apology in his eyes. Adam reaches out and grabs my hand, sadness written all over his face.

"It's okay," I say, squeezing Adam's hand. "I already know."

Michael nods. "After she died and Adam killed himself, you gave me something." He pulls a crumpled envelope from inside his uniform. "You told me one day I'd meet your younger self and that I should give this to you. And here we are."

I take the envelope from him and turn it over in my hand. It weighs nothing, has yellowed edges, and looks like it's never been opened. I tear into it and find a single item inside: a black-and-white photograph. From the angle, it looks like it was taken from a security camera. The photo shows a guy with a Dodgers baseball cap, a light-colored windbreaker, and a large backpack walking through a crowd of shoppers. A time stamp marks it as taken on Black Friday at 2:58 p.m. in the Beverly Center—a shopping center not far from Miracle Mile.

"Who is that?" Adam asks, peering over my shoulder.

"You both believed it was one of the men who released the virus," Michael says.

My breath catches. With this photo, we might be able to do something to prevent the virus. If we can find this man, maybe we can trace him back to the rest of the White Outs and stop them.

"I waited fifteen years to give that to you," Michael says. "I hope you can use it to stop all of this from happening."

My head snaps up. "I died fifteen years ago? How?"

"We were investigating near the Aether building. You thought there might be something there, some clue about the virus, I don't know. We never found it 'cause we were attacked by a large group of the Infected. You gave me the photo, told me to join the Militia, and wait for your younger selves to show up. Then you fought the group alone so I could escape." His voice gets a bit choked up. "I didn't want to go, but you told me I had to protect the photo, no matter what else happened. And that's what I did."

I step forward and rest my hand on his arm. "Thank you."

He pulls me into a hug. "You saved my life. I'll never forget that."

I hug him back, emotion crowding my throat, making it hard to speak. When we break apart, I stare at the photo again. The man in the Dodgers cap doesn't look like an obvious neo-Nazi or the kind of guy who would murder thousands of innocent people, but I suppose you can never really tell.

I'm not sure how we'll track him down, but this photo is enough to get us started. I shove it in my backpack and check my watch. "Adam and I need to get downtown. We only have an hour before the window opens to send us back to the present."

"Not a problem," Michael says. "I can get you both out of here."

The door bangs open, making all three of us jump. Four large men in uniform walk in, followed by an old, wrinkled man with white hair who wears a crisp black suit over his thin frame. He must be in his eighties by now, but there's no mistaking who it is: Vincent Sharp.

Michael squares his shoulders and gives a salute. "Mr. President. I wasn't expecting you."

"It was worth a trip from Napa to meet our newest guest." He turns toward me with a wide smile. "I'm glad you could finally make it, Elena. Guess we should have fixed that problem with the accelerator, eh?" He laughs softly, like we're all in on some big joke and not a time-travel experiment gone wrong.

I study him carefully. On one hand, the Vincent in the present sent me here to rescue Adam, and according to Paige, we're going to make it back. On the other, Vincent's men threw me in a prison cell and have been making Adam work on a cure for the past few months. I don't know if I can trust him, but he might be our best chance of getting out of here.

"We need to get back to the Aether office before the aperture opens," I say.

"Of course," Vincent says. "But first I need Adam to finish making the vaccine for us."

Adam furrows his brow. "I tried. I've done nothing but work on it for two months. But it's impossible."

Vincent walks around us at a slow pace. "Is it? Or have you been taking your time, hoping Elena would rescue you?"

"No! If I could do it, I would. But I'd need more time and more resources, and even then it might not be possible."

"My men tell me otherwise. They say you're close." Vincent pauses in front of us and sighs. "I'm sorry, but I can't let you leave until you finish it."

I clench my fists. "Is that why you're keeping us here?

He clasps his hands behind his back. "I kept Adam here because it was the safest place for him until you arrived—and it allowed him to help us at the same time. And I promise to get you to the aperture as soon as Adam fulfills his side of the bargain."

"Adam wouldn't be stuck in the future in the first place if it weren't for you."

"You're right," Vincent says. "He'd be dead."

I glance at the scar on Adam's chin and scowl, before turning back to Vincent. "You sent me here to get Adam. You're waiting for us back in the present. You know we succeed in coming home on time. You might as well let us go already."

"What I know is that the future can be changed. You taught me that. But don't worry. My younger self will keep opening the aperture for a few more hours in the present, which gives us a few weeks, thanks to the time dilation. If you don't return, he'll send someone else to rescue you. Or maybe he'll give up. Hopefully, it won't come to that."

"Send Elena back, at least," Adam says. "She can't help with the vaccine. She doesn't need to be here."

I throw him a sharp glance. "No, I'm not leaving without you."

Vincent shakes his head, his face heavy with sadness. "I know my methods seem harsh, but please try to see this from my perspective. In the past thirty years, the human race has been brought to extinction because of a virus. A virus Adam helped create. A virus he can help me stop now." He spreads his hands. "I've done everything I can to keep people safe and to rebuild this world, but it's not enough. I need your help to stop the virus for good."

"We're going to stop it," I say. "Once you send us back to the present, we'll prevent the virus from ever getting out in the first place."

He looks at me with something like pity. "You tried that already. I know because I helped you. But it didn't work. It will never work. This future is inevitable. The only thing we can do is find a way to stop the virus, and I need the vaccine for that."

Adam's head drops. "I can't do it. I wish I could. Believe me. But I can't. I'm sorry."

"Sir," Michael says, stepping forward. "I've been guarding Adam the entire time he's been here, and I believe he's telling the truth. Maybe we should consider sending them back."

Vincent looks at him for the first time. "Major Duncan. You've been a loyal soldier all these years, but somehow I'm not surprised to hear you take their side. Too much of your father in you, perhaps." He waves his hand. "You're dismissed."

Michael stiffens but doesn't back down. "Keeping them here isn't right, sir. If we help them get back to the present, there's still a chance they can change all this."

Vincent gestures at the guards behind him. "Get him out of here. Maybe a few hours in lockup will remind him how important our work here is."

Two of the guards reach for Michael, who starts to step back. "Sir—"

One of the guards grabs his arms and yanks them back, while another slaps handcuffs on him. I debate trying to intervene, but there are two additional guards hovering on either side of the room. Michael doesn't fight back, and all Adam and I can do is watch while they drag him out of the room. He gives us one last stoic look as the door shuts.

04:01

"I suggest you start working," Vincent says. "The sooner you finish the vaccine, the sooner you can return home."

He spins on his heel and walks out of the room, with a short nod to the two soldiers he left behind. They watch us with bored expressions from either side of the door, making sure we can't escape.

Adam glances over the microscope and lab equipment in front of him. He looks exhausted. Vincent wants us to make a vaccine, and while I understand his motives, Adam says it's impossible— and we don't have time to waste.

I pull Adam into a hug and whisper in his ear. "We're going to get out of here. Just follow my lead." He gives me a slight squeeze to show me he understands before we break apart.

"Get to work," one of the soldiers snaps.

Adam turns back to his microscope, while I begin a slow inspection of the room, searching for another way out or for anything to use as a weapon. Paige and Zahra must surely be wondering what's taking me so long, though they'll wait until they get a signal from me before doing anything. But I need to take care of the guards first.

They're both heavily armed and a lot bigger than I am, but I doubt they'll kill me or Adam. Vincent wants to keep us alive for now. Regardless, I need to be quick and use the element of surprise because I'll only get one shot at this.

I lean against the counter near Adam, like I'm checking out what he's working on, then push one of the nearby beakers over the edge, making it look like an accident. The glass beaker hits the floor and shatters loudly, making one of the guards swear.

"Oh God, I'm sorry. I'm a little shaken up." I bend down to clean up the sharp pieces of glass, but one of the guards rushes forward.

"Leave it," he orders.

He's too late though, because I've already grabbed a large, sharp piece of glass. As I straighten up, he grabs my arm, yanking me away from the mess. Without hesitation, I jerk my hand up and stab the glass into his neck. His eyes widen, and blood begins to gush out of his throat, but I can't stop to think about what I'm doing. I grab the gun at his hip, just as his partner yells something at me. I line up my target, exhale, and shoot the man between his eyes. The loud shot fills the room and then is immediately replaced by heavy silence while Adam stares at me like he's never seen me before.

"Jesus," he says, his face pale. "You killed them."

"It was us or them, and I'm always choosing us." I search the guards, taking their keys and weapons, including a large knife. I can only hope that this lab is sealed and no one heard the gunshot, but either way, we need to hurry before more soldiers arrive.

"Yeah, but…" He's staring at the guy I stabbed in the neck, whose blood has made a thick puddle on the floor. "Damn."

I swallow the sourness in the back of my throat at the sight of the dead man's face and hand Adam one of the guns, then shove the other in the back of my pants. "You've seen me kill people before."

He glances at the gun in his hand like it might come alive and bite him. "Those were in self-defense."

"And this wasn't?"

He opens his mouth like he might argue with me, but then he notices something. "Your hand."

I look down at it. Blood rushes out of a deep cut, which begins to throb now that I've noticed it. I must have sliced it open on the glass when I stabbed the first guard.

Adam grabs the knife from me and cuts off a clean piece of the guard's shirt, then carefully wraps it around my hand. I can feel his shock and disapproval even while he bandages me with quick, confident movements.

"None of the deaths matter," I say. "Once we change the future, none of this will exist anymore."

"They matter. Yes, if we stop the virus, these guards will be alive and won't remember any of this." He finishes up, and his deep-blue eyes slowly rise to meet mine. "But you'll remember."

The truth of his words shakes me, but I can't stop to think about that now. I'll do whatever it takes to get us back to the present. Once we're there, after we stop this future from happening, then I can deal with what I've done.

Hopefully I'll have some humanity left when that time comes.

"We need to hurry." I unzip my backpack and pull out the iPhone that the guard at the gate examined. I switch it on, then text a message to Zahra: Ready.

"Does that actually work?" Adam asks.

"Sort of. Zahra's got it rigged so it can send messages to her."

The phone vibrates, showing a new message. Incoming.

I shove the phone in my backpack. "Let's go."

The guard's keys unlock the door. I slowly it ease it open, checking the hallway. Another soldier patrols at the end, his back to us.

"Come on," I tell Adam, gripping the guard's knife in my hand.

He clutches the gun but looks vaguely sick. I can only hope that if the time comes, he'll do what has to be done.

When the patrol turns the corner, I sprint down the hallway, with Adam behind me. I'm on the guard in a flash, covering his mouth with one hand and stabbing the knife into his neck with the other. He dies before he even fully registers I'm there. Adam gives me a sharp glance as I drop the guard to the ground, but I ignore it and keep going.

I start to backtrack along the way I remember coming from the prison, using the map in my head. If this base has security cameras watching us we're going to be in a world of trouble soon, but I can't worry about that. One thing at a time.

A loud rumble suddenly shakes the walls and the ground, raining plaster down on us. Adam and I stop and cover our heads, crouching down until the noise fades and the tunnel stops shaking.

"What was that?" Adam asks.

"That was our ticket out of here, courtesy of Paige and Zahra."

"They're alive?"

I nod at Adam and gesture for him to follow me slowly. Shouts sound nearby, along with the rush of heavy footsteps. A siren begins blaring in the distance, somewhere above us. We head for the stairs, but don't see any other soldiers along the way. They all must have gone to deal with the explosion our friends created as a distraction. Exactly as we planned.

We sneak up the stairs as quickly as we can, until we emerge in the hallway of the first floor of the building. A soldier is running down it, but he slows when he sees us. I ready my knife until he yells, "We've gone into lockdown. All civilians are ordered to get to their safe houses."

"We're heading there now," I say. "What's going on?"

"An explosion along the east wall. That's all I know." He takes off again, raising his gun, his boots thumping against the carpet.

Once he's gone, Adam grabs my arm. "What about Michael? We have to find him."

I hesitate, glancing back the way we came. I have no idea where Michael is being kept or what they've done to him. He might be in the prison where they locked me up earlier, or he might be somewhere across the base—there's no way for us to know. Rescuing him would take time, time we don't have, and could get us captured again. But leaving him here might be sentencing him to death.

"Elena?" Adam asks.

I shake my head, even though the decision pains me. "We don't have time."

"We can't just leave him here." But Adam's face falls because he knows I'm right.

"Once we change all this, it won't matter anyway," I say, partly to reassure myself. "But we need to get back to the aperture to do that."

Adam nods, his face grim. "Lead on."

We both glance back one more time before heading through a door that leads outside. It's pure chaos out here, with soldiers and civilians running around and yelling. Smoke fills the air, making our eyes water, and we cover our mouths with our arms. Gunfire sounds in the east. I share a wary look with Adam and pray they're not shooting at our friends. No one notices us in all the confusion. We sprint across the grass between the buildings, past the spot where people were eating, now abandoned. Past the empty jungle gym. Past chunks of wall and debris that have scattered onto the grounds as we get closer to where we're supposed to meet. An old tree in the corner between two of the buildings.

As we approach, there's movement in the smoke, and three figures emerge wearing all black. They're heavily armed and even have swords and baseball bats attached to their backs. Their faces are covered with gas masks, but I know who they are. Jesse keeps guard, while the two women step forward.

"You did it," Zahra says, raising her mask. "Hello, Adam. Long time, no see."

Paige grabs Adam in a quick hug. "It's so good to see you again."

Adam glances between them all. "Thanks for the rescue. How did you get in?"

"We need to get going," Jesse says over his shoulder.

Paige nods. "We blasted a hole in the east wall, then tossed some smoke bombs inside, then sneaked over the north wall when everyone was distracted. We can escape in the same place."

She leads us through the smoke with confident, silent steps, making me wonder if she's been here before. More gunfire sounds from the east, along with shouts and screams. But they're not shooting at us.

"Halt!" someone yells behind us.

We freeze and turn toward the sound, raising our weapons. Five soldiers stand with the smoke curling around them and their guns pointed directly at us.

"Lower your weapons," the soldier at the front says.

"Not going to happen," Zahra replies.

Five against five, and all of us have guns. I'm debating the odds when we hear a snarl nearby. It's hard to see anything in the smoke, but we all glance around, though we keep our weapons trained on one another.

An Infected woman grabs one of the soldiers and snaps her teeth onto his neck. He screams and tries to fight her off, but before anyone can help him, more of the Infected emerge from the smoke. The soldiers turn their guns on them and begin firing, while we use the distraction to start running. There's more gunfire and screaming behind us, but I don't stop to look back, even though my stomach twists at what I just saw.

Paige peers around the edge of a building before turning to the rest of us. "We have a problem. Our escape route has been overrun with Infected. Seems the noise of the explosion attracted them. A *lot* of them."

"Shoot our way through?" Zahra asks.

Jesse shakes his head. "Too many. We'd never make it out."

"We don't need to make it out," Paige says. "Only Adam and Elena do."

"No." I don't want my friends dying for me if I can help it. "He's right. It's too risky."

"How much time before the aperture opens?" Zahra asks.

I check my watch. "Forty minutes."

"Dammit," Paige says. "That's barely enough time to get you back to downtown."

"I might know another way out of here," Adam says.

He heads west, and we follow close behind him, guns ready to shoot anything that moves in the smoke. We pass a dead soldier with an Infected chewing on his arm, which Paige shoots in the head with one blast of her shotgun. She pumps it and reloads, and we continue on, past dead bodies, both of soldiers and Infected. So much death, and all of it because of us. *None of their deaths are real,* I remind myself over and over as more cries fill the courtyard. *None of this will ever happen.*

Adam leads us to a large building that looks like an airplane hangar. He grabs the door handle, but it's locked. I reach around inside my backpack for the guard's keys, while the others form a protective circle around us.

A raspy breath is the only warning we have before we're attacked. Hands reach for us, teeth gnash together, but by then it's already too late. They're upon us.

Paige's shotgun rings out, followed by other gunshots echoing in the smoke. I raise my own gun to shoot the Infected closest to me, but another one slams into my side, making me stumble. I'm dragged down onto the grass, and I lose the gun. Fingers reach around my ankle, and I kick, kick, kick, scrambling to get away, terrified I'll feel their teeth on me at any second.

There's a gunshot nearby, and then the fingers around me loosen. Adam reaches for my hand. "You okay?"

I nod as he helps me to my feet. "There are too many of them."

"We have to get in that door."

I scramble to find the guard's keys, while the others keep firing around us. Adam stands at my back and shoots another Infected that gets too close. I try one key in the door, and then another, and another. Someone screams, and I nearly drop the keys, but I keep going, my hands shaking.

Finally I find the right one and throw open the door, rushing inside. "Hurry!"

Adam crowds in after me, and we slam the door shut as soon as the others get through. Two Infected come with us, but we deal with them quickly and then step back. We're in a large garage full of armored cars and trucks, but there don't seem to be any soldiers inside.

"I saw this place when I first arrived here." Adam heads for a nearby cabinet and grabs a set of keys. He leads us to a large armored SUV. Paige grabs the keys from him and hops in the driver's side, while the rest of us pile in.

All of us except Jesse.

"Get in," Zahra says. "There's enough room for all of us. Barely."

"I can't." He's covering his arm, but now he removes his hand, showing the bloody gash underneath. "I've been bitten."

"No," Paige cries. She starts to jump out, but Jesse holds up a hand to stop her.

"Someone has to open the gate," he says. "Go. Get them out of here."

Paige's lip trembles, but she nods. Her fingers tighten around the steering wheel as she swallows, and then she starts up the car. Jesse hops onto the bumper, grabbing the back of the car for a short ride to the gate. A garage door clicker along the driver's visor opens a huge door at the end of the hangar, and we drive through it, leaving safety behind.

The smoke has dissipated a little, but that only makes it worse because now we can see the destruction around the base. Bodies are scattered in every direction. The Infected shuffle through the courtyard, while soldiers hunker down along the edges to fight them off. For a brief moment, I wonder what happened to Vincent. Did he escape all of this, leaving his people behind? Or did he watch as his base fell because he wouldn't let us go?

When we near the gate, Jesse jumps off and sprints to the control room. There's one person guarding it, but Jesse knocks him out quickly and slips inside. Now we wait.

"I'm sorry," Zahra says to Paige. "I know he was your favorite trainee."

Paige nods, wiping at her eyes. I glance at Adam, who stares out the window with a grim expression. Wombat—Jesse—has been in every future we've been to, always helping us in some way. Once, as a friend of Future-Adam's who got us fake IDs and hit on Zoe. In another timeline, he worked for us at Future Visions and dated our daughter. Now he's giving up his life to make sure we get out of here, even though he barely knows us. I was upset about him dating Ava at first, but not anymore. If we fix all this and return the future to the way it should be, I'll gladly give him my blessing—because in every timeline, he's proven himself to be a good guy.

The gate begins to open, and Paige grips the steering wheel tighter. Jesse steps into the doorway of the control room and gives us a farewell salute, before a bullet strikes him in the shoulder. He staggers but manages to yell, "Go!"

Paige slams her foot on the accelerator the second the gate is open wide enough, and we haul ass through it, tires screeching against the pavement. Gunshots fire after us, shattering the back window, but Paige doesn't slow. When the bullets stop, Adam and I turn to glance behind us, but Jesse isn't in sight.

"We left him behind," Adam says.

"We had no other choice," I say.

This future isn't real, I tell myself over and over. It's. Not. Real.

But it sure as hell feels real.

04:47

Paige pulls up outside the Aether building with a screech of tires. I fire off another round at the three Infected following us. One drops, but then my gun clicks empty. I reach around in my bag, looking for more ammo, but come up empty. I toss the gun aside. "I'm out."

Adam fires at one of the remaining Infected, but his shot misses. I knew I should have made him come to the shooting range with me. "I'm out too," he says.

As we come to a stop, Zahra leaps out of the car and shoots both Infected in the head. Her time at the range has definitely paid off. "We're clear."

The rest of us get out of the car, but Paige moves a little slower than before. Blood trails from a wound on her leg.

"You okay?" I ask her.

"I'll get over it." Paige glances back the way we came, back toward the base where we left Jesse, and then shakes her head. "How much time left?"

I check my watch. "Eleven minutes."

Another group of the Infected emerges from a building across the street and begins loping toward us. I count five of them, but then three more jump out of the shadows and trail behind. As they approach, I grab the knife I took off the guard and grip it tightly. Zahra reloads her handgun with her last rounds of ammo. Paige can't have much ammo left either. Taking on all of them is going to be tough.

Paige pumps her shotgun. "We've got this. You two get inside."

I glance back and forth between the Infected and our friends. Leaving them here now, outnumbered and with barely any ammo, will be signing their death sentences. And no matter how much I tell myself that none of the deaths here matter, it's different when it comes to my two best friends.

"We can't leave you with them," I say, as the Infected get closer and closer.

Paige removes the baseball bat from her back and hands it to Adam. "Don't worry about us. Just head to the aperture."

Zahra rests her hand on my shoulder, looking me in the eye. "You need to go. Get back to the present and make things right."

My throat is tight, but Adam speaks for me. "We will," he says. "We'll fix all of this."

Paige and Zahra take up positions outside the Aether building, ready to defend us with their lives. They both have to know they'll never make it out of here, but they're sacrificing themselves so we can escape. So we can undo everything that's happened in this future.

"We won't let you down," I promise them.

"Go!" Paige yells before firing her shotgun at the first Infected. It drops to the ground, and she shoots another. Zahra begins firing too.

"Come on!" Adam grabs my arm and yanks me inside the building just as the Infected attack. I stumble after him and over some debris, the broken glass crunching under my boots, trying to ignore the sounds of combat behind us.

As we near the stairwell door, I make the mistake of glancing over my shoulder. The Infected have surrounded our friends, and Zahra's ammo clicks empty. She drops her gun and pulls out her sword as one lunges for her. A choked cry escapes me, but there's nothing I can do but keep going. Especially since some of the Infected have broken off from the main group and are rushing toward us, their jaws snapping, their eyes glazed and hungry.

Adam slams one with the baseball bat, right in the face, with a ferocity that surprises me. I give a hard kick to the one coming for me and send him sprawling back, then turn on the other with my knife. Cold, rough hands grip my arm, tugging me toward them.

I yank my arm free and yell, "Run!"

Adam rushes ahead and throws the door open. I fight off the one nearest me with a slash of my knife to its throat, then turn and run toward Adam as fast as I can.

But just as I slip through the door, hands grab onto my backpack and yank it off my shoulder. "No!"

Adam is already closing the door behind me. I reach for my backpack, but it's already being dragged away and ripped open, as the Infected search it for food. The door shuts and locks, and the only light comes through the cracks around it.

I reach for the door handle. "The photo was in there! We need to get it back!"

Adam grabs my hand to stop me. "We can't. We've got to hurry if we're going to make it to the aperture in time, and there's no way we'd survive against all of those things."

The Infected pound on the door with metallic thuds, and I know he's right, but I also feel sick to my stomach at the idea of going back without that photo. Adam and I both saw the man in it, but without the photo, we can't show it to anyone else or use it to warn people.

"How will we change things without the photo?" I ask.

"We'll have to rely on your memory." Adam rests his hands on my shoulders to steady me. "We'll figure it out. We always do."

I nod, but I'm not sure I agree with him. Things are so much worse than they ever were before, and we have so little information to go off. But we'll worry about that once we return to the present. Our time in the future is running out.

We rush down the stairs, trying not to trip over our own feet as we descend into darkness. The basement is pitch-black, and we move through it by touch and instinct. Without my lantern, it's so dark it's almost painful. My eyes keep trying to make sense of shapes but can't latch onto anything real. My heartbeat pounds in my chest, while my mind tries to convince me that we're not alone, and that something is going to jump out at me. I rely on the sound of Adam's feet shuffling against the laminate floor, the feel of desks and office chairs and computer keyboards, and the smell of dust and mold and decay.

Finally, we reach the smooth metal of the accelerator and feel our way along it until we find the door. We step inside, moving to the center, and bump into each other in the dark. Adam wraps his arm around me, and I bury my face in his shoulder as we wait for the aperture to open.

"Paige and Zahra…" I whisper.

"I know," he says, his voice rough.

"We have to change this future. For our friends. For our daughter."

He rubs my back slowly. "We'll fix it. Whatever it takes."

The golden light appears around us like dust sprinkling the air. We straighten up, and I'm so relieved to be going back to the present that I want to cry. But as the light thickens, I hear something moving outside the dome. Footsteps.

"What—" I ask, turning toward the accelerator door. Have the Infected managed to find their way in? They won't be able to return with us to the present, at least. Only people who have traveled forward in time can go back, according to Dr. Campbell.

The world explodes into light. For a split second, I see a dark figure standing in the doorway of the accelerator. And then we're gone.

THURSDAY

There's a third person in the accelerator with us.

It should be impossible, but I sense their presence beside us as my eyes adjust to the fading light. I can't make out many details yet, except for a vague feminine outline. I grip my knife tighter, just in case. Maybe Dr. Campbell was wrong, and one of the Infected did return with us. Or someone else.

The accelerator door opens. Something hits the floor near my feet with a loud flash. Smoke begins to fill the air, turning it to a murky gray almost immediately. I cough and cover my mouth, but the gas seeps into my eyes and nose, burning me up from the inside out. The dark figure darts away while my head spins and my knees hit the floor.

I reach for Adam before the void swallows me.

* * *

I open my eyes. I'm lying on the floor of the accelerator, and my chest hurts. Scratch that, my *everything* hurts. I feel like I got run over by a truck, multiple times. Plus my eyes are damp and scratchy, like I've been crying or something. Returning from the future always results in some physical side effects, but never as bad as this.

My first thought is that I'm suffering from future shock. But as I sit up, the moment before I blacked out comes rushing back to me. The third person who came with us from the future. A woman. She threw some kind of smoke bomb at us that knocked us out, and then she escaped.

Adam coughs beside me. "You okay?"

"I think so." A million questions rush through my head about who attacked us and why. And where they are now.

My legs still feel unsteady, but we both manage to get to our feet. Faint traces of smoke linger in the air, causing us to cough and squint our eyes. The accelerator door is still open, but it's oddly quiet outside it. I step out of the machine carefully, keeping my eyes and ears peeled for any hint of danger. The mysterious person could still be out there. But all I see are the scientists and the CEO of Aether Corporation on the floor, and all I hear is the low hum of computers and electrical equipment.

Adam moves to check on the others, who aren't moving at all. "They're still alive, but knocked out like we were. Some kind of gas maybe that put us all to sleep for a few minutes. But who would do this?"

I glance around the room, looking for anything out of order. Was something stolen? If it was, I can't tell. "There was someone else with us in the accelerator."

Adam's head snaps up. "Impossible. Only those who travel to the future can return through the aperture."

"Then Dr. Campbell was wrong…" A new thought occurs to me, and my eyes narrow. "Unless someone else went to the future with you?"

Adam's brow furrows. "You know I went alone."

"Sorry. It's a little hard to trust you at the moment." My voice comes out harsher than I intend, but now that we're safely back in the present, my frustration with him is creeping back in. Ever since I found out he quit school and went to the future alone, I've worried there's something else he isn't telling me, some secret he's keeping from me. I'm not sure that will ever go away.

He sighs. "I assume you went alone too?"

"Of course I did. I wasn't risking anyone else's life."

The sound of movement and a sharp intake of breath distracts us from whatever we're about to say next. Vincent is sitting up, rubbing his forehead. "What happened?"

"We're not sure," Adam says.

"Someone knocked us out and then took off," I say, while Vincent slowly gets to his feet.

The other scientists are waking up too, stretching their limbs with pained expressions. Adam helps Dr. Walters up, offering his arm to help steady the older man. Dr. Kapur wears a deep frown and mutters something about how we should all be checked out immediately, but we all ignore him.

Vincent brushes off his suit and surveys the area with clear eyes. "Nothing appears to be stolen, but I'll check the video from the security cameras. Whoever did this won't get away with it."

"But who would do this?" Dr. Walters asks.

I hesitate but decide it's better to tell them the truth. "Someone might have come back through the accelerator with us."

"Is that possible?" Vincent asks. He's moved to one of the nearby computer terminals and is typing something on the keyboard, his eyes intent on whatever is on the screen.

Adam shakes his head. "According to Dr. Campbell in one of

the futures we visited, no. She tested it out but couldn't send anyone back in time."

Dr. Walters pushes his glasses back on his nose. "That's correct, but there might be one exception. It could be someone who previously time traveled, perhaps. Like your older selves."

"They were both dead in the future we visited," Adam says. "But I guess it could be someone else."

I shoot Adam a sharp look, hoping he gets the hint to stop talking. I don't want him to tell Vincent anything about our time in the future, especially since the only people who fit with what Dr. Walters is saying would be Zahra or Paige. One of them might have come back to help us or to escape the hell of that future. I can't imagine them attacking us and running off, but maybe they're suffering future shock or have some motive I can't quite understand. Either way, it's better if Vincent knows as little as possible.

And now that my head's clearing, I notice there's one person missing from the room.

"What happened to that girl with the ponytail who was here?" I ask.

"Nina?" Vincent asks with a frown. "That's none of your concern."

That girl was about the same height and build as the person I glimpsed in the accelerator. Vincent planned to send her to the future to rescue Adam or wanted her to go with me. Maybe he sent her after me because he didn't trust me to get Adam back on my own or because he wanted someone he could better control to bring him intel from the future. I'm not sure why she'd attack us and escape, but it wouldn't surprise me if she decided to betray her employer.

"Did you send her to the future to get us?" I ask.

He types something else into the computer. "Don't be absurd. Even if I did, Nina would have no reason to attack us."

I spread my hands. "It's the most likely explanation. Unless someone figured out a loophole to travel back in time."

"Impossible," Dr. Walters says.

Vincent examines my dusty, bloodstained clothes. "Why don't you tell us what happened in the future so we can all figure this out?"

I cross my arms and give him a level stare. "You know I'm not going to tell you that. The plan was that I rescue Adam and then we all go back to our agreement of staying the hell away from each other."

"Let me examine you at least," Dr. Kapur says. "You look like you've been through hell."

"None of this blood is ours," I say.

His lips curl. "Very well, but we don't know what was in that gas."

He makes it sound as if he wants to help us, but I know better. Behind those beady little eyes, he's thinking of all the data he can collect on us after our fifth trip to the future. All I want to do is go home, but Adam nods. "It's probably a good idea if we're checked out," he says. "Your hand might need stitches."

I completely forgot about my bandaged hand. I sigh. "Fine. But make it quick."

Dr. Kapur leads us into a room that looks like a tiny doctor's office. He gestures for us to sit on the exam bed. "Elena first," he says.

I let him check my heart, lungs, and blood pressure, but hold up a hand when he reaches for the needles. "Hell no. I remember what you did last time you said you were taking blood."

Last time he did an exam on us, he injected us with something that made us pass out. We woke up shortly after and found we were locked inside the accelerator. I don't trust him with needles around me after that.

He scowls. "That was different. I promise I only want to run some basic tests."

I cross my arms. "Thanks, but no thanks. I'm perfectly fine."

I use the time to lean against the wall and close my eyes. My head's been pounding ever since I woke up, and it doesn't seem like it'll get better anytime soon. But my eyes snap open when Dr. Kapur says, "Hmm." He checks his notes and glances at Adam. "That can't be right."

"What is it?" Adam asks.

"It says you've lost eleven pounds."

Adam stares at the floor. "Strange."

Dr. Kapur shakes his head. "I must have recorded it wrong."

"That must be it," I say.

Adam and I both know it's not an error though. My chest tightens thinking about what Adam must have endured during those seventy-three days. What did they even eat in that Militia base? Not much, it sounds like.

Dr. Kapur finally declares us healthy and lets us leave, but when we walk out of his office, Vincent waves us over.

"I have the security footage ready," he says.

We move beside him and check out the screen, which shows a black-and-white view of the basement with the accelerator on one side. Vincent clicks his mouse, and the video begins to play. Vincent and the two scientists stand outside the accelerator while the door opens, but Nina is nowhere in sight. There's a sharp, blinding flash from inside the machine, which makes the image scramble. When the feed comes back again, the men are unconscious on the floor while a woman walks past them without hesitation. She's wearing dark clothes that completely cover her body, including a hood that hides her face, and the camera never gets a good angle on her. Almost like she knew it was there.

"Not much to go on," I say. The clothes remind me of what Paige and Zahra were wearing in the future, and they did use smoke bombs to infiltrate the militia, but I can't believe it was either one of them.

"I'll have security see what else they can get," Vincent says. "Whoever it is, we'll find her."

"Any idea why she was here?" Adam asks. "Did she take anything?"

"Not that we can tell. I'll let you know when we have more information." He shuts off the screen and turns to us. "Until then, be careful. We don't know what she wants or where she went."

"We will."

He nods but eyes Adam carefully. "Did you find the information you were seeking in the future?"

"Unfortunately, no," Adam says.

"I'm sorry to hear that."

I study Vincent's face, but he seems genuine. I've never trusted him, but since the death of his son, he's changed and become more subdued. And even though his future self locked us up and tried to force us to make a vaccine for him, I understand why he did it—especially after seeing the mayhem the Infected unleashed upon the base. He was trying to protect his people and save the world, and I can't fault him for that when I'm trying to do the same thing.

* * *

I unlock the door to the apartment, and Max rushes toward us, his tail wagging at top speed. Adam gathers the dog in his arms and buries his face in his fur. It's been only a few hours since I left, but for Adam, it's been months.

"I missed you so much, little guy," he says. Max responds by trying to lick Adam's face all over.

"What was it like, living there for so long?" I ask.

Adam releases Max and straightens up. "In some ways, it wasn't too bad. The Militia had food, water, and electricity, although all of those things were carefully rationed out. I was free to move around inside the base, when I wasn't locked in the lab. But the Infected were outside the walls at all times, and the people inside had a weariness to them I've never seen before, even the children. Like they expected death to come for them at any moment."

"Were you scared?"

"I was scared I'd never see you again." His eyes meet mine, but there's hesitation in them. "Now I'm scared you'll never be able to forgive me."

"I'm not sure I can." I wish I had a better answer, but I have to be honest with him.

His brow furrows, his face pained. "I don't deserve your forgiveness anyway."

Neither one of us moves from the entryway. We stare at each other, waiting for the tension between us to break or for one of us to say something more. We need to have a conversation about what he did and about our future, but I'm not ready for it yet. Neither is he. We're both exhausted, physically and emotionally, and we're still wearing our bloodstained clothes. I can't even remember the last time we ate, and Adam's already too skinny as it is. We need to shower and grab some food before we do anything else.

"You should shower first," Adam says, as if reading my thoughts. "I'll feed Max."

"You sure?" Yesterday I would have invited Adam to join me, but not anymore. Maybe never again. "It's been a long time since you were home…"

"I'm sure. You need it more."

I glance down at myself. "Good point."

I head into the bathroom and shut the door, then lean forward on the sink and stare in the mirror. I barely recognize myself. Blood has dried in my tangled hair, dust has caked onto my skin, and my eyes are dark and haunted. Somehow my clothes are even worse. I strip them off and toss them in the trash. Those bloodstains will never come out. I know that from experience.

The hot water washes off all the grime, blood, and physical traces of that terrible future, but it will never erase my memories of it. My mind replays flashes on a loop I can't seem to shake away from. Walking through ruined, abandoned Los Angeles. Driving away from Wombat, knowing we were leaving him to die. Watching the Infected surround Paige and Zahra, while Adam and I got away.

Every memory reminds me of how important our task is now that we're back in the present. Our friends sacrificed everything to make sure we made it back here safely. Even though we don't have the photo, we'll have to find a way to stop that future from ever happening—no matter what it takes.

But the worst memories are the ones that remind me of what I am. A killer.

The sick squish when I bashed the Infected's head in with a baseball bat. The warm spray of blood when I shot those guards. The cold feel of the knife slicing the other guard's throat.

Adam was right. Their deaths might never happen in the future. But they happened for *me*.

I sink down to the floor of the shower and curl up into a ball, letting the water hit my back. The memories go back, back, back to six months ago, when I shot Jeremy in the chest in front of the accelerator. The look on his face before he fell haunts me, even now. He would have killed me and Adam, along with Vincent, but still. He was my age, and I ended his life without a second thought.

Then back, back, back to one year ago, when I fought with Lynne on the beach for my life. I had to get the gun from her to stop her from killing me or Adam, to stop her from getting away with the murders of Trent and Zoe. But the gun went off. She fell into the pale sand. I can still feel the trigger sliding between my fingers. I like to think it was an accident, but it wasn't. Not really.

And back, back, back even further. To the moment that defined my life, that I try to never think about, that I keep locked away in the back of my mind in a thick safe. Somehow the memory still manages to get out anyway, now and then. Papá, drunk and angry, going for my poor mother with a baseball bat. Me, just seven years old, darting in front of him. Not thinking about anything but protecting the person I loved most. The look on his face of pure rage before the bat came down on me instead. And then Mamá, pulling me away, tucking me behind her, taking the rest of the blows. Protecting me until her very last breath.

Papá is in prison for being a killer. And me? I'm not any better than him. Maybe I should be locked up too.

"Elena?" Adam's voice breaks through the darkness of my mind. "Are you okay?"

The water is cold, and my limbs are stiff. I don't know how long I've been in here. Adam reaches inside and shuts off the shower, then wraps a towel around me and carefully helps me to my feet. I stumble out and he pulls me against his chest, wrapping me in his warm strength.

While he rubs circles along my back, I bury my face in his shoulder. All I can do is hold on to him as he slowly restores life to me. "I know," he says. "I know. And I'm so sorry."

It's true. He's the only one who will ever understand what I've been through or what we're up against. I don't know what will happen between us, or if I'll ever trust him again, but right now we need each other. It's his fault we're in this mess, but if he hadn't gone to the future, we'd never have known what horrible fate awaited us, and we'd never have had the chance to change it.

I draw in a deep breath. The past is in the past, and the future isn't written yet. There's still time for us to make things right, but we have to work together to do that.

I pull back. "Your turn for a shower."

"It can wait," he says with concern in his eyes as he looks me over.

"I'm fine. And you definitely need one." I retreat to the doorway, but then turn around. "I'll order us some food while you're in there. Your choice. Anything you want."

"Pizza." His answer is immediate. "Really hot, greasy pizza."

That gets a small smile out of me. "Done."

Once the shower is running, I order Adam's favorite pizza and sit down with my laptop. Max curls up at my side while I begin searching the Internet. I'm not sure how much I'll find, but it seems the obvious place to start.

After a few minutes, I want to throw my laptop against the wall. There's no record of any neo-Nazi group called the White Outs, and everything else I searched for came up blank or led me to a dead end. I should have gone back for that photo. I'm almost tempted to go back to the future to try to get it somehow. Almost.

"Find anything?" Adam asks. He's thrown on some jeans and a thin black T-shirt, but his dark hair is still wet and messy, hanging over his eyes. With him in those clothes, I can tell how thin he's gotten, and my heart aches for him all over again.

I force my eyes back to my laptop before I say or do something I shouldn't. "No. I don't think the White Outs exist yet. Or at least there's no record of them online."

"Hmm." He slides on his glasses and curls up beside me on the couch, rubbing Max's head. "Maybe we should ask Zahra if she can dig up anything."

I shake my head. "I don't want to involve her or anyone else. Not yet at least."

"Why not?"

"They've been through so much over the last couple months, and their lives are finally getting back to normal after Jeremy's death. I don't want to ruin it all by telling them what the future has in store for them. Not yet anyway."

He slowly nods. "Maybe it's better to keep it between the two of us for now. Especially since we don't know who came back from the future with us or why. Getting them involved might put them in danger."

"Exactly. Once we know more, we'll tell them everything."

Our dinner arrives, and for a few minutes, we do nothing but eat. Adam tears through the BBQ chicken pizza like he hasn't eaten in days. For all I know, he hasn't.

When he catches me watching him, he gives me a sheepish grin. "Sorry. We couldn't exactly order delivery over there."

"No kidding. Eat as much as you want."

He finishes his slice and wipes his hands on a napkin. "Every night in the future I'd lie in bed, unable to sleep, wondering if I'd ever make it home. Thinking about all the things I missed. You. Max. Family and friends. And yes, pizza."

I hand him another slice. "You had to know I would come for you."

That haunted look is back in his eyes. "Some days I hoped you would. Other days I prayed you'd stay far away from that nightmare."

I set my plate down, my appetite gone. "What are we going to do?"

"I don't know. But we have a few years to figure it out."

"We need to track down the man in that photo. My future self must have believed he was a part of this, otherwise why would she include it?"

"Maybe we can trace him back to the White Outs. But how do we find him without the photo? It'd be a lot easier if we had a name."

I'm silent, staring at the empty pizza box, because the only thing I can think of is something I don't want to consider. But Adam already knows. He can read it on my face.

"You want to go to the future again," he says quietly.

"I don't want to go, but it's the only way."

"No. After last time, I swore I'd never mess with time travel again."

"It's the only way. We go ten years into the future, to the Beverly Center on that Black Friday. We track this guy down and find out who he is. Then we come back and stop the White Outs now, before they have a chance to get the virus in the first place."

Adam's mouth hangs open. "You can't be serious. Even *if* we could convince Vincent to let us go to the future again, and even *if* Dr. Walters could fix the accelerator so we arrive at the correct time, going to that mall on that exact day might be a death sentence for us. What if we contract the virus ourselves and bring it back to the present?"

"It's the only way," I say. When Adam doesn't look convinced, I go on. "We'll be careful. We won't confront the guy or anything. Even if we could stop him, the virus will be released all over the country, so there's no point. We'll just watch from afar and get the information we need, then come back right away."

He tears his hand through his damp hair, and I can see the wheels turning in his head. He must come to the same conclusion I did because his shoulders slump and he sucks in a long breath. "God, Elena. Are we really doing this? Again?"

He's been through so much, I can understand why he doesn't want to get back in that accelerator ever again. I rest my hand on his knee. "You don't have to go."

His glance is sharp. "And let you go alone? No way." His hand finds mine, and he threads our fingers together. "We're in this together."

"Together," I repeat. "Until the very end."

FRIDAY

I barely sleep that night. Adam, on the other hand, sleeps like the dead. I suspect he didn't get much rest while he was stuck in the future.

Once the sun wakes us up, I get sick of tossing and turning and head to the kitchen to grab some coffee. Adam walks out of the bedroom an hour later wearing nothing but a pair of sweatpants, and my eyes travel over his bare chest and broad shoulders. Even though he's lost some weight, he still makes my pulse race. Heat rushes through me, and I force myself to look away. My heart is bruised and my brain knows better, but my body doesn't seem to get the message.

"Morning," he says.

I grumble something in response, but he's used to that. I tend to be grumpy in the mornings. What can I say?

"Have you thought of anything else we could do?" he asks while he pours some cereal for both of us.

"No. Have you?"

He sighs. "No. I guess we need to talk to Vincent."

"I have class today. And an English paper due tomorrow. But how am I supposed to focus on any of that?" I stare at my cereal.

"How can I pretend everything is normal, knowing what's going to happen? I want to spend every minute of the day trying to stop it."

"I know. I keep thinking we need to do something to warn people. Give them time to prepare. But who would believe us?"

"No one. I barely believe it myself."

I take a bite of cereal, but it tastes like cardboard, and I end up swirling my spoon around while we sit in silence. Adam devours his breakfast, just like he did the pizza last night.

"You should go to your class," he says between bites.

"And what will you do?"

"Head to the lab, probably."

To work on genicote, no doubt. Even though it might one day become a virus that kills everyone. My fingers tighten around the spoon. "Ken told me you dropped out of school. Were you ever going to tell me that?"

Adam rubs the back of his neck. "Of course I was going to tell you."

"Yeah? When?"

"I don't know. I didn't think it was that big a deal. It's not like I need those classes. I can make genicote without them now." He lets out a sad laugh. "Not that I want to anymore. Now that I know what it becomes."

I shove my cereal away. "Genicote isn't all you're supposed to do with your life. Or have you forgotten? Developing a cure for Alzheimer's. Helping Ken cure Huntington's. Creating Future Visions with me." All the original anger and frustration with Adam is boiling up in me again now that we're safe. "We had a plan, and you threw it all away without even telling me."

He stares into his empty bowl. "I'm sorry. It was a mistake—one of many, it seems. I should have discussed it with you first."

"Yeah, you should have. I thought we were a team."

"We *are* a team."

I stab my finger at his chest. "If we were a team, you wouldn't keep secrets from me."

He opens his mouth to answer, but I don't want to hear it. He'll say he's sorry, that he made a mistake, but so what? That doesn't change what he did. Or the fact that I can't trust him now.

I spin on my heel and head into the bedroom, slamming the door behind me. I throw on some clothes quickly and grab my bag, shoving my textbooks inside. Then I walk out of the apartment without another word, worried that if I even glance at Adam, I'll start another fight.

I don't know how it's possible to love someone so much you'd die for them, while at the same time to be so upset with them you can't even look at their face. But it is.

* * *

I make it through class somehow, although it's tough to listen to anything the teacher is saying. Some crusty old book that a long-dead white guy wrote seems pretty inconsequential compared to the upcoming destruction of life as we know it.

Afterward, I meet Adam at Aether's office in downtown LA. He's standing in the lobby, hands shoved in his pockets, staring out the window. I wonder if he's picturing this building in the future, with all the broken windows and debris, or the Infected climbing through it to get to us.

"How was class?" he asks.

"Fine," I mutter. "Did you go to the lab?"

"Yeah, but it was a waste of time. I'm no closer to making genicote safe than I was before I went to the future. All I did was stare at my samples and think how they're going to bring about the end of the world. I debated destroying them, but then I thought about all the lives they could potentially save if I find a way to fix this. Except I have no idea how." He sighs. "And so the spiral continues."

"We'll figure it out. But first we need to find the man in that photo."

Adam nods, and we head to the front desk. We're given security badges and sent to Vincent's floor. Once there, the receptionist waves us right in, even though we don't have an appointment.

"My two favorite time travelers," Vincent says from behind his desk. He gestures for us to sit down in front of him. "Do you have information on who came back from the future with you?"

"No, not yet," Adam says.

"That's unfortunate. My security team hasn't found anything else either, but I'm confident something will turn up soon."

Sure, unless the person who came back was working for him in the first place. But we have bigger things to worry about right now.

"We're here because we need your help," I say, though it kills me to speak the words. I suppose his future self was right about us working together after all.

Vincent's eyebrows shoot up. "Is that so?"

"We need to visit the future again," Adam says.

Vincent stares at us for a long moment, then lets out a short laugh. "Wow. You're serious."

"Very," I say. "And this time we want to go ten years into the future."

Vincent steeples his fingers on the table. "Forgive me, but I must be having a bit of déjà vu here. Except last time when you demanded I send you to the future a second time, it resulted in my only son's death." His eyes rest on me, and I feel a pinch of guilt.

"Sorry, but the answer is no."

"We wouldn't do this unless it was absolutely critical," Adam says. "But we really need to use the accelerator again, this one last time."

"Each time you visit the future, something terrible happens to you or the people you're with. Now someone's come back from the future with you, and we have no idea who they are or why they're here. Why in the world would I send you again?"

I lean forward, palms flat on his desk. "You owe us. We've kept all your secrets. We rescued your other team from the future. We saved your life."

"And despite the fact that you killed my son and destroyed my other accelerator, I allowed you both to return to the future one more time. That makes us even. But now? We're done."

"What if we tell you what we saw in the future?" Adam asks.

"No—" I start, but Adam's look silences me. This is all we have to bargain with, but knowledge of the future is a powerful gift and curse. Those of us who have time traveled have an unspoken promise to never tell anyone else what we've seen or what might come to pass. The one exception was when I told Dr. Campbell that her husband was going to be killed and how to stop it. But she risked everything to help us, now and in the future, and she deserved to know.

Vincent leans back in his chair casually, but his eyes dance with interest. "I'm listening."

Adam glances at me again before speaking. "In ten years, a neo-Nazi terrorist group is going to release a virus that will wipe out the world. Billions will die. Civilization will crumble. And thirty years in the future, they're still trying to rebuild and stop the virus."

"You saw all that?" Vincent asks. He's wanted our knowledge of the future since the very first time he sent us there, and we've never given him anything. Until now.

Adam nods. "We did. And we think we can stop it. But we need to go to the day the virus was released to find out who did it."

Vincent stands and moves to the window, looking out at the city. "And what happens to me? Do you know my fate?"

Adam hesitates. "You're still alive. You run a survivor's colony out of Napa."

I wait for him to say more, but he doesn't go on. It's way more than I'd like Vincent to know about his future as it is.

Vincent seems to ponder this for a moment. "Did you see me while you were in the future?"

"Yes," Adam says.

"And?"

He looks at me again, and I nod for him to continue. "You...you said you helped us try to stop the virus."

Vincent frowns. "And failed, it seems."

My hands clench into fists in my lap. "We won't fail this time."

"Maybe, maybe not." He rubs his chin, considering. He doesn't believe us. As Adam said, who would?

"We can give you the exact date the virus will be released," I blurt out. "Along with the locations. That way you'll be able to prepare long in advance."

"Very well," he says. "I'll send you to the future one last time. But I want to be kept in the loop about all this from now on."

"You'll help us?" Adam asks.

"I will. Regardless of what you think of me, I don't want the world to end any more than you do. After all, that would be bad for business." He sits down at his desk. "Give me a few days while Dr. Walters works on the accelerator's navigational computer. I'll let you know when it's ready."

I'm impatient to get going immediately, but even I can admit this delay is unavoidable. We need the accelerator to send us to the exact day the virus was released and no later. If it's off by even a tiny bit, Adam and I could get the virus ourselves. If it's too early, the trip will be for nothing.

And we only have one shot at getting this right.

* * *

When we get back to the apartment, Max does his little happy dance, not noticing the tension between me and Adam. This is the first time we've been alone together since the morning, and I'm not sure how to act around Adam. My anger has faded, but the underlying issues are still unresolved.

Adam grabs Max's leash to take him outside. After a second's hesitation, I follow them out to the grass in front of our apartment.

"After I went to the lab, I visited my mom," Adam says while Max sniffs around. "She told me to say hi."

We had dinner with his mom a few days ago. At least, a few days ago for me. Not for Adam though. He's always been close to his mom, maybe because his dad was never around, so I can understand why he'd visit her right away. He risked everything to save her life, after all.

"How's she doing?" I ask.

"She's good. Still no sign of the cancer returning."

We lapse into silence. I cross my arms and gaze down the street, hating this awkwardness between us. It's never been like this before, even when we disagreed about things. I'm starting to worry we might never go back to the way we were before.

Max leads us farther down the street, peeing on every bush or flower he sees, while I search around for another safe topic. "How much time do you think we need in the future?"

Adam tilts his head to consider. "Maybe three or four hours? We know what time that guy will be there, but we need time to get in position and—"

Something cold jolts down my spine, some primal instinct that yells, *Danger!* I catch movement out of the corner of my eye. Someone in all black. A flash of metal.

"Get down!" I shout, grabbing Adam's arm at the same time the shot is fired.

The bullet rips into him, knocking him back, his blood spraying against my cheek. We both drop to the grass while Max barks frantically around us. Adrenaline races through my blood as I yank Adam and Max behind a parked car, blocking us from the shooter's line of sight.

Adam's face is twisted in pain while he tries to stop the blood rushing out of his side. But he's alive. Thank God he's alive.

I peer over the hood of the car, but the shooter is gone. It's not safe out in the middle of the street like this, so I slide my arm around Adam and help him to his feet. "C'mon," I say. "We need to get inside, fast."

I drag him back into our apartment building, and Max rushes in after us. The door clicks locked, securing us in the lobby. I check the street again, then turn around. Adam slouches against the wall, holding his hand against his wound, his face growing paler every second. Blood drips down onto the carpeted floor. I rush toward him, although I'm not sure what I can do.

"Oh God, you've been shot," I say. "I'll call an ambulance."

"No!" He hoists himself up with a groan. "It's not that bad. Just help me get into the apartment."

"Are you crazy? We need to get you to a hospital!"

"All gunshot wounds have to be reported to the police. What are we going to tell them? That someone from the future is trying to kill us?" He shakes his head. "Please, Elena. I can handle this. Trust me."

My phone is already out of my pocket, but I hesitate. "I can't lose you, Adam."

"You won't. The bullet only grazed me. I think." He checks it again, but all I see is blood. Thick, red, and leaving him way too fast. "Call Ken. He was his team's medic. He'll know what to do."

I still think this is a terrible idea, but I dial Ken. Adam knows a lot more about this stuff than I do. He's been trained in first aid and volunteered at a hospital for a long time. If he says it isn't that bad, I'll try to believe him.

"Hey," Ken says, as soon as he picks up. "Did you find Adam?"

"Yes, but he's been shot. Can you get to our apartment fast?"

"He...*what*?"

"Just hurry. Please. And be careful on your way in because the shooter might still be out there."

"I'll be there in five."

I hang up. "He's on his way."

Adam nods, and I lift his arm around my shoulders to help him up. He groans with every step, but we make it back to the apartment after a few minutes. Max hovers around our feet the entire time, obviously worried about his favorite human.

Adam has me take him to the bathroom, where he sits on the closed toilet seat with a grimace. "Grab my first aid kit and some towels."

I fetch some of our old towels, the ones we use to wash Max, then get his kit out from under the sink. My hands are shaking, but I manage to use the scissors to carefully cut off Adam's shirt. As it falls away, my panic increases. Adam was shot in the ribs. *Oh God, oh God, oh God.*

The buzzer stops me from changing my mind and calling an ambulance. Ken's outside, and I rush him in to see Adam.

"Oh crap," he says, as he enters the bathroom. "What happened?"

"Long story," Adam says, his voice weak. "Short version is: I got shot."

"Well, yeah, I can see that." He wastes no time in opening the first aid kit. "You should really go to a hospital. And call the police."

"We can't," I say. "Can you help him or not?"

He inspects Adam's wound. "I think so. The bullet only grazed him. I just need a few minutes to stitch him up."

He starts cleaning the injury, and the sight of it makes my head dizzy. Considering how many people I've killed, you'd think a little blood wouldn't faze me, but it's different when it's coming out of the person I love.

"Go," Adam says to me. "We're okay in here. Make sure the apartment is secure."

I reluctantly nod. I don't want to leave, but Adam must know that if I stand here and watch, I'm going to lose my mind worrying over him. There's nothing I can do to help anyway. They've both been trained in saving people's lives. I'm only good at ending them.

I check the locks on the front door, then head to the windows and draw the curtains. There's no sign of the shooter anywhere, but she could still be out there. Lying in wait. Maybe I need to increase our security. Or get a gun.

The bathroom door's been closed, but I hear Adam let out a soft, pained sound. Oh God, what are they doing in there? The two of them aren't doctors. What if the bullet hit something bad and they don't know it? What if the wound gets infected? What if Adam's lost too much blood?

I'm so worried I can barely stand still. I want to pace. To run. To punch something. Like the person who shot Adam. Or a wall. I'm not picky, really. All this nervous, anxious energy is swirling inside my stomach, and I need to let it out somehow. Otherwise I'll have a panic attack. I haven't had one in six months, but I can feel one coming for me now. The tightness of breath. The rapid beating of my heart. The feeling that the world is spiraling out of control.

Max whines from outside the bathroom door. I kneel down and bury my face in his fur. "It's okay. Adam's going to be fine," I tell him, although I'm consoling myself as much as him. I take even breaths and hold on to the dog until the panic attack recedes into the background again.

After the longest ten minutes of my life, Ken opens the door. "All done."

I release Max and straighten up. "Is he okay?"

Adam has a large bandage over his ribs now, on the left side, but the bleeding seems to have stopped. "I'm fine, Elena. Or I will be. I promise."

Ken helps Adam to his feet. "You're not fine. You've been shot. You should really go to a damn hospital."

"Not going to happen," Adam says.

"Fine, then I'm putting you in bed. You need to get some rest. Doctor's orders."

Adam grunts as Ken half carries him into the bedroom. "You're not a doctor."

"Hey, I'll get my PhD before you at this rate."

Adam chuckles, then makes a face as he's carefully lowered onto the bed. I hover on the side, ready to jump in and help if they need me. Max hops on the bed and curls up against Adam's good side.

Ken pulls something out of his own bag. A bottle of pills. "Take two of these. They'll ease the pain and help you get some sleep."

Adam takes the bottle and frowns. "Do I want to know where you got these?"

"Probably not." Ken's been arrested for this kind of thing before, though he claimed he got the illegal medication for his mom. At this point, I don't care where he got the pills, as long as they'll help Adam.

Adam tries to shove the bottle back at Ken. "I can't take these."

My hand rests firmly on his shoulder. "You're going to take them and get some rest, or we're going to the hospital. No arguments."

He sighs. "All right, all right."

Ken leaves the room to give us some privacy. As Adam takes the pills, I can't stop staring at the bandage on his ribs. If the bullet had been slightly to the side, Adam would have been hit in the heart. I came so close to losing him today.

"Hey," Adam says, drawing my eyes back to his face. "I'm going to be okay. The bullet just grazed me. Really."

I push the slightly too long hair away from his eyes and then let my fingers trail down his cheek. "You better be okay. I can't do this without you."

He smiles faintly. "I find that hard to believe. You're the most capable person I know."

"I'm serious." My throat is tight with emotion. "I need you, Adam."

"I'm not going anywhere. I promise."

I cup his face in my hands, staring into his blue eyes. "When you went to the future and didn't come back, I was so scared. Angry too, but mostly scared I'd never see you again. I realized then I'd do anything, *anything*, to get you back." I draw in a ragged breath.

"But none of that compares to how terrified I was today when you got shot."

His eyelids flutter, the drugs already kicking in, dragging him into sleep, but he runs his fingers through my hair. "I'm sorry. I don't deserve you, not after what I did. But I'm going to spend the rest of my life trying to be the kind of man who does."

My chest tightens. I used to think I didn't deserve Adam and that he could do much better than me. But maybe we do deserve each other, flaws and all.

I press a long kiss to his forehead. "Get some rest."

He mutters something, but his eyes are already closed. I watch him for a moment, making sure he's breathing normally, before shutting the door on my way out.

Ken is cleaning up in the bathroom, but he pauses and looks me in the eye. "What's going on, Elena?"

"I wish I knew," I mutter. I collapse onto the couch, suddenly exhausted. Ken brings me a glass of water, and I give him a grateful smile. "Thanks."

He nods and sits across from me. "Tell me everything that happened after you left the lab yesterday."

God, was that only yesterday? It feels like a century has passed since I went searching for Adam. I debate how much I can divulge, since we planned not to tell the others yet. But Ken is already involved, and has been from the moment I met him at the lab and told him Adam was missing. He might already be in danger just by being here and helping us. He deserves to know the truth.

I sit up and look him in the eye. "If I tell you, you have to promise not to tell Paige or the others. Not yet, anyway."

A deep frown settles on his face, but he leans forward. "I won't tell them."

"Adam was working with Aether, just like you thought. He went to the future on his own and got trapped there. I rescued him, but this time someone came back with us through the aperture." I hope I'm not making a mistake by telling him all this, but it feels good to talk about it.

"What?" He shakes his head, shocked. "Who was it?"

"We're not sure. I never got a good look at the person, although I'm pretty sure it's a woman."

"What does she want?"

"I don't know for sure." I glance back at the bedroom door and grab my unicorn necklace. "But I'm starting to think maybe she wants to kill us."

Ken's brow furrows. "But…why? And how could someone come back with you? I thought that was impossible."

"I have a theory that Vincent sent someone else after us who's gone rogue for some reason. But Dr. Walters said it might be one of our future selves. Maybe Future-Zahra or Future-Paige. But I can't imagine why they'd try to shoot us. They saved our lives in the future."

"What exactly did you see in the future?"

I take a long swig of water, then press the cool glass to my forehead, which has started throbbing. Or maybe it's been throbbing ever since Adam was shot. I might need some of those painkillers too. "I saw the end of the world."

"Tell me," he says softly.

I bow my head and blink back the memories, as fresh in my mind as when they happened. Then I lay it all out for him. The pandemic. The Infected. The Militia. I even tell him about his own fate.

When I'm done, he looks as shaken as I've felt ever since Adam went missing.

"I know," I say. "It's a lot to take in."

"No kidding." He stares at nothing, his eyes empty. I wait in silence for my words to sink in. "How do we stop it?" he finally asks.

"We have a plan. We're going to the future again, to the day the virus was released, so we can find one of the people who was responsible for it. Once we know who he is, we can find him in the present and trace him to the rest of the White Outs. Then we can find a way to stop them before they ever get their hands on genicote."

His eyes widen. "Sounds risky. What if you get infected?"

"We won't. We'll be careful."

"How soon are you going?"

"I'm not sure. Hopefully soon. We're waiting for Dr. Walters to fix the accelerator."

He glances at the bedroom door with a frown. "Adam's in no shape to do anything like that. But I'll go with you."

"You'd do that?"

"To save the world? Um, yeah. Definitely."

We go over a few more details before Ken leaves. As soon as he's gone, I debate moving something heavy in front of the door, but then I imagine us having to leave quickly and being trapped inside. Zahra's security system will have to be enough.

I turn it on, then use my computer to check the recordings from the cameras outside our apartment. It takes me a few minutes to figure out how to access it, but I refuse to call Zahra for help. Then I play the video from a few hours ago. It shows us walking Max down the street, but we move far enough away from the apartment that we're off camera. After two more minutes, we hurry into the apartment building, Adam leaning heavily on me with his hand against his side, and Max in a barking frenzy. The entire shooting was off screen, and the camera never captured even the slightest glimpse of the attacker. She must have known exactly where the camera was and how to avoid it. Just like at Aether.

With a sigh, I close my laptop and head into the bedroom to check on Adam. Max lifts his head, thumps his tail against the bed once, then relaxes against Adam's side. I stand beside the bed for a few minutes, watching Adam's chest rising and falling, listening to the soft sound of his breathing. His glasses are on the table beside us, and he always looks younger without them. Sometimes I forget he's only nineteen, barely a few months older than me, except when he's sleeping.

I curl up behind Adam, sliding an arm around his waist, fitting myself against him. He stirs in his sleep, pulling me closer. I don't know if I'll be able to sleep, but if nothing else, I'll lie here all night and watch over him.

I almost lost him today. A few inches, and he would have been gone forever. It doesn't matter if he was the target or if I was, because either way, I'm going to find the person who shot him—and make sure they never hurt us again.

SUNDAY

The next two days are pure torture.

Look, I'm just not good at waiting. Adam's the patient one. But me? I like to rush into things. Once I make a decision, I want it done yesterday. Yes, this has gotten me into trouble in the past, and yes, I'm trying to do better. But it's really freaking hard sometimes.

Unfortunately, all we can do is wait. Wait for Adam to heal. Wait for the accelerator to be finished. Wait for the attacker to strike again. And try to go about our normal lives at the same time.

It's the weekend, so I'm spared from going to class at least. In between taking care of Adam and working on my English paper, I spend hours going over all the security footage, just in case the shooter walked by our apartment at some point. She didn't.

Adam and I stay in the apartment as much as possible, and I make sure to walk Max only within sight of the security cameras, just in case. But by Sunday we're both restless.

"Time to change your bandage," I tell Adam. Ken did it the last two days, but he can't make it today, so it's my turn.

Adam's sitting in bed with his laptop, his glasses low on his nose. "That's okay. I can do it myself."

"I don't mind." I sit beside him on the bed. "Shirt off."

He grins as he lifts his shirt off his head. "Ah, I see. You just want to get me naked."

"Keep dreaming." I run my hand along his chest, then lightly push him back into the pillows. He grimaces slightly, and I instantly feel terrible. "Sorry! Did I hurt you?"

His face relaxes and he smiles. "Nah. Besides, I'd never complain about you touching me."

I brush his hair away from his eyes. "Don't get any ideas. I'm still mad at you."

"I know." But we both know that's not really true anymore. It's hard to be upset with the person I love more than anything after watching him get shot.

A large, dark bruise covers his ribs, spreading out beyond the bandage. I gently ease the tape off, trying not to hurt him again, but swallow hard when I see the gunshot wound and bruised skin underneath. "You said this was just a graze."

He adjusts slightly to give me better access to his side. "It is. Kind of. The bullet took a nice chunk of skin out, but it didn't hit anything major and didn't lodge inside my body. I'm lucky, really."

Lucky is right. Seeing what the bullet did to him up close makes me even more grateful he's alive and even more determined to keep him that way. I carefully clean the wound with the stuff Ken gave us. Adam hisses but doesn't flinch away. His skin is hot to the touch, but Ken did a good job with the stitches, and there isn't any bleeding now.

"You're going to have a big scar here," I say as I put the new bandage on.

"Good. It'll add to my rugged appeal."

I can't help but laugh. Rugged is the absolute last thing I would call Adam. Not that I mind or anything. I've always loved his sexy geek look. "You don't need scars to impress me."

"Good to know." He closes his eyes, his voice faint.

I take his hand in mine, worried again. Will I ever stop being worried about him? "Are you okay?"

"Just tired. It's nothing." Tired is right. He's barely gotten out of bed for the last two days, but Adam knows more about this stuff than I do. If he says he's fine, then I have to believe him. I'm sure his body just needs a lot of rest to heal.

My phone rings, and I pull it out of my pocket. An unknown number. "Hello?"

"The accelerator is ready," Vincent says. "Can you come in tonight?"

I glance at Adam. Now that the waiting is over, I'm not sure we're ready. But what choice do we have?

"We'll be there."

* * *

Adam insists on coming with me to Aether, even though I'm not sure he should be out of bed yet. If I were in his position, I'd insist on going too, so I eventually cave and let him tag along.

By the time we get there, Ken's already in the basement, chatting with Vincent. Dr. Walters stands nearby, working on the accelerator.

Ken takes one look at Adam and frowns. "You look like hell, man. You shouldn't even be here."

"I'm fine," Adam says. He's really not though. His eyes are glazed, his face is pale, and every step seems to pain him.

"He insisted on coming, but I think he needs more time to heal," I say.

Vincent looks Adam over. "What happened?"

I cross my arms. "That woman who came back from the future shot him."

"I'm okay," Adam quickly says. "It wasn't that bad, and Ken patched me up. I can still go to the future. Really." But he rests a hand on the nearest desk as if he needs it to help him stand.

"Kapur!" Vincent calls.

The older Indian scientist pokes his head out of his office. "Yes, sir?"

"I need you to examine Adam." Vincent gives Adam a sharp look. "Don't bother arguing. I'm not letting you go to the future until Dr. Kapur checks you out."

Adam sighs, but he relents and lets Dr. Kapur remove the bandage and inspect the wound. The doctor grunts, then shoves a thermometer in Adam's mouth and checks his lungs and heartbeat. He grabs the thermometer, and his forehead wrinkles as he checks it. "As I expected. You have a fever." He glances at Ken. "Did you give him antibiotics?"

"Um, no."

Dr. Kapur clucks his tongue. "Gunshot wounds have a high chance of becoming infected." He gives all of us scathing looks. "You really should have brought him to me first."

Ken holds up his hands in surrender. "Hey, I told Adam to go to the hospital."

Dr. Kapur checks the injury again, poking it with a gloved finger, and Adam cringes. "Yes, definitely starting to get infected. I'll prescribe some antibiotics, but you need to stay in bed for the next couple days."

"Fine," Adam says, his voice weary. "After we get back."

Dr. Kapur shakes his head. "Definitely not. You're not well enough to travel to the future. The physical strain might kill you."

"Then we need to delay this trip until I'm better."

"We can't do that," Vincent says. "I've already shuffled my schedule around to accommodate this second trip of yours. You go now, or you don't go at all."

"Ken and I can do this," I tell Adam. I'm relieved he isn't coming, actually. One less thing for me to worry about.

Adam looks miserable, and not just because he seems like he might pass out at any second now. "I hate the idea of you going to the future without me."

"Now you know how I feel."

His head drops. "Guess I deserve that."

I hug him gently, careful of his side. "It's better this way. Someone who's seen the future needs to stay in the present in case we don't come back. If we fail, you're the only one who can stop the virus."

"Don't say that." He touches my face. "You can't fail. I can't do this without you."

"We'll be back safely before you know it. I promise."

He nods and pulls me close again. "Be careful. I love you."

I press a kiss to his cheek. "I love you too."

I step back and join Ken near the accelerator. We grab the backpacks we've both prepared and slip them on. I turn toward Vincent and Dr. Walters. "Ready."

Dr. Walters enters the date and time we gave him into the accelerator and then opens the door for us. He looks almost as tired and run-down as Adam. Once again I wonder why he's here helping Aether after being so adamantly opposed to more time travel. I'd ask him, but not with Vincent standing right there.

"Good luck," Dr. Walters says.

"This is your last trip," Vincent says. "Make it count."

Adam watches with sad eyes as Ken and I step inside the machine. I give him one last lingering look before the door shuts behind us.

The accelerator is claustrophobic with two of us in it, barely big enough for us to stand shoulder to shoulder. Ken moves to the center, gripping the straps of his backpack, and I settle in beside him.

"I can't believe we're doing this again," Ken says. "Another five hours in the future."

"Let's hope it's our last trip."

I'm not sure how much more time travel my mind or my body can take.

00:00

The future slowly comes into focus. I'm standing beside Ken inside the accelerator, but the door's already open. Vincent waits just outside it, looking a little older, a little grayer, but just as self-assured as in the present.

"Impressive," Vincent says. "I've never actually been on this side of it before. You simply appeared out of nowhere."

"What are you doing here?" I ask.

"I'm here to help you." He steps back. "Let's go. No time to waste."

Ken and I shuffle out of the accelerator, and Vincent leads us to the elevator. Unlike my last trip to the future, the lights are on in the basement, and it looks nearly identical to when we left it. Assuming Dr. Walters got the navigation working, we've only gone ten years forward this time.

"Where is everyone?" Ken asks as we step into the elevator.

"It's the day after Thanksgiving." Vincent gives us a knowing glance. "I gave my employees the entire week off and made sure they knew there would be no overtime if they came in. The building should be completely empty."

"You didn't warn them about what would happen today?" I ask.

"No. I debated it for a long time, but wasn't sure anyone would believe me. Or if they did, and word got out that I knew about the virus in advance, the authorities might investigate me and not look for the real perpetrators. Instead, I gave my employees an early Christmas bonus in the hopes they'd use it to get out of the city for a while. Or at least be able to buy supplies when things start going to hell. It's not ideal, but it's the best I could do." He shakes his head. "And if you succeed, none of this will matter anyway."

"That's the idea," Ken says. "Do you know where our present-day selves are?"

"I haven't spoken to any of you in years. I imagine you're all doing the same thing I am—preparing to ride out the end of the world."

The elevator opens to the parking garage, and Vincent strides out, expecting us to keep up. He's wearing a charcoal-gray suit and shiny black shoes, still playing the role of corporate big shot even though there's no one around but Ken and me.

Vincent stops beside a dark-silver sedan that looks exactly like a car from the present. "You can use this car while you're here. Everything you might need is inside already, including updated maps of the Beverly Center. I've also included some other electronic devices you might find useful, along with some money in case there's anything else you need."

"Thanks," I say, as he hands me the keys. He's helping us, just like his future self said he would. But Future-Vincent also said we would fail.

He gives me a sharp nod. "I won't be here when you get back, but there's a security badge inside the car that will get you in and out of the building."

"Where are you going?" Ken asks.

"To my vineyard in Napa. Thanks to your warning, I've spent the last ten years preparing for what's to come. Just in case you're unsuccessful in stopping it." His gaze shifts to a large pickup truck across the parking lot. "I'm heading up there as soon as you're on your way."

Napa. Where, twenty years from now, he rules as President of West America. A horrible sinking feeling drags my stomach down. He only did this because of us, because we told him about the future. A self-fulfilling prophecy we created. We're responsible for it all. Not just the virus and the end of the world, but the Militia too.

And if this future is any indication so far, we're not any closer to stopping it. This timeline is on the same track as the last one we visited. Nothing has changed yet, although maybe that's not a bad thing. The whole point of us coming here is to observe. If something changed, like maybe the date or time they release the virus, our entire trip might have been pointless.

We just need to make sure this trip is successful.

00:20

While I drive, Ken studies the map Vincent gave us. I traveled this same path with Future-Paige on our way to the Miracle Mile refuge, except now the streets are packed with cars. A stark reminder of how important our mission is and what will happen if we screw it up.

Ken looks up from the map and glances out the window. "Ten years doesn't look any different from the present. I thought it'd be more futuristic or something."

I shrug. "Not that much has changed since we were kids either. And in this timeline, Pharmateka was never created because Jeremy is dead, and Vincent seems to have switched his focus to surviving instead of making Aether some big tech giant."

"I suppose," Ken says. "I wish we had more time to look around. Probably sounds crazy, but I actually enjoyed my trips to the future. When they didn't end in death, anyway."

"Let's hope this one doesn't either," I mutter.

My fingers drum on the steering wheel while we stop at a red light. We have almost two hours before the time stamp on the security footage, which should give us plenty of time to scope out the mall and get in position, but there are still so many things that could go wrong. What if we can't get any information about the guy in the hat? What if he's already released the virus by the time we find him? What if one of us gets sick?

Ken glances at my impatient fingers. "Are you worried about Adam?"

"Of course." Although my concern for Adam is the least of my problems at the moment. He's relatively safe back in the present, while the two of us are here, mere minutes away from the beginning of the end. It's strange being in the future without him, but it's a relief too. If we fail, Adam will still have a chance.

"He'll be fine," Ken says.

"I'm more worried about making sure we find this guy and don't get infected at the same time."

Ken shoves the map back in the bag. "Me too. But I talked to Adam about the research he did on the mutated virus while he was in the future, and it seems to spread from direct contact with bodily fluids. Be careful what you touch, and you'll be okay."

"What if someone sneezes on me?"

"Then you're probably screwed." He gives me a weak smile that he probably thinks is reassuring. "We're both going to be fine. Really."

As I drive, I keep talking to distract myself from the anxiety threatening to take control of me. "Did you tell Paige about any of this?"

"What? No. Of course not. Why would you even ask that?"

"I thought the two of you…" I look over at him and shrug.

His shoulders slump. "Unfortunately not. Even if we were, I wouldn't tell her. Not yet."

"What happened? I thought you were going to ask her out."

"Yeah, but my mom's been sick and Paige just broke up with her boyfriend and we've both been really busy and…" He trails off, staring out the window at the buildings we pass by.

"Sounds like a lot of excuses to me."

"Easy for you to say." He glances back at me. "What about you and Adam? You still mad at him?"

"I don't know."

He gives me a pointed look, but I ignore him as I pull into the mall's parking structure. All of LA seems to be inside it already, creating a massive traffic jam full of honking, impatient people. We creep along behind the other cars, and just when I begin to worry we'll spend all our time in the future looking for a parking spot, someone backs out in front of us. I quickly squeeze our car in the spot before someone else can steal it.

We take a few minutes to go through the equipment Vincent provided. The smartphones he's given us are paper-thin, transparent, and flexible—likely a precursor to the flexis we saw in another timeline. We also find two tiny wireless earpieces with built-in microphones that look like something out of a spy movie. They fit into our ears discreetly and sync with the phones, allowing us to talk to each other. And at the bottom of the bag, he's left us some antibacterial hand gel. I can't imagine it will do much against a bioengineered super virus, but I guess it can't hurt either.

I glance at the map Vincent provided, memorizing it instantly. From the photo, we know the exact time the guy with the hat will be in the mall, but not the exact place. There was a women's clothing store behind him in the photo, but not the name of it. Vincent's map shows all the current stores with the locations of the security cameras, and he's marked two places he thinks are the most likely spots, which are on either side of the mall.

I point to the location on the left. "I'll take this one. You grab the other."

Ken fits his earpiece in and nods. "Got it." He gets out of the car, but then hesitates. "If we find the virus, should we bring it back? If we can do it safely?"

I consider it for a moment, but then shake my head. "No, it's too dangerous. We can't risk infecting people back in the present."

"But what if we could make a vaccine? Or find a way to stop it?"

"What if we can't?"

He sighs. "I guess you're right. I just wish there was something more we could do."

We divide the money and then split up, heading in opposite directions through the mall and trying to blend into the crowd. The Beverly Center has multiple levels of shops and restaurants and is completely enclosed, although the skylight roof lets in plenty of light. It's already been decorated for the upcoming holidays, with fake snow and mini Christmas trees covered in gold tinsel and twinkling lights. A huge ice palace sits in the middle of the first floor, with a long line of families waiting to visit Santa. And to top it off, they're blasting Christmas music.

It's only March back in the present. I am so not ready for all this holiday spirit.

Stores line either side of the bright, white walkway, with advertising for Black Friday sales all over their windows. People swarm the place, most of them holding shopping bags, and many of them dragging kids along with them. Everyone's wearing bell bottoms, so I guess that trend is back in a big way. I try to keep my distance as much as I can, but it's so crowded I end up brushing past people more often than I'd like. Once the virus gets out—assuming it hasn't already—this place is going to be in big trouble.

I find the security camera pointed toward an H&M and scope out the area. "I'm in position," I say, hoping the earpiece picks it up.

"Me too," Ken says. "Now what?"

I check my watch. We still have an hour. "Now we keep our eyes peeled for the guy."

I walk over to the railing and glance down at the levels below me, then turn around and check out the walkway on either side. No way to know if the guy is already here, wandering around, releasing the virus. All we can do is wait.

I stroll into one of the nearby stores and buy a black cardigan so I have a shopping bag, allowing me to blend in better. Plus it's Vincent's money, so why not? Afterward, I grab a pretzel from one of the vendors and then find a bench where I can survey the area while pretending to play on my phone.

With every minute that passes, I become more and more convinced this was a terrible plan. There are so many people here that it's going to be nearly impossible to find the right guy. And I haven't even considered how we'll get out of here safely.

A pregnant woman sits beside me on the bench while I finish my pretzel. She gives me a tired smile and rubs her large stomach. Emotion clogs my throat, and I look away. She's already dead, along with her unborn child, and she doesn't even know it yet. Everyone here is, and there's nothing I can do to help them. Not in this time period, anyway.

"I think I see him," Ken says through my earpiece. "Dodgers hat, windbreaker, backpack, right?"

I jump to my feet. "Yeah. What's he doing?"

"Heading into Victoria's Secret." Ken snorts. "Definitely a terrorist. Or at least a creep. No normal guy would ever go in there alone."

"He could be buying something for his wife or girlfriend." I head for the escalator. "I'm on my way. Don't lose him."

"I've followed him into the store," Ken says. "Now I'm just as big of a creeper. A single douchebag looking at women's lacy underwear. Hey, I bet Paige would look good in this."

I roll my eyes. "Stay focused, please."

"Sorry."

I walk through the mall as fast as I can without drawing attention to myself. My shopping bag bangs against my thigh. The crowd surges around me. Are any of them already infected? I hold my breath, keeping my hands tucked away, dodging around anyone that gets close.

"The guy's in the corner of the store," Ken says. "Wait. He's pulling something out of his bag. I'm going in."

"No! That's not part of the plan." My voice comes out too loud, and the person in front of me on the escalator gives me an odd look.

"I can stop him right now!"

"That will only alert them that we're on to them."

It's too late. Ken's already gone in. "Stop what you're doing right now!" he says.

"Excuse me?" a man's voice asks.

"The virus! Leave it!"

"What are you talking about?"

"Just…give it to me!"

There's a shuffle through our earpiece, and I pick up my pace, sprinting now. I reach the store in time to see the two men struggling over the backpack. The cashier woman shouts for security into a phone, while I rush inside. Ken pushes the guy with the Dodgers hat down, grabs the backpack, and dashes out of the store without even sparing me a glance.

"What the hell are you doing?" I ask Ken through the earpiece, while keeping an eye on the guy with the hat. He stands up and looks around, his mouth hanging open.

"I'm checking what's inside this bag," Ken says, his voice breathless.

One of the salesladies asks the man if he's okay, and he nods. A security guard walks into the store and starts asking the guy some questions. I pretend to check out a red lacy nightie, keeping my head down.

"Shit," Ken says. "There's nothing in here!"

"What do you mean, nothing?" I ask. "Has he already spread the virus?"

"No. I don't think he's the right guy. There's nothing in his backpack except some Black Friday coupons and a shopping list."

"Oh God." My head spins. I have to grab the clothing rack for support as my knees try to give out. Future-Elena was wrong. That picture she found wasn't a clue at all. "If he's not the right guy… then it could be anyone."

2:08

Another security guard arrives as I try not to have a full-out meltdown while surrounded by bras and thongs. They talk to the Dodgers hat guy again and then leave the store, glancing around like they're looking for something. Someone.

"Security is after you," I tell Ken. "Better lie low."

"Will do. But how are we going to find the right guy?"

"I don't know." I stare across the mall at all the people walking around, wondering which one of them might be a terrorist. "Just keep your eyes peeled for anything suspicious, and maybe we'll get lucky."

"Okay," Ken says, but he sounds just as hopeless as I feel.

We can't give up yet though. If we fail here, there's nothing we can do in the present but wait for the White Outs to show up sometime in the next ten years. By then, it might be too late.

As I'm standing there, trying to figure out what the hell to do next, a white guy with a shaved head and a big, bushy beard walks past me. He bumps into the guy with the Dodgers hat and raises his hand in a brief apology. His sleeve slides back, and I catch a split-second glimpse of a swastika tattoo on his arm.

The shock of seeing a tattoo like that momentarily stuns me, but then I shake it off. This could be the guy we're looking for. Maybe Future-Elena's clue wasn't as worthless as I thought.

He has a backpack, and he heads inside an electronics store I've never heard of called Charge Mart, which is packed with people. I trail after him at a safe distance, pretending to check the price of a camera, then picking up a cell phone case like a normal shopper might, although I keep my eye on him the entire time. But he doesn't look at any of the things on sale…No, he watches the people around us with the slightest smirk on his face. It's barely noticeable, almost like he's quietly amused at something, but it creeps me out like nothing I've seen before.

This has to be our guy.

"I think I see our target," I quietly tell Ken.

"Really?" he asks through my earpiece.

"Yep. Swastika tattoo, shaved head, and carrying a backpack. I've followed him into a store called Charge Mart."

"Be careful. I'll try to be there soon, but security is on my tail."

The guy in question stops in front of a row of paper-thin big-screen TVs, next to a family with a mom, a dad, and two little girls. They're black, and the girls can't be older than seven at most. One of them holds a polar bear stuffed toy, and the other has a Pokémon backpack.

The man with the beard and the tattoo watches the family intently, while the parents debate between two of the TVs and the girls bounce around beside them. They look happy, the kind of loving family I always dreamed of having, and my heart squeezes painfully at the way he eyes them like they're his next meal.

I can't get involved. That's not part of the plan, and besides, it's way too risky. Getting too close to him could get me infected with the virus too, and I can't bring it back to the present under any circumstances. Even if I stop him, dozens of other men just like him are releasing the virus at other shopping centers across the country at this very minute. If I interfere, they'll know someone is on to them, which might make them change their tactics and make it harder for us to stop them. Anything I do now can change the future—and not necessarily in a good way.

But how am I supposed to get information on him without confronting him?

The younger girl with the bear drops it, and the older one picks it up and hands it back to her, then gives her a hug. The man with the beard and the tattoo watches it all.

I swallow hard. Maybe I'm wrong. Maybe this isn't the guy. Maybe these little girls won't be among the first ones to get sick. Maybe this perfect family won't be dead within a week.

He opens his backpack and reaches inside. Panic shoots through me, and I'm in motion before I know what I'm doing. I have to stop him. I can't just stand there and do nothing. That's just not who I am. And maybe I can't save everyone, but I can save this one family at least.

I spot something on the wall near the row of TVs and change course. A fire alarm. I shatter the glass with my elbow and pull the handle. Lights flash. A shockingly loud siren blares. With a sharp hiss, water sprays down on us from the ceiling.

People scream and begin running for the exit. The dad grabs one girl, the mom grabs the other, and they take off. Away from the guy with the shaved head and out the door. They might still get sick in the days to come, but maybe they'll be among the lucky ones. For now, they're safe.

The man begins walking toward the exit, his smirk now replaced by a slight frown. I stalk toward him, moving quickly, and when

I'm close enough, I bump into him, hard. His backpack falls to the ground, and I grab it, then dash behind the nearest row of shelves, heading back into the store in the opposite direction from everyone else.

"What's going on?" Ken asks.

I glance behind me. The guy is looking for me, and I duck down, dashing to the next aisle. "I pulled the fire alarm. I've got the guy's backpack now."

In the corner of the store, behind the video games, I open up the backpack and look inside. There are five white canisters that look like asthma inhalers, all of them unmarked. Is this the virus? I can't tell, but I try not to touch any of them. I search around in the bag, but don't find anything else of interest. No wallet. No phone. No information on who this guy is. Dammit!

The guy rounds the corner and fixes his steely eyes on me. He no longer looks amused. "What are you doing?"

"You can't do this," I say, holding up the backpack.

He takes a step toward me, his face darkening. "Give me that. Now."

"It doesn't work the way you think. The virus, it targets everyone, regardless of skin color." The words slip out, and I can't seem to stop them. Even though I know reasoning with him isn't going to work.

He laughs, but it's a dark, menacing sound. "You stupid girl. You have it all wrong."

He lunges for me, and I try to jerk back, but his big, meaty hand wraps around my arm. I swing the backpack at him until he releases me with a grunt. In that split second, I have to decide: run or fight. The smart move is to run, but I still don't know who he is.

Fight it is.

I drop the backpack and raise my fists, getting into the stance drilled into my head during hours and hours of kickboxing and self-defense classes. He reaches for me again, but I sock him in the face, a quick jab with each fist. He stumbles back, stunned, and I throw a front kick straight against his chin as hard as I can. He falls against the display behind him, scattering video games everywhere, and then hits the floor, facedown. He doesn't move again.

Hmm. Guess he wasn't so tough after all. Not a fighter, just a disgusting man with a terrible mission. I reach around in his pants, hating every second I have to touch him, until I find his wallet. Bingo.

"Hey!" a security guard yells at me. I pocket the wallet and slip away, and only when I'm out of the store do I realize I left the backpack behind. There's nothing I could do with it, even if I took it—we already decided not to bring the cure back to the present. At least I got what we came for, and now we can track this guy in the present. Maybe then we can find who he's working with and shut them all down.

"I got the guy's wallet," I tell Ken. "Heading back to the car now."

"You got it? Nice work. Meet you there soon."

I walk through the mall at a brisk pace, glancing around me for any security guards or other threats. A kid with red hair is coughing nonstop outside the Disney Store. Is that the first sign of the virus or just a regular cold? The swastika guy had five of those inhaler things. Did he release the virus already in different stores?

I walk a little faster.

As soon as I'm in the parking garage I start sprinting, then once I get inside the car, I tear open the bag Vincent provided until I find the antibacterial gel. I pour that slimy stuff all over my hands, rubbing my fingers together rapidly until it evaporates, and then debate covering the rest of my skin with it too. Only then do I realize my hands are shaking.

All of those people back there are probably going to die. The redheaded kid. The pregnant lady. The family with the two girls. Even the guy with the Dodgers hat. None of them will likely survive the week. And I just...left them there. With a terrorist and a backpack full of death. But what else could I do?

Our best bet is to make sure Ken and I get back safely with this guy's wallet so we can make sure this day never happens at all. But even though I know that, and I don't think I was actually infected, I can't seem to calm down. I've been in some seriously scary situations in my life. I've had many moments when I thought I was going to die. But all of those things I could see coming and could fight back against. A virus is invisible and deadly silent. It could be inside me now, and I wouldn't even know it. How can I fight against that?

I force myself to take long breaths until my heart rate slows, then I open up the man's wallet. It's dark brown, and the leather's cracked and worn, like he's been using it for a long time. Inside I find a driver's license, a couple credit cards, some money, and a couple receipts. Nothing all that interesting, but at least we have a name and address.

Harrison Weiss of Van Nuys, California—we're coming for you.

03:44

It takes Ken another twenty-eight minutes to get back to the car. I sit inside it, engine running, staring at the clock until he finally opens the passenger door.

I'm backing out of the parking space before he even has his seat belt on. "What took you so long?"

"Sorry. Got caught by security, but I managed to get away. Told them it was all a misunderstanding, and they finally let me go." He looks over at me. "You got something?"

"Yeah." I toss the wallet into his lap, and he opens it up, checking out the contents.

"Hot damn." He takes out the driver's license and holds it up. "What happened?"

"I tripped the fire alarm and grabbed his backpack. There were these asthma inhaler things inside that I thought might be the cure. He confronted me, and I punched him, then took his wallet."

"Wow. You punched a neo-Nazi. Nice job."

I stretch my hand out with a dark smile. "Definitely the highlight of this trip."

Ken relaxes back into the seat. "I can't believe we did it. We really did it." But then his face drops. "But all those people…"

"I know." My throat tightens. "I wish we could do more."

"We're doing everything we can."

I nod, but then glance at him. "Do you think we're infected?"

"No, probably not. How long until the first symptom?"

"A nose bleed at four hours."

"I guess we'll know soon enough then."

We're quiet for the rest of the drive back to the Aether building, grappling with our thoughts of what we saw and what we still have to do. We were lucky today, but there's still so much to be done before we can celebrate. And so much we still don't know.

I park the car, and then we take the elevator down to the basement. Vincent's truck is gone. He didn't care whether we got the information we wanted or not, because for him in this timeline, it's already too late. Presumably he's on his way to Napa to prepare for the end of the world.

For once, we're not out of time. In fact, we have another forty-two minutes until the aperture opens. Maybe we could have explored the city or tried to do more, but right now, with the virus being released across the country, Aether's basement is the safest place for us.

I wonder what our older selves are doing right now and how they prepared for this day. Are they hiding out with a ton of food and water stored away? Are they in a bunker here in LA? Or somewhere out of the city, like on a farm? If our plan fails, I'll be making those decisions in the upcoming years too.

Ken sits at one of the desks and plays with the phone Vincent gave us, so I slump into a chair and do the same. I pull up a news feed first, but there aren't any reports about the virus yet. They won't know about it for a few more days probably, and by then, it will be too late. I run a search on the White Outs and find a Wikipedia page, along with a few news articles on them from the last four years. Unfortunately, there's very little known about them, including who leads the group or when it was started.

They seemed to have sprung up out of nowhere, using message boards and social media to covertly attract new members and spread propaganda. Two years ago, they caught media attention when one of them shot up a Jewish center in Boston before shooting himself. A year later, another one of their members bombed a mosque in Missouri and was arrested by police. I take note of the attackers' names, but find little else of use. A search on Harrison Weiss also reveals nothing helpful.

I search for myself next, but don't find much except a college graduation announcement from a few years ago. My social media profiles are private, and none of my passwords work. The strangest thing is that I'm using my last name in all of them, not Adam's name as I did in the other timeline. Upon closer inspection, I can't find a single mention of our wedding or any pictures from it. It should have happened by now. I saw pictures of it in the other future. The two of us on a beach, looking happy and free, ready to begin the rest of our lives together. But in this timeline it never happened.

What changed between us? Was it because of what Adam did? Was I never able to forgive him?

"When we get back, I'm going to ask Paige out," Ken says.

My head snaps up. Maybe he saw something in his future he didn't like either. "Oh yeah?"

He leans forward, his brow furrowed. "After what we went through today, knowing how close we were to the end, I don't want to wait any longer. If we only have ten more years before everything goes to hell, I want to spend them with her." He rubs the back of his neck. "I mean, assuming she's interested."

"It's about time. Zahra and I were starting to think it would never happen."

He grins slightly. "Me too. But I'm done making excuses. And you should talk to Adam too."

"Yeah, maybe." I scowl, looking away. My situation with Adam is totally different.

I check my watch. "It's almost time. We should stay in the accelerator for a few hours when we get back to make sure we're not infected."

Ken groans. "I hate that you're right."

"Tell me about it. I'd rather be anywhere but stuck inside Aether."

We hop to our feet and head inside the accelerator to wait for the aperture to open, leaving everything behind except for the wallet. None of the electronics will work once they go through the aperture anyway.

The golden light appears, ready to take us home. I close my eyes as the future vanishes.

SUNDAY

I open my eyes. If it wasn't for the accelerator door being closed, I'd still think I was back in the future. But when the door clicks, I yell, "Wait! Don't open it."

My voice echoes across the metal walls around me, but the door stays closed. A speaker crackles on around us and Vincent's voice asks, "Is there a problem?"

"We don't know if we've been infected or not. Since the first symptom shows up after about four hours, we'll wait in here until then to make sure it's safe."

There's a slight pause. "And if you're infected?"

I swallow hard. "Then I guess you can send us back to the future. Permanently."

Ken gives me a miserable look, then sinks to the floor, leaning back against the accelerator's walls. Settling in for a long wait. "Wish we'd brought a book or something."

"Or a pillow."

"What are you doing?" Adam's voice asks through the speaker.

"Making sure no one in the present gets the virus," I say.

Adam sighs. "Are you okay?"

"We're fine." I slouch against the nearest wall. "Are you?"

"Yeah. Dr. Kapur fixed me up. I should be better after a couple days of antibiotics."

I relax a little, knowing he's okay and only a few feet away. Hearing his voice relieves a lot of the tension in my shoulders. I didn't realize how wrong it felt to be on a mission without him until now. "We'll be out of here soon, and then we can go home."

"I'll be right out here the entire time."

Vincent's voice comes back on the speaker. "You can use these four hours to tell us what happened in the future. Did you get what you wanted?"

I hesitate, debating how much to say out loud. Our deal was that we'd keep him in the loop from now on, but I don't know who's listening or who I can trust. "We got something."

"Well, what is it?"

"We found the man who was going to release the virus, and I managed to steal his wallet, but we didn't learn much more about the terrorist group." I pull out the wallet and flick through it again. "His name is Harrison Weiss. He lives in Van Nuys, or at least he will in ten years."

"Got it. We'll see what we can find. Anything else?" Vincent asks.

"We talked to your future self. You…helped us. Gave us supplies and a new map. Then you said you were heading up to Napa to wait out the storm. Since we told you about the virus, you had plenty of time to prepare."

There's a pause before he answers. "Good to know."

After that, there's nothing to do but wait and see if we're dying. I'm so tense that every muscle in my body aches, and I can barely breathe under the tight metal dome that seems to keep getting smaller and smaller. Ken seems a lot more relaxed, lying on the floor and staring at the ceiling. I don't know how he can be so calm, but then again, waiting has always driven me crazy.

About halfway through the four hours, I get up and start pacing, until Ken tells me to quit it. After that, I sit down again and study Harrison's wallet for the tenth time, as if some new clue will reveal itself. I play with my unicorn necklace and worry about my relationship with Adam. I think through the news articles on the White Outs, wishing I'd been able to get more info. I mentally list the symptoms of the virus over and over in my head and begin to overanalyze everything. Is that twinge in my neck from sitting funny, or because I'm infected? Ken just coughed. Does that mean he's sick?

Finally our prison sentence is up and, with no signs of a nose bleed, we're released from the accelerator. I step outside with a relieved sigh, and Adam throws his arms around me. I hug him back carefully, making sure not to touch his wounded side, even though I want to squeeze him tight and never let him go.

"Thank God you're okay," he says, touching my cheek.

"I'm fine. And very ready to go home now."

"Me too." We break apart, and he nods to Ken. "Glad you're both okay."

He clasps Adam on the shoulder. "Told you we'd make it back safely."

"So you did," Vincent says. "Congratulations on a successful mission."

"Did you find anything on Harrison Weiss?" Ken asks.

"Nothing of interest so far. We'll let you know."

Beside him stands a woman in all black with her arms crossed, a dark ponytail on her head. Nina.

"What's she doing here?" I ask.

Vincent gives me an exaggerated look. "She works here."

Nina returns my look. How long was she out here? Is she the one who shot Adam? She matches the body type, she'd know how to avoid cameras, and I'm pretty sure that's a gun on her hip. But why would she come after us? Is she trying to get back at Vincent or double-cross him somehow? Or did she visit the future and learn something that made her think the only way to stop what will happen is to kill us?

I catch Dr. Walters's eye, from where he stands at the back of the room, but he just shakes his head. I make a note to talk to him alone sometime to see what he knows. And why he's helping Aether.

* * *

Dr. Kapur wants to run tests on us, of course, but we can't get out of Aether fast enough. Ken and I don't have the virus, and we've time traveled enough to know we won't suffer any other problems, so there's no reason for us to stay.

Back at the apartment, Adam crashes on the couch with Max on his lap. I pull the brown leather wallet out of my jeans and toss it to him.

"So what really happened there?" Adam asks as he goes through the wallet.

I sink beside him onto the couch, running my hand over Max's fur. "The truth? It was horrible. Walking around the mall, knowing all the people there were going to die, and there was nothing I could do to stop it, and that by being there I might be a victim too…" I shake my head, unable to go on.

"I can only imagine. But you *are* doing something to stop it." He holds up the wallet. "How'd you get this?"

I give Adam a quick rundown of everything that happened, from chasing down the wrong guy, to checking this man's backpack, then fighting him and taking his wallet. When it's over, I lean my head against his shoulder. "I was terrified the whole time that I was infected and didn't know it. I've never felt so powerless in my entire life."

"If you'd gotten infected...I don't know what I would have done." He rests his head against mine. "I was so worried about you the entire time you were gone. It took every ounce of willpower not to run after you into the accelerator."

"I'm glad you stayed behind. It was easier knowing you were safe."

He runs his fingers through my hair. "I got a taste of what you must have felt when I was missing. You were only gone for minutes, but it felt like an eternity. I couldn't breathe the entire time. And I was gone for hours." His hand slides to my cheek, and he turns my face toward him. "I'm so sorry, Elena. If I could go back and undo it all—"

"Then we wouldn't know about the virus." I search his eyes, and then my gaze dips to his mouth, so close to mine and so familiar. The urge to kiss him is strong, along with the desire to forgive him and put this past us, but I'm not ready yet. I pull away instead. "How's your side?"

Disappointment flashes on his face, but then he shrugs. "It hurts, but I'll heal." He flips open the wallet and riffles through it. "There's not much in here."

"I know. His phone would have been more useful, but I didn't find it on him."

He holds up the driver's license, examining it closely. "I'm surprised you told Vincent his name."

"I wasn't going to, but then I thought, why not? Maybe he can find something we can't."

Adam grabs his laptop and searches for the guy's name online. We scroll through Facebook profiles and Twitter accounts, but none of them look like the guy I confronted. Either he's really private, or his driver's license is fake and we'll never be able to find him.

I'm about to give up, when Adam says, "Hang on. I found something on LinkedIn."

"People still use that?"

"Yep. A guy with his name works for some pharmaceutical company I've never heard of, called Aceso Pharmaceuticals. It's out in the valley, near where his address is in the future."

"A pharmaceutical company?" I lean forward to look over his shoulder. "They could be the ones who create the virus. We should head over there tomorrow and check it out."

Adam's eyebrow arches us. "And then what?"

"We'll see if this Harrison Weiss is the same one I met in the future. If it is, we can follow him. See who he's working for and what they're doing." I spread my hands. "Do you have a better idea?"

"Unfortunately, no." He sighs and closes the laptop. "I just feel like we're grasping at straws here."

"Me too. But we have a name and a place where he might work. It's a start." I don't say my next thought out loud—that if we can't find the right Harrison Weiss, then Ken and I risked our lives in the future for nothing.

MONDAY

I head to class in the morning and try to pretend my life is normal and that I'm not thinking about mysterious shooters, neo-Nazi terrorists, or the upcoming demise of civilization. My grades are going to suffer this semester since staying focused is nearly impossible at the moment. I'll do the best I can though. I spent most of my life worried I'd never make it to college, and I don't want to waste this opportunity. Besides, I saw my graduation announcement in the future, so I must get through this somehow.

After class, I pick up Adam, who's slept away most of the day, thanks to the powerful antibiotics Dr. Kapur put him on. I study him closely as he gets into the car. He's moving carefully, like his side is still hurting him, but his color is better. He's wearing a dark suit with a gray tie, he's shaved his face, and his hair has been tamed. I've never seen him in a suit before, and it's hard to look away from the handsome, confident man in front of me.

"You look nice," I say. "Going somewhere special?"

He adjusts his tie with a grin. "Maybe I just wanted to look good for you today."

We drive over the hill into Van Nuys to check out the address on the man's driver's license first. A quick scan of the last names at the apartment building shows this is probably a dead end. Harrison must not be living here yet.

Our next destination is Aceso Pharmaceuticals. I pull into the parking lot of a run-down strip mall with a doughnut and kabob shop, a shoe repair place, and a dry cleaner. "Is this the right address?" I ask, as I turn off the car.

"Yeah. I think it's on the second floor," Adam says.

I lean back and survey the place. "Now what?"

"I came up with a plan while you were gone." He holds up a folder he brought with him. "I'm going in."

"By yourself?" I already hate this plan.

He rolls his eyes. "Yes, by myself. I printed out my résumé, and I'm going to ask if they have any positions available right now. They'll probably say no, but maybe I'll learn something about them or get a glimpse of this Harrison guy. That way I can confirm whether it's him or not."

I grab the folder from Adam and open it up, then scan the paper inside. I have to admit, his résumé is pretty impressive. He graduated from college with degrees in biochemistry and molecular biology by the time he was eighteen, interned for three years for some of the biggest pharmaceutical companies around, and even volunteered at a children's hospital for two years. He probably could get a job at a place like this, if he wanted.

I close the folder and hand it back to him. "Just be careful."

He leans over and presses a soft kiss to my cheek. "I will."

He gets out of the car, brushes off his suit, and then heads for the stairs to the second floor. I watch him and touch the spot on my cheek where he kissed me, then clutch my origami unicorn pendant. He's going to be fine, I tell myself. Nothing bad is going to happen.

I keep an eye on the parking lot while he's gone, watching out for Harrison Weiss or the woman in black. The minutes tick by, and I begin to worry something's gone wrong. Dozens of scenarios play through my head about what might have happened to Adam, each more ridiculous than the next. For all we know, this place is full of neo-Nazis bent on destroying the world, and Adam just walked in there without any protection.

After forty-five minutes he steps outside, and relief flows through me. He slips back into the car and closes the door, then turns to me. "Well, that was a bust."

"What happened?"

"After making me wait for thirty minutes in their lobby, I found out they're not hiring right now, but they said they'd keep my résumé on file. I didn't get a glimpse of Harrison Weiss. And I found out they make diabetes medicine."

All the breath rushes out of me. "Another dead end."

"Maybe. He might still work there, but even if he does, I don't think they're involved with any neo-Nazis or the virus. At least, not yet anyway." He glances over at the doughnut and kabob place. "I haven't eaten all day. You want something?"

"Sure."

We head into the small shop, which does in fact sell both doughnuts and kabobs. A strange combination, but it works for some reason.

As the guy behind the counter rings us up, the door chimes and a man walks in. He's wearing a polo shirt, has medium-brown hair, and is average height and weight. The kind of guy who blends in easily and is perfectly forgettable.

Except that I've seen him before.

His head isn't shaved. He doesn't have a beard. There's no swastika tattoo on his arm. But it's definitely the same guy.

"Hey, man," the guy behind the counter says. "The usual?"

"Please," Harrison says.

I give Adam a sharp nudge with my elbow, and he looks over at the guy. His eyes widen, and he glances back at me. I nod and wonder what we should do, feeling awkward and way too visible. But the man completely ignores us, and we step outside without him giving us a second glance.

Once we're back in the car, Adam asks, "That was him, right?"

"Yeah, it was. He looks a lot different though." I rest my hands on the steering wheel, but they're shaking. His menacing voice comes back to me. *You stupid girl. You have it all wrong.* It's hard to believe that guy is going to become the man I will face in ten years, but somehow, he will.

"Okay. This is good." Adam stares out the window as Harrison heads back up the stairs to the office. "We know where he works now. We can wait 'til he leaves and then follow him home."

We dive into our food and then wait. The sun goes down. Cars pull in and out of the lot. We change stations on the radio over and over. Until finally, Harrison Weiss walks out of the office and gets into a white sedan.

I start up the car. "Here we go."

I trail behind him at a safe distance, and within fifteen minutes, he pulls into a parking space of a small apartment building. Unlike our building, there's no lobby or gate, and anyone can walk right up to each apartment's door. We park a safe distance away on the street and watch as he unlocks one of the apartments and slips inside. Lights flicker on, and he appears at one of the windows, then opens it to let in some air.

We get out of the car and move closer, sticking to the shadows and avoiding streetlights. Once we're close enough, we catch a glimpse of Harrison sitting on a couch, watching TV with a beer in his hand.

"What do we do now?" Adam asks.

"I don't know." I study the man for another minute. "I guess I thought we'd find something more. Some connection to the White Outs. Some clue he's a neo-Nazi. Or some hint he's working on the virus."

"Maybe he hasn't gotten involved in any of that yet."

I drag a hand through my hair. "There has to be something. We can't watch this guy for the next ten years."

Adam's face is grim. "We might have no other choice."

"We could get Paige to break into his apartment to look for evidence. She's good at that stuff."

He shakes his head. "We agreed not to involve our friends yet. And I'd rather not resort to breaking the law unless we have no other option."

"Could you get into his office somehow?"

"Probably not. It'd be pretty suspicious if I showed up again so soon."

A dark thought occurs to me. "We could just…kill him."

Adam looks at me like I've gone mad. "What? No."

"Think of all the lives it would save. We'd be changing the future for the better."

His voice rises, his face incredulous. "And destroy our only link to the White Outs. Not to mention, we'd be killing an innocent man."

I set my hands on my hips. "Innocent? In ten years that man is going to help release a virus that will kill millions of people. He may be innocent today, but he's going to be a murderer soon."

"We can't condemn him for something he might do in the future. Remember when everyone thought you were going to become a murderer too?"

"This is different! I was *there*, Adam. I saw the way he looked at that black family. I found the virus in his backpack. I even spoke to him about it." I'm shaking again, remembering that moment like it's happening right now.

Adam sighs. "Right now he's just a lonely guy with a crappy job who's trying to unwind after work. He hasn't done anything wrong yet. Until that changes, there's nothing we can do but watch and wait."

"Dammit!" I stomp back to the car, my shoes tearing at the grass under me. I hate that Adam's right and that we're out of options again. Desperation and frustration are warring for control of me, and everything we do seems to end in a dead end. We have to do *something*. But what?

* * *

We're halfway back to our apartment when Adam's phone gets a notification. He pulls it out of his pocket and frowns at the screen, his eyebrows drawing together.

"What is it?" I ask.

"The smoke alarm's gone off at the lab. Probably a false alarm, but maybe we should check it out. Just in case."

My fingers tighten around the steering wheel. "Maybe Ken's working late?"

"I'll text him and ask."

I switch direction to head toward Adam's lab, although my gut twists at the idea. His lab represents everything causing distance between us. He hasn't been there since he was shot, and I thought he might have finally broken free of genicote's clutches.

Adam's phone buzzes again, and he lets out a long, strained breath. "Ken's not at the lab."

Uh-oh. "Then we need to be careful. This could be a trap."

He stares out the window, his knee bouncing slightly. "It's possible, although the lab's security alarm didn't go off. I would have gotten a notification."

I open my mouth to reply, but as soon as we turn onto the street, it's clear there is something wrong. Thick, black smoke rises from the lab and sirens blare nearby, getting closer and closer. Two fire trucks show up in front of the building at the same time we get there. Adam makes a choking sound as I throw the car into Park, and then we both jump out, running for the smoking building.

We're stopped by a firefighter in his full gear. "You can't go in there!"

Adam's eyes are wide, and he gestures frantically. "That's my lab! All my work is in there!"

"And we're going to put out the fire as fast as we can. For now, we need you to stay put." He gives us both a stern look and turns back to his team.

Adam starts forward again, but I grab his arm and yank him back. "There's nothing we can do."

His mouth falls open, but no sound comes out. He shakes his head, his face as pale as the moon above us.

We're forced to stand at a safe distance and watch while a dozen firefighters shout orders to one another, grab a long hose, and head for the building. They have to break down the door to get inside, and then they vanish into the smoke.

I wrap my arm around Adam, and he leans against me. I can only imagine how awful this must be for him, to watch all his hard work go up in flames, not knowing if any of it will make it through the night—or who's responsible. Even though I wished he would spend less time in the lab, I never wanted this.

* * *

It's two hours before the fire's out, and another two hours before they'll let us into the building to look around. By then, we've already talked to investigators from both the fire department and the police, but they have no information for us and we have nothing for them either. Everyone seems to know a big, fat nothing about who started the fire or why.

Adam leads the way through the broken-down door into the charred ruins of the building. The lobby's walls are singed, and the smell of smoke clogs my nose, but the damage only gets worse the farther inside we get. We step over debris and broken glass as we head into the main part of the lab.

"My God," Adam says as his eyes take in the destruction. He takes a tentative step inside, his shoe crunching on a broken beaker. "All my research. All my samples. Gone."

The lab is a hollowed-out, blackened husk of what it used to be, almost completely unrecognizable from the sterile white space I visited a few days ago. The fire must have started in here because only rubble and ash are left on the linoleum floor.

"I'm sorry," I say, even though it's not nearly enough.

Adam bends down and sifts through the wreckage. His face is devastated as he picks up a piece that used to belong to a computer, then tosses it aside. He continues like this around the entire room, though I'm not sure if he's searching for anything specific or just trying to salvage whatever he can. When he reaches one side of the room, he pauses for a long time before finally rising to his feet.

"Who would do this?" he asks.

"I don't know." I nudge what remains of a chair with the toe of my shoe. "Do you think they took the cure?"

His empty eyes sweep across the room again. "I can't tell, but I wouldn't be surprised."

"Can you salvage anything?"

"No. Thank God I gave Chris a backup of all my files with some of the vials of genicote, in case something like this ever happened."

"You should warn Chris. Whoever did this might go after him next."

Adam nods, his face grim. "I'll send him a message, but he should be safe. The only people who know about the backups are the three of us."

"Maybe, but we don't know who you might have told in the next thirty years." A piece of the drywall crashes to the ground, making us both jump. "We should get out of here."

Adam's mouth is set in a thin line, but he nods and reluctantly leaves the room with slow steps. It's almost midnight by now, and we're both exhausted and covered in ash, but once we're in the car, I wait to start it.

"I couldn't get into the lab when you were missing," I say. "You changed the security code on the door."

He takes off his glasses and wipes them clean with his shirt. "I changed it after I met with Aether in case they were watching me. I was going to tell you the new code. I just forgot."

"Who else knew it, other than you and Ken?"

"That's it." His frown deepens. "I changed the code to our daughter's birth date, thinking no one in the present would know the significance of those numbers except you and me..."

"But someone from the future might be able to guess it," I finish for him.

That seems to rule out Vincent or Nina, at least. Future-Zahra or Future-Paige are starting to look more likely. I find it hard to believe they'd shoot us though. Maybe we're facing two different threats.

Of course, there's one other person who could do this. "Could it be Ken?"

"I considered that, but he said he was with Paige when I texted him, so it seems unlikely," Adam says. "Besides, he has no motive for destroying the cure when he's worked on it with me for months. After all, he's modifying it to work for Huntington's disease too."

"Good." I didn't want to believe for a second it might be our friend, but I had to consider every possibility.

"The only thing I can think of is that someone stole the cure in order to create the virus, which means the terrorists are already planning their attack…or someone from the future is trying to stop the virus before it's even been created by destroying the cure now."

"I think you're right." I sit up a little straighter. "Maybe we should do the same thing."

Adam glances at me with a weary expression. "What do you mean?"

"We know Harrison Weiss is involved, right? What if we go, I don't know, five years in the future or something. Once there, we can break into his apartment or the place where he works and look for clues. If that pharmaceutical company is the one who stole the cure and developed the virus, we can destroy their lab with all the vials and all the data, just like someone did here."

His eyebrows dart up. "How will we know which year to go to?"

"We can try five years. Then seven years. We'll keep trying 'til we find something. We have a time machine; we might as well use it."

Adam looks at me like he doesn't know who I am anymore. "I can't believe that after all we've been through, you want to go to the future again. Multiple times."

I drag a hand through my tangled hair. "I don't *want* to go, but I don't know what else we can do at this point."

"Assuming Vincent even lets us use the accelerator again, which I doubt, we'd need a much better plan than just picking a time and hoping we find something. Especially since every time we use the time machine our risk of future shock goes up."

"We've been fine so far. We have another year or so until we're old enough for future shock to affect us, which is why we have to do this now. What's our other option? Sit around and wait for the end of the world? Or for someone to come after us again?"

Adam stares out the window at what's left of his lab. "I don't know. And I don't think we should decide tonight either."

He's probably right. We've had a long day, it's past midnight, and he's still recovering. Maybe in the morning we'll have a genius idea for what to do next.

But I seriously doubt it.

TUESDAY

The door opens, and Adam's mom beams at us. "Come in! Come in!" She gestures for us to step inside, and Max rushes forward to bounce at her feet.

"Hey, Mom," Adam says, giving her a hug. "You look good."

She does look a million times better than the first time I saw her, when she was at death's door thanks to the cancer ravaging her body. She's no longer so thin she looks like a twig that might snap at any second, and her hair's grown back in soft waves. Even her skin looks brighter. It's hard to imagine that was a year ago and that the cancer is completely gone now. She was the first person Adam ever cured, although she doesn't know what he went through to save her.

"Thank you, dear." She gives me a hug next. "It's so great to see you, Elena."

"You too," I say, squeezing her back. Parents usually hate me, with my tattoos and attitude, but Adam's mom has treated me like family from the moment we met. I figure it's because Adam never brought home a girl until me.

Max demands Adam's mom's attention, and she bends down to give him a back rub. "Hello, little man," she says. "I heard you're going to be staying with me for a little while."

"Just until our schedules settle down," Adam says. "We're so busy with school and stuff right now, and I hate to leave him in the apartment alone for so many hours."

That's a lie, of course. We both decided Max would be safer with his mom, what with Adam getting shot outside our apartment and his lab getting torched. What if someone breaks into our apartment next, and Max is the only one there? Neither one of us could handle it if the dog got hurt because of us.

"We really appreciate you looking after him," I add.

She straightens up and smiles at us. "It's no trouble at all. Really, you're doing me a favor. I miss having him around. I was just thinking I should get myself a dog of my own now that Adam's moved out."

"That's a good idea," Adam says.

She pats the back of the couch. "Now sit down and tell me everything that's going on with you two. I'll get something to drink."

Great, time for more lies. Neither one of us wants to lie to his mom, of course. But we can't exactly tell her what we've really been up to in the last couple days. Or what we're planning to do next.

Not that we have much of a plan. I don't have class on Tuesdays, so we spent hours debating what to do about Harrison Weiss. The only thing we can come up with is watching him like a hawk for the next few years…or going to the future again. Neither plan is a good one.

While Adam's mom is in the kitchen, his phone rings. He frowns at the screen. "It's Vincent."

"Maybe he has some news," I say.

"Hello?" Adam asks into the phone. I can hear Vincent's voice on the other side but can't make out what he's saying. But from the crease in Adam's forehead that gets deeper and deeper, I'm guessing it isn't good.

"Okay. We'll head over now." He ends the call.

"What was that about?" I ask.

"Vincent wants us to come in. The accelerator's been destroyed."

* * *

The basement inside Aether's building smells faintly of smoke. Flashing red lights guide our way to what used to be the accelerator. Vincent is standing beside the giant hulk of scrap metal, his arms crossed as he gazes into the wreckage. Nina waits against the wall with a blank expression, while Dr. Walters hovers over a computer screen with a frown. The place looks a lot like Adam's lab did—blackened walls, scattered debris, and mangled hardware—but the damage here was contained to the accelerator, as though the fire started within it. None of the desks or other equipment were touched.

Up close, the accelerator looks like a soufflé that has fallen in on itself. The roof of the dome has caved in, and debris is scattered along the basement floor. It's gone—along with our last chance for visiting the future again.

"What happened?" Adam asks.

Vincent slowly lifts his head toward us. "A small explosive was placed inside. Just big enough to blow up the accelerator without harming the rest of the building. We're lucky in that way, at least. None of my employees were harmed."

"Can it be fixed?" I ask, despair running through me.

"Ask him," Vincent says, gesturing to Dr. Walters. "Maybe you'll get a better answer than I did."

Dr. Walters shakes his head, looking as tired as ever. "I'm afraid not."

"You were able to fix the other accelerator when it was tampered with," I say.

"Yes, but that was when Dr. Campbell sabotaged it. She made sure it wouldn't hurt anyone. This…this was done with brute force. It can't be repaired."

"You could build another one," I say, grasping for something, anything.

"Says the girl who destroyed the other one." Vincent shakes his head. "There's nothing I can do to help you. I suggest you take your own advice and start preparing for the end of the world. Or, if nothing else, go out and enjoy the next ten years before it all falls apart."

"Did anyone see who did it?" Adam asks.

"No," Vincent says. "But security tapes show it was the same woman in black who came back from the future with you."

"How did she get in the building without anyone noticing?" I ask.

"I'm not sure, but my people are looking into it."

"Can we see the video?" Adam asks.

Vincent gestures at the woman standing against the wall. "Nina would be happy to show you."

"Of course," she says, but her tone is clipped. She moves to a desk and types something onto the screen. Adam and I move behind her as she pulls up the footage. As we watch, smoke fills the area and renders the people around the accelerator unconscious, much like it did when we returned from the future. The woman in black moves through the basement and steps inside the accelerator, presumably setting the charges. The mysterious woman then leaves the same way she came, but the camera only catches brief glimpses of her through the smoke. Nina fast-forwards the image by five minutes, and then we watch the blast shake the accelerator from the inside, before the domed ceiling crumbles and debris and dust blast out of it.

"Not much help," I say, turning away from the screen.

"Did you find anything about Harrison Weiss at least?" Adam asks Vincent.

"No more than you did, I suspect. Single white male, works for a small pharmaceutical company, lives alone." Vincent spreads his hands. "Until he actually does something suspicious, he's as innocent as you or me."

Except that none of us are innocent. Not at this point.

"You're welcome to look around some more, but I have a meeting now that I can't miss." Vincent gives us a nod and then steps inside the elevator, leaving the ruined accelerator behind. For all I know, it's the last time I'll ever see him. The thought doesn't make me as happy as I once believed it would.

With the accelerator gone, there's nothing we can do but watch and wait, even though it goes against every fiber of my being to do nothing. I need to act. I need to resist. To fight. That's what I am, down in my core: a fighter. But there's no one to fight, and no way to defend against a future that hasn't happened yet.

Dr. Walters moves to stand beside us. "I'm sorry it all turned out this way." He offers his hand to Adam, who shakes it. Then he turns to me and shakes my hand next, his eyes sad. "Take care of yourselves."

We take the elevator back to the parking garage level. Disappointment creeps into my bones, and exhaustion rolls through my blood. My legs must weigh three hundred pounds each as I walk to the car.

I slide into the seat and sigh. "Now what?"

"Now we go see Dr. Walters." Adam holds out his hand. A small post-it note rests inside, with unfamiliar handwriting.

Meet me at my house in two hours.

The smallest flicker of hope lights inside me as I start the car.

* * *

We grab a quick bite to eat and then drive to Dr. Walters's house. After spending an eternity finding a parking spot, we make our way to his front door, through grass that looks like it hasn't been mowed in weeks. He opens the door before we even knock.

"Come inside," he says, gesturing fiercely at us. He shuts the door as soon as we're in his living room. "Sorry. I don't want anyone to see you. You never know who might be watching."

Once I might have thought he was being overly paranoid, but not anymore. "No kidding," I say.

"Where's Armando?" Adam asks, glancing around for Dr. Walters's husband. We met him six months ago, last time we were here, and the house seems empty without his warm, charming presence.

"That's why I asked you to meet me." Sadness flickers over Dr. Walters's face as he leads us to his sofa. We sit down, and he takes an old, brown recliner across from us. "He's in the hospital."

"What happened?" I ask.

"Lung cancer. From his smoking days." His voice is so weak it's hard to hear him. "I always told him those cigarettes would kill him. I made him quit years ago, but it wasn't soon enough."

"I'm so sorry," Adam says.

"Is that why you were working for Aether again?" I ask.

Dr. Walters nods. "There's nothing the doctors can do, they say. I went to Vincent because I didn't know what else to do.

169

I thought maybe he'd know of some experimental treatment or something." He wrings his hands in his lap. "Instead he told me about you, Adam."

Adam sits up straighter. "Me?"

"He said you were working on a cure. That you were close to having it ready. And that all you needed was to go to the future one more time."

"Jesus," I say under my breath. "Vincent knew all this time."

Dr. Walters sighs. "Yes. He convinced me to finish the accelerator for him in return for him getting the cure. But when you came back, you didn't get the answers you were looking for. So he had me send you again. And now the accelerator's been destroyed."

"You should have come to me," Adam says. "I could have helped you."

"You have the cure?" he asks, his eyes widening. "It's ready now?"

"Yes," Adam says with reluctance in his voice. "I wanted to run more tests, to make sure it was safe before I let anyone use it, but if Armando is running out of time, I can get it to you now."

Dr. Walters leans forward and takes Adam's hands, his face relieved. "That is the best news I've heard. Thank you so much."

"I'm glad I can help. I liked Armando a lot."

"I don't know what I'd do without him. He's my rock. He grounds me. Like you and Elena do for each other."

Adam and I glance at each other, and he clears his throat. "I'll bring by the cure tomorrow."

Dr. Walters nods. "In return, I'll help you out as well." He leans back in his chair. "Earlier today it sounded like you wanted to return to the future. Is that true?"

"Yes," I say. "It might be the only way to stop the horrible future we saw from happening."

He lets out a long breath. "I hesitate to tell you this, but…there's another accelerator."

My jaw drops. "What?"

"A third one?" Adam asks.

"Yes." Dr. Walters glances around, like he's worried someone might be listening in or spying on us. "But maybe it's better if you let this go. The time machines I've created have done nothing but bring about death and destruction."

"They also allowed us to save people's lives and right future wrongs," Adam says. "And this time we're trying to save the entire world."

"Then perhaps my greatest invention won't be my greatest regret after all." Dr. Walters sighs. "When I first created the accelerator with the dream of sending people to the future, I designed three separate prototypes, but only the first one was ever finished. Six months ago, you blew up the original accelerator, along with the building it was in out in the desert. But Vincent wasn't ready to let Project Chronos die, even though it got his son killed. While one team worked on the second accelerator in the Aether building, another team built a new facility in the desert, in the same spot where the old one stood. He moved the third accelerator to that facility."

My fingers tighter around the edge of the couch. "He lied to us."

"Of course he did. He wants to keep this one for himself. It allows only a single person to go forward in time, and he plans for Nina to use it, since he's too old to avoid future shock. Of course, that's assuming she hasn't used it already."

I lean forward, my heart racing. "Maybe that's how she went to the future without us knowing. Then she returned with us through our aperture."

"It's possible," Dr. Walters says. "But I don't know if that accelerator is ready or not."

"If not, how long will it take before it's ready?" I ask.

"I'm not sure. I'll need to go there and assess it. Maybe a few days."

"A few days." I exchange a glance with Adam. "That would work."

Adam frowns. "But only one of us can go."

"We'll worry about that later," I say. Except we both know that person is going to be me. Adam might argue with me or try to prevent me from going, but he's still injured. I'll have to return to the future one more time—alone.

WEDNESDAY

Boom.

My gun clicks empty. I'm tempted to reload, but my time is up and I need to get to the valley soon. Paige is already done, chatting with Rob up front, and Zahra's packing up too. I took a little longer today because I wanted to make this practice session count.

I grab my rented gear and head to the front desk. The rows of guns along the back wall catch my eye. I'm tempted to ask about buying one for protection, but not with Zahra and Paige here.

"Take care, ladies," Rob says with a wave as we step outside.

It's another perfect Southern California day, the kind that makes other people jealous of us for living here. But today I can't enjoy it.

"You okay, Elena?" Paige asks me.

I realize I've been standing in place too long while scanning the area for a possible attack. We seem to be safe, so I snap out of it. "Just tired. Didn't sleep much last night."

"Neither did Paige." Zahra nudges her in the side. "Tell Elena where you were last night."

Paige's smooth cheeks flush a pretty shade of pink. "Ken and I went out on a date."

"Finally," I say, smiling for the first time in days.

Zahra laughs. "I know, right?"

I lean against my car. "So how was it?"

"It was really good." A smile lights up Paige's face. "I had no idea he felt that way about me. I just thought he saw me as a friend, but he said he's had a crush on me from the moment we met."

Zahra shakes her head. "It was painfully obvious to all of us."

Paige shrugs. "I've always gone out with guys who made it clear from the beginning what they wanted."

"AKA, sex," Zahra says, making a face.

"All your previous boyfriends sound like jerks," I add.

"They were. But I'm done with jerks now." She stops at her car and smiles at me. "How are things with Adam? He still working all the time?"

"He's been home a lot more lately." It's not a lie. Adam is home a lot now, thanks to his injury and his lab being destroyed.

"Oh good!"

We chat a little longer about school before going our separate ways. I hate keeping secrets from them, but telling them what's going on is not an option right now. There's nothing they can do to help us, and knowing what the future might hold will only prevent them from living their lives happily. If Adam, Ken, and I haven't made any progress soon, then we'll tell the others to allow them to prepare for the worst possible scenario.

Until then, it's better if only the three of us know what's to come.

* * *

I crumble up the hamburger wrapper in my lap and toss it in the backseat. "I wish this guy would do something suspicious already."

Adam takes a sip of his soda. "We might be waiting a long time. It could be years before he gets involved with the White Outs. And you said they weren't in the news for another six years."

I groan and shove another fry in my mouth. We've been watching Harrison Weiss through his windows for over an hour, after tailing him from his office to his apartment, and so far he's done nothing but sit on his ass in front of the TV with a beer in his hand. The most excitement we've had was when he got up to microwave a frozen pizza. If the next few years of my life consist of spying on this guy every night, I might die of boredom before the virus hits.

"How did shooting go today?" Adam asks.

"Pretty good. Although I felt bad about keeping secrets from Zahra and Paige."

"Sometimes we have to keep secrets to protect the people we care about."

I tilt my head toward him. "It's not the same as what you did. Not even close."

"That's not what I meant." He sighs. "Tell me what to do to make things better between us, and I'll do it. I'll do anything."

"I can't. There's no easy fix for this." I toss the rest of my food in the takeout bag, my appetite gone. "You know how hard it is for me to trust people after everything I've been through with my family and foster care. I finally opened myself up to you, and then you betrayed that trust. I don't know how to move past that."

"Then I'll keep trying to win your trust again for as long as it takes." He reaches across the center console and tentatively takes my hand. "I'm not giving up on us."

I don't want to give up on us either, but I can't deny that in most of the futures I've been to, Adam and I aren't together. For some reason we can't seem to make it work long term, even with our daughter in the picture. We're completely different people from different backgrounds, thrown together because of the strange circumstances we've been thrust into. I'll always love Adam, and I know he loves me too, but maybe we're just not meant to be.

Adam's phone rings and lights up the dark interior of the car. "Hey, Chris," he answers, before putting it on speakerphone. "Did you get the genicote for Dr. Walters?"

"No," Chris says. "Someone broke into my house. *My house!*"

Adam's fingers tighten around my hand. "What?"

"Is everyone okay?" I ask. "Shawnda? Michael?"

"Yeah, we were all out of the house at the time, thank God."

"What happened?" Adam asks.

"They destroyed your backups and all the samples I had of the cure."

"No," Adam says softly. All the life seems to drain out of him at the news that his life's work has all been destroyed.

"What the hell is going on?" Chris asks. "First your lab, now this. Who's doing this? Is my family in danger?"

"We don't know," I say. Adam stares out the window with the same emptiness on his face that I saw back at his lab.

"There's something you aren't telling me, isn't there?" Chris asks.

"We have to tell him," I say to Adam, who barely nods. Chris could be in danger now, along with his family. The time for keeping secrets is over. "Meet us at that twenty-four-hour diner near your place in fifteen minutes. We'll tell you everything."

* * *

As we walk into the diner, I check out everyone inside, looking for any signs of trouble. Two people are on an awkward date in the corner. A college kid works on his laptop with a textbook beside him. A tired-looking woman sits at the counter with a milk shake. None of them look like threats, but you never know. It's not paranoia when people are really out to kill you, after all.

I pick a seat in the corner where I can keep an eye on everyone and watch the windows. Adam slides into the booth with me, but he doesn't study the other people here or look for the nearest exits like I do. His brain doesn't work that way, and he's too depressed about the loss of all his research. Good thing I'm here to look out for both of us.

Chris walks in, spots us across the room, and then scoots into our booth. "Hey."

We order some drinks from the waitress. As soon as she's gone, I ask, "What happened exactly?"

Chris scans the room with the same suspicion as me before speaking. "Shawnda and I took Michael to visit my mom. We were gone maybe three hours. When we got back, the place had been broken into, but nothing in the rest of the house was touched. Just the stuff you gave me, Adam. That was it."

"Did you call the police?" I ask.

"No. I wasn't sure if you'd want me to."

"Good. What about the security cameras Zahra installed? Did they get anything?"

"Unfortunately no. I checked them, but all I saw was a dark figure, maybe a woman, and only for a few seconds. Whoever it was got into my house without tripping the security alarm either."

I wish we could narrow down the suspects some more. Future-Zahra could easily hack in and deal with his alarm, since she set it up in the first place. Future-Paige was a master of stealth, and even her younger self is known for stealing. But it could also be Nina, working on her own or for Vincent, especially since he's known about the cure all this time.

"They did the same thing at the lab," I say.

Chris turns toward Adam. "Is that it then? All your research just...gone?"

"Not quite," Adam says. "I have another backup in a storage unit outside the city. No one knows about it but me. It's small and not quite up to date with all my most recent work, but it's something."

Chris nods. "Who else knew about the stuff at my place?"

"The three of us. That's it."

The waitress brings our drinks. All of us ordered coffee, since it seems like it's going to be a long night.

Chris takes a quick sip of his coffee. "I told Shawnda to take Michael and go stay with her parents for a few days. Seemed like the safest move. Now I think it's time you two tell me what exactly is going on."

I run my finger along the rim of my mug. I'm not sure telling Chris anything is the best idea, but he is our oldest and most trusted friend. He's been with us from the beginning, and he has a family to take care of. If there's anyone who deserves to know, it's him.

"We went to the future again," I say.

Chris practically chokes on his next sip of coffee. "You did *what* now?"

"It's my fault," Adam says. "All of it."

We tell Chris everything that happened. The fate of the world. Meeting his son. My trip to the near future with Ken. Everything.

He runs a hand over his shaved head when we're done. "Holy shit."

"I know," I say. "It's a lot to take in."

He stares into his coffee mug for a long time while he absorbs everything we told him. A week ago, we had a party to celebrate the anniversary of our first time-travel trip, but we were also celebrating being done with time travel and Aether Corporation forever. Now we've just told Chris that not only are we not done with those things, but that he and his wife have only ten years left to live.

"Thank you for telling me. About Michael and everything else." He downs the rest of his coffee and slams the mug down. "Who do you think came back from the future with you?"

"It's either one of Vincent's people or Zahra or Paige. Everyone else was dead in the future."

"Why would Zahra or Paige attack you or destroy the data about genicote?" Chris asks.

"Maybe they think it's the only way to stop what is coming," Adam says, his voice glum.

"You said Vincent knows about genicote. Could he be behind the attack on the lab?"

"It wouldn't surprise me," I say. "Except the same person seems to have destroyed his accelerator too."

Chris snorts. "Hard to be sad about that."

I take a long sip of coffee before answering. "Unfortunately, we needed that accelerator. But we've learned there is a third one we can use instead."

He stares at me for a beat. "Please tell me you are not going to the future again."

"We have no other choice. We think we know who is responsible for developing the virus, so we're hoping if we go to the future again, maybe five or seven years from now, we can destroy it before it's released."

"That's a terrible plan," Chris says.

I spread my hands. "We're open to suggestions."

He shakes his head. "I thought we were done with Aether and time travel and all this bullshit. I'd hoped we could move on. But it's going to haunt us for the rest of our lives, isn't it?"

"That's why we didn't want to involve you in this," Adam says. "You have a family to look after. You can put this all behind you."

"Not if the world is going to end in ten years. I can't sit back and let that happen."

"We'll let you know if we need help," I say. "At the moment, there's nothing you can do but look after your family and let us know if you see something."

"All right. But once you have a real plan, let me know." Chris checks the time. We've been sitting here for over an hour. "I should get going."

We pay our bill and then head out into the parking lot. Our cars are parked next to each other. Mine's a little Honda I bought used, while Chris has a big SUV, decked out with all the options and shining silver rims.

"Tell your family we said hi," Adam says, as we stop beside the cars.

"Will do." Chris gives Adam a man hug, slapping him on the back. "Wish we could have hung out under better circumstances, but it's always good to see you two."

"Be careful, okay?" I give Chris a quick hug. "Watch your back."

"You know I always do. Always have."

He turns toward his car, but then he pauses, his eye catching on something behind us. Adam and I both turn to look as a bullet whizzes past our heads and slams into Chris's car.

"Move!" Chris yells, shoving us both aside with his powerful arms. I manage to scramble behind Chris's car, but Adam is slowed down by his injured side. Chris moves to help him.

Another shot rings out. It hits Chris in the chest, making his entire body go rigid, before he stumbles back.

"No!" I yell, my heart lurching into my throat.

Adam and I grab Chris's arms and help him behind his car, which offers some protection from the shooter. But once there, his legs seem to give out on him, and his head lolls. He slides down the side of his car to the ground, leaving a trail of blood across the door.

"Chris?" My voice is high-pitched, almost shrieking. I don't recognize it at all.

Adam rips off his own sweater to press against the blood rushing out of the wound. I glance over the car, looking for the shooter, but the roof is clear. They're gone.

Chris's eyes are glazed, his mouth open slightly. *Oh God, oh God, oh God.* This is so much worse than when Adam was shot. I scramble for my phone and dial 911. But then the phone slips from my trembling fingers as Chris reaches for me.

"Tell..." Chris stops to cough, wincing at the pain. "Tell my family I love them."

"We will." A tear rolls down my cheek.

"Love you guys too," he manages to get out, and my heart twists even more.

Adam clasps Chris's other hand. "Hang on, man. Help is coming."

But Chris is already fading away.

There's nothing we can do but watch as our friend bleeds out in front of us. His eyes go from bright to dim, and his chest stills. A choked sound escapes me, and the tears flow freely, for both me and Adam.

It's not the first time I've seen Chris dead, or even the second, but it's the only time I can't fix it. When he died in the future, I still had hope. I knew I could change his fate. But not this time. This is the present, and there's no going back this time. What happens here is final.

Emotion fills my lungs and I have a hard time breathing. "Oh God, what are we going to tell his family?"

"I don't know," Adam says softly, then wipes at his eyes. His fingers are coated red, and he leaves a streak of Chris's blood across his eyebrow. "I don't know."

The ambulance shows up two minutes later, but it's too late. As people come out of the diner to gawk at the scene; the police arrive and section off the area. Photographs are taken. Chris's body is removed. And we're questioned for hours, for the second day in a row.

When they let us go, we make it back to the car and climb inside, but both of us are such a mess it takes a minute to find our keys. Adam's driving this time, but he can't seem to turn on the car. He just sits there, staring ahead at nothing.

I place my hand over his. "Let's go."

He snaps out of it and glances at me, then inhales sharply. "Where?"

Good question. Our apartment isn't safe. Not if the attacker is willing to shoot us out in public. But we can't go to any of our friends' places either. I won't risk any of their lives.

"Just drive."

* * *

We stop at an ATM and get as much money as we can. Then we drive across town, to some area I've never been to before, and get a cheap motel for the night. It faintly reeks of mold and has sheets with yellowing edges, but neither one of us cares.

I flop onto the bed, and Adam sinks into a chair. We've barely said a word to each other since Chris was shot. Maybe because there are no words. Not for this.

I stare at the ceiling and try to struggle with the fact that Chris is no longer in this world anymore. He was one of my best friends, and now he's just…gone.

Because of us.

The police must have told Shawnda by now that her husband isn't coming home tonight. She's going to be a single mom. Michael will grow up without a father. Exactly what Chris was trying to prevent all this time. And now there's no way to prevent it, because there are no do-overs anymore. The present is permanent. The past is impossible. And the future...the future seems hopeless.

Adam's voice rouses me from the darkness. "It's my fault. All of it. The pandemic. The future. And now Chris's death too."

I roll onto my side to face him. His hair is a mess, his shirt is covered in dried blood, and his eyes are red. God knows when the last time he shaved was. "You couldn't have known any of this would happen."

"Maybe not, but it all comes back to me. I brought the cure back to save my mom. I took the other sample from Jeremy. I rushed to develop genicote as fast as possible. I went to the future to try to make it safe." His voice is haunted, and his eyes stare at nothing. "Now someone's come back to stop me. They destroyed my lab. Then they used Chris as bait to get us out in the open." He bows his head. "He took a bullet meant for me."

I open my mouth to reply, but then I play through both attacks in my head again. He's right. Both times the attacker went for Adam. The first time, I managed to get him out of the way so the bullet only grazed him. The second time, Chris protected him, sacrificing his own life to save his friend.

Adam was the target all along.

"Maybe this attacker has the right idea," he says.

"What?" I sit up quickly. Something in his voice scares me.

He runs a shaky hand through his hair. "If I die now, the cure will never be finished. The virus will never be created. No pandemic. No end of the world. That entire timeline will never happen."

My throat tightens. "What about all the millions of lives you'll save by curing cancer?"

"It's not worth it. Not with the potential for it to be used as a weapon that wipes out billions."

I grab his hand, but he won't look at me. "But that future isn't set. We can still change it. We have time."

"Every time we try to change the future, we only make it worse."

"That's not true. We stopped Lynne. We stopped Jeremy. We can stop this too."

He stands up and begins pacing the tiny room. "I don't think we can. We saw this happen in every future we went to. Every single one. I always make genicote in order to help people, and it always ends up being used as a weapon. And each time we change the future we speed things up, so it happens sooner and sooner." He stops and meets my eyes. "The only way to stop it for sure is with my death."

I've never seen him like this before. Guilt hangs over him, mixed with grief and desolation. He's talking like he's given up completely. Like his own death would be a better solution than trying to fight back.

"No." I stand up and clench my fists. "I refuse to accept that your death is the only way out of this."

"Elena." His voice softens, and he touches my face. "If I have to die to prevent that future and save you and everyone else…so be it."

My heart breaks at the thought of losing him. I rest my hand over his, pressing his palm to my cheek. "No, Adam. I can't do this without you."

"You've always been the stronger one. Once I'm gone and the last traces of genicote are destroyed, all of this will end. You'll be safe again. Everyone will."

"What about Ava?" I ask softly.

"I…" He falters, his eyes full of memories. Ava is the gift we never imaged we'd receive. A perfect mix of Adam's intelligence and my strength. I know he would never do anything that would jeopardize her life.

He buries his head in his hands. "I don't know."

I dig my fingers into his shirt. "If you die, our daughter will never be born. I can't accept that. Can you?"

"No." His breath rushes out of him. "But I don't know what else to do."

I press my forehead against his. "Don't give up yet. Not on us. Not on our future. And not on yourself. Please."

His fingers tangle in my hair, holding my head close. "I don't want anyone else to die because of me."

"I know, but we'll find a way. We always do. Together." I press a kiss to his cheek. "And maybe it's time we got some help."

THURSDAY

Getting out of bed the next morning is the hardest thing I've ever done. I spent most of the night crying or passed out in a tangle of sheets, and when I finally get out of bed, I'm still a wreck. I don't think Adam slept at all. Every time I glanced over at him he was staring at the ceiling with a haunted expression. But once the sun shines through the motel's dingy yellow curtains, I make him get out of bed too. I don't know how we're supposed to move on after Chris's death, but we can't sit around and wait for the shooter to find us either.

I get dressed and eat something from a vending machine, but my movements are routine and I'm not really in the present. I'm stuck in the past, watching Chris get shot over and over again. Wondering if there was something I could have done to prevent it. Wishing there was a way to redo it all.

As much as I'd like to mourn Chris longer, we don't have that luxury. Especially because our friends might be in danger. They need to know what's going on so they can protect themselves, both now and in ten years. And maybe, if we're lucky, they can help us figure out how to stop the pandemic from happening at all.

By the time Adam and I arrive at Zahra and Paige's apartment, Ken is already there. He's sitting next to Paige with his arm draped over the top of the couch behind her. He's not touching her, but he's not exactly being subtle either. As we spread out around the living room, I feel a pang of homesickness for our apartment and for Max. I miss our life before all of this happened, when I thought I was done with time travel forever.

"Is it true?" Paige asked, her eyes glistening. "Is Chris really dead?"

Word travels fast, it seems. I lower my head as grief wraps itself around my heart again. "He is."

Paige buries her face in Ken's shoulder and cries softly, while he pats her back. Zahra simply looks stunned, her eyes wide, her mouth open.

"I can't believe it," she manages to say. "We didn't know Chris as well as you did, or for as long, but he was still one of us."

"His poor family," Paige says, wiping her eyes.

"Was it the same person who shot you?" Ken asks, glancing at Adam's side with a frown.

"We think so, yeah," Adam says. "Both times the person was trying to kill me. Chris…" His voice breaks. "He saved my life."

"What are you talking about?" Zahra asks, her head snapping back and forth between Adam and Ken. "Who's trying to kill you?"

I draw in a breath and begin to explain it all, leaving nothing out from the time Adam went to the future to Chris's death last night. It gets easier to tell this story every time, even though the story itself keeps getting worse. But our friends are our only hope. If anyone can figure out what to do next, it's them.

Paige and Zahra ask questions along the way, and then they fall into stunned silence as they absorb it all.

Paige breaks the silence first. "Why didn't you tell us any of this until now?"

"We wanted to tell you, but we thought you would be safer if you didn't know," I say. "We planned to tell you eventually though." My stomach twists as I realize these are the same words Adam said to me to justify keeping his own secrets. I've done the same thing I've been unable to forgive him for, for the same reasons.

Zahra scowls at me. "We're supposed to be a team. We should have been involved from the moment you got back from the future, if not sooner. Hell, we should have been there to help you rescue Adam in the first place."

"You told Ken and not us. Why did you leave us out?" Paige glances at Ken, who she's scooted away from on the sofa. "And how you could keep this from me?"

"We had no choice but to tell Ken," Adam says. "We needed his help when I got shot."

Ken's head drops. "I wanted to tell you. Believe me, I did. But they made me promise not to say anything, and I agreed with them. It was too dangerous."

"You should have come to me right away," Zahra snaps. "I could have found all sorts of info on this neo-Nazi guy for you or on the place he works."

I lean forward, meeting her stern gaze. "That's why we're here now. We need all of your help because we're out of options. And with this mysterious attacker coming for us over and over, we seem to be out of time too."

Paige stretches out her legs, which end in bright-pink running shoes, and gets a thoughtful look on her face. "What if we break into the place where this neo-Nazi guy works and check if Adam's samples are there?"

"That's illegal," Adam says.

"Barely," she scoffs. "We won't actually take anything. We'll just do a little recon. Maybe Zahra can get into their computers too."

Paige has always been partial to stealing, so it's no surprise she's come up with this idea. Probably why she gets along so well with Zahra, who has no trouble hacking into off-limits computers. I often think they would have gotten along well with Trent, if he survived. He also had a knack for breaking and entering and a disregard for laws and authority.

Zahra grabs her laptop and pops it open. "You've been watching this guy for days, and he hasn't revealed anything yet. It can't be a coincidence he works for a pharmaceutical company. Once I'm inside, I can find out everything."

I hesitate, but there's really no better idea I can think of. "What about the person trying to kill Adam?"

"You can crash in our apartment until we figure out who they are," Paige says.

"I don't think—"

"Trust me, Zahra has this place sealed up like Fort Knox. No one is going to get close to Adam without us knowing it."

I sigh. "Fine. We'll stay here for a few days."

"One thing at a time," Zahra says. "First up, we break into Aceso Pharmaceuticals."

"How soon can we go?" Adam asks.

Zahra's dark eyes gleam. "Tonight."

* * *

We spend the next hour making plans, and then we split up. I head back to our apartment to pick up fresh clothes for me and Adam, along with some other things we might need. The tricky part is making sure I'm not followed on my way back to Zahra and Paige's apartment. I spend an extra hour driving all over the city to make sure I don't have a tail, just in case.

When I get back, the apartment smells like disinfectant or some other strong chemical. Adam and Ken are in the kitchen, wearing paper masks over their noses and mouths while they lean over something on the counter. They're so engrossed in whatever geeky stuff they're doing that they don't even hear me come in.

"Hey," I say. "I got you some clothes and everything else you wanted."

Adam glances at me over his shoulder. "Thank you. I'll change when we're done here."

"What are you doing?"

"Adam's showing me how to make chloroform," Ken says, in the same voice someone might announce they're going to Disneyland.

"Have fun with that."

"Oh, we will," Adam says.

They return to whatever they're doing, but I linger in the doorway and watch them work for a minute. Adam made chloroform with Trent on our first trip to the future too, allowing us to break into Aether Corporation's building. My heart tightens painfully in my chest thinking about all we've lost since then. Adam and I are the only ones left from our original team. Zoe, Trent, and now Chris…all gone, their lives snuffed out way too soon.

How much more will we lose in the fight to save the world?

I leave them to it and take a much-needed shower. As soon as I'm alone, the grief overwhelms me again, and my tears mingle with the running water. I cry so hard that my chest hurts and my sinuses burn. But this time I manage to shake myself out of it. Chris wouldn't want me to stand around crying over him. No, he'd want me to get out there and find whoever's responsible for this. He'd want me to make sure the future is safe for his wife and son. As I shut off the water, I silently swear to myself that I will do whatever it takes to avenge Chris's death and take care of his family.

By the time I'm dressed, Zahra and Paige have returned, and everyone's converged in the living room.

"We're back," Paige announces. "And we've brought pizza!"

"My heroes," Ken says, gazing with fondness at Paige, but she turns away from him.

Zahra rolls her eyes and sets the pizza boxes down on the coffee table, then grabs some plates and napkins for everyone. The guys practically launch themselves at the food, so I guess I'm not the only one who is starving.

"How'd it go?" I ask after we've all served ourselves and settled around the living room.

Paige picks at her slice of pizza. "We didn't find anything suspicious in his apartment. I was super disappointed."

"Did you have any problems?" Ken asks.

"Nope. Breaking into his place was easy peasy. He'll never even know we were there."

I shake my head. "It's disturbing how good you are at that."

She shrugs, grinning at me. "We all have our own skills. Mine happen to be a little bit shady, that's all."

"Was there anything on his computer?" Adam asks.

"Not much," Zahra admits. "I found some right-wing extremist websites in his browser history, but it seems like he's just perusing for now." Her mouth twists into a scowl. "You should see what they say about people like me. I need a serious brain cleanse after looking at that stuff."

"I'm sorry," I say. "That must have been tough to read."

She waves it away. "It is what it is. I've dealt with that stuff my entire life. Anyway, I get the feeling he's testing the waters, but might not actually join up and go full white supremacist for a few years still."

Paige grabs another slice of pizza. "He's like one of those men who shoots up a mosque, and then the neighbors all go, 'Well, he seemed like such a nice guy.' But all along he's been hiding that racist, hateful garbage inside him and it was just waiting to be let out."

"Except he's going to help release a pandemic that takes out the entire world," I mutter.

"Not if we stop him first," Zahra says. "How'd you guys do?"

"Ken and I are almost finished with the chloroform, but we need a few things from the store," Adam says with a nod from Ken. "We can make some smoke bombs too, if that will help."

"Can't hurt," Zahra says.

I wipe my hands on a napkin. "I'm all set. I got everything we needed from the apartment, and no one followed me."

"Good," Zahra says. "I'm going to dig up some blueprints for the building Aceso Pharmaceuticals is in. We'll move around midnight."

We finish up, and everyone gets back to work. Zahra buries herself in her laptop, completely oblivious to anything else going on around her. Ken heads back into the kitchen, with one lingering glance at Paige, who ignores him. Adam makes a list of supplies they need, then sends me and Paige off to get them.

We head to the nearest supermarket and browse through the aisles, grabbing all the household cleaners and other things Adam needs. It's shockingly similar to when Zoe and I did the same thing to prepare for our Aether Corporation break-in. I pause and lean on my shopping cart, overcome with memories of Zoe's shy smile and her bright-blue hair. She was small, like Paige, and scared of dark, enclosed spaces, but she was brave enough to crawl through the air ducts anyway. I barely knew her before she was killed, but we both grew up in foster care and we understood each other in a way that is missing with Zahra and Paige. They both grew up with loving, upper-middle-class families. But Zoe? She was like me. Same with Chris and Trent. They knew what it was like to have the people you love ripped away from you, to live in a new house every year, and to worry about where your next meal might come from. They knew what it was like to live in fear every single day.

I miss them so much. But the three of them are gone, and there's nothing I can do to change that. I have to move on and do whatever I can to protect the friends I still have left.

"Hey," I tell Paige, who's grabbing some granola bars. "I'm sorry for dragging Ken into this before and not telling you and Zahra about it. But don't take it out on him. He cares about you a lot."

She gives a big, dramatic sigh. "I know. I just thought he and I were connecting, that we had something real, and then I find out he wasn't being honest with me."

"I get that. After Adam went to the future on his own without telling me, I was so mad at him. I'm still not sure I can forgive him." I draw in a long breath. "But you should give Ken a chance. He was only trying to help us out."

Paige rests a soft hand on my shoulder. "What Adam did was wrong. But if you were in his shoes, would you have made a different choice?"

"I don't know," I admit.

"You did the same thing to me and Zahra by keeping us out of the loop for our protection. I forgave you anyway, and Zahra did too, because we both know you were only doing what you thought was best."

"That was different," I mutter.

"Was it?" She cocks her head, her blond ponytail twitching. "All I'm saying is, we've all made mistakes. But our motives came from a place of love. That has to count for something."

I open my mouth but don't know what to say. She steps forward and gives me a tight hug, and I hug her back just as hard, emotion clogging my throat.

When she steps back, I wipe at my eyes and give her a fake scowl. "Why are you so damn nice all the time?"

She gives me a wink. "Mainly because I know it makes you and Zahra crazy."

* * *

Getting into Aceso Pharmaceuticals is a lot easier than breaking into Aether's building was. Paige picks the lock on the front door of the office. I knock out the sole security guard with chloroform, and then Zahra hacks into the security system and wipes out all traces of us. The whole thing takes less than five minutes. It's almost too easy.

"I think we might have over-prepared for this mission," Ken says.

I survey the drab, gray lobby again, just in case. "No such thing."

"Don't jinx us!" Paige tells Ken. She raps on the nearest door-frame. "Knock on wood."

I lead them farther into the office, going first in case there's another security guard lingering around or someone working late tonight. Zahra and Paige are good with guns, but I'm the only one on the team who can throw a punch properly. The office isn't very big, just one hallway with a few labs and other rooms leading off it, and I'm relieved that it appears to be empty and no one's working late.

The others split up to search the different labs, while I remain on lookout. The lack of security makes me think we won't find much, and that this place has nothing to hide, but I could be wrong.

After a few minutes, Adam emerges from one of the labs and leans against the wall near me, his face tired. "There's nothing here. Nothing related to my work, to the cure, or to the virus."

"Not yet, at least," I say. "They might have something in another few years."

"Maybe. But I don't think they're the ones who destroyed my lab."

"What kind of research do they do here?"

"They're working on drugs to treat diabetes. One of them releases insulin through an inhaler or a spray so the person won't have to give themselves shots. Genius, really."

My heart skips a beat. "An inhaler?"

"Yeah, like the kind they use for asthma."

"Show me."

He leads me into the other room, to a cabinet full of small, white inhalers. Nearly identical to the ones I saw in the future in Harrison Weiss's backpack.

I pick one of them up and inspect it. "This has to be it."

"What do you mean?" Adam asks.

"This inhaler thing. It's very similar to the ones Harrison Weiss had the virus in."

"Hmm." He picks one up. "There's nothing dangerous in these inhalers now, but perhaps in a few years they're used to release the virus instead."

"When we go to the future again, we can check. Now we have something to look for."

"Guys, I found something," Zahra yells.

I pocket one of the inhalers, and we head over to the lab she's in. Paige and Ken walk in a step behind us.

"What is it?" Paige asks.

Zahra's face is grim. "I tapped into this place's finances to see who was funding it. Took some digging, but then I found it. The number one contributor is Vincent Sharp."

My stomach starts to free-fall. The world narrows to a sharp point, an arrow pointing to the truth. And it all leads back to Vincent. "Are you sure?" I ask.

"It makes sense," Paige says. "Vincent's wife had diabetes before she died." When we all turn to her, she shrugs. "Jeremy told me once. My dad has it too."

"Vincent's behind it all," I say, even as I struggle to believe it. But it all makes sense now. I hold up the inhaler. "We found this in the other lab. It's nearly identical to the one I saw in the future on Harrison Weiss."

Paige gasps. "You think Vincent is responsible for the virus in ten years?

Adam's face has gone pale. "He knows about genicote. He knows about the virus in the future. He knows we were looking at Harrison Weiss." He looks up and meets my eye. "You're right. It has to be him."

"Hang on," Zahra says. "I dislike Vincent as much as anyone, but we don't know if he's involved yet."

"Yes, we do," Ken says. He's gripping the table in front of him like he might fall if he lets go. "Oh God."

Paige is immediately at his side. "Are you okay?"

He looks up at her. "I—I have to tell you something. Something bad. Something that will make you look at me differently."

"What are you talking about?" she asks.

"I've done something terrible." He sinks down into an office chair and buries his head in his hands. "I've been working for Vincent for the last couple months."

My jaw drops. "You what?"

"What do you mean, working for him?" Adam asks.

Ken looks up at us with grief-stricken eyes. "From working with Adam, I knew genicote could be the key to stopping Huntington's. Vincent offered me funds and supplies to try to create a cure for Huntington's disease, and I said yes. Not only because I know I'll die from it in twenty years, but because my mom is dying from it right now. She doesn't have much time left. Even if she's cured now, she won't be the same, but at least she'll be alive. I didn't want to work with Vincent, not after what we all went through, but to save my mom, I didn't have any other choice."

Adam's motivation for stealing the cancer cure from himself in the future was similar—to save his mother's life. But that action triggered a chain of events that resulted in the deaths of Trent and Zoe and almost led to mine and Chris's too. Now Ken's decisions have led him down a similar spiral, all in the name of saving someone he loves.

"Why didn't you tell me this?" Adam asks. "I could have helped you."

Ken bites his lip, looking away. "The last few months you've been uh...kinda difficult. Every week you became more and more obsessed with creating the cure. I didn't want to get in the way of that...but I also saw you starting to fall apart. I thought it might be better to keep this to myself until you got yourself together again."

"But why would Vincent help you out like that?" Zahra asks.

"In return for my research, Aether would retain all the rights to the drug and would be able to sell it. They'd have a monopoly over the market because no one else has anything like it. I don't care about the money though. I just want to save my mom. I want to live past the age of forty. And I want to make sure I can have kids one day without worrying about them getting this horrible disease too." He looks at Paige and swallows.

"Why didn't you tell us?" Paige asks.

"I knew none of you would be happy about me working with them, not after what happened with Jeremy and our last trips to the future. But Vincent seemed different after his son's death, like he wanted to make a difference in the world and put the time-travel thing behind him forever." He sighs. "But I was wrong. He hasn't changed at all."

I thought Vincent had changed too. He acted like he cared about Adam, and the fate of the world, and his people in the future, but he had us all fooled. The only one he cares about is himself. "We've all made mistakes with Vincent," I say, since I'm just as guilty as Ken is. "But what does this have to do with the virus?"

He meets my gaze with haunted eyes. "Because I've done something terrible. Something I didn't realize was bad at the time, but now, after learning the truth about this place and Vincent..." He trails off and shakes his head.

"What is it?" Paige asks.

"Were you the one who destroyed Adam's lab?" I ask. "Or the backup at Chris's place?"

"No! Why would I do that?" He glances around at all of us, his eyes pleading. "Come on. You know that wasn't me. I'd never destroy Adam's research."

Zahra crosses her arms. "Then what's this terrible thing you did?"

His head drops. "I brought the virus back from the future."

"You did *what*?" I ask. "We both agreed that was a bad idea!"

"I know. I know. And I felt really bad about it, but Vincent had already convinced me to do it."

"Of course he did," Zahra mutters.

Ken holds up his hands in surrender. "Just let me explain. Please."

"We're listening," Adam says with a frown.

"When you told me about the zombie-like people you encountered in the future, the symptoms sounded a lot like an advanced case of Huntington's disease. I began to wonder if the pandemic you said wiped out the world was actually caused by *me*. Not Adam. When the opportunity came to visit the future with Elena, I thought I might be able to find out the truth." He rubs the back of his neck.

"Before you two arrived at Aether that day, Vincent pulled me aside. He said if I got the virus and brought it back, we could work on a way to stop it before it became a problem. We'd find a cure or a vaccine now, so that the pandemic never happens."

"I waited for you in the car for almost thirty minutes," I say, thinking back to our time in the future. My fists clench at my side. "You got the virus then."

He nods. "It was easy. You knocked the guy out, and his backpack was right there. I grabbed the five canisters he had and brought them back to the present with me."

"Are you crazy?" Paige asks. "You could have gotten yourself killed! Or spread the virus yourself! What were you thinking?"

"I thought I was doing the right thing. I only wanted to find out how the virus was created and then find a way to stop it. That's all. I swear!"

I shake my head and turn away, too upset with him to even look at him anymore. His actions have jeopardized not just our lives, but the lives of everyone in the world. Maybe he did it with good intentions, but that doesn't excuse what he did or how he betrayed us.

Adam stares at Ken over his glasses, his arms crossed. "Did you get a chance to study the virus?"

"Yes, but as you suspected, it's a modified version of genicote," Ken says. "It has nothing to do with Huntington's disease after all. And as far as I can tell, there's no way to stop it."

"And now Vincent has it," I practically growl.

Ken swallows. "Yes. I'm sorry."

"What about the White Outs?" Paige asks. "Were they ever a real thing? Or was all of that another lie?"

"They're real," I say. "Or they will be in a few years. I saw lots of news articles on them when Ken and I were in the future. And Harrison Weiss was definitely one of them."

Zahra frowns. "Assuming Vincent really is behind the virus, he probably used them to release the virus. He knew the media would be all over it."

"And he knew we'd be in the future asking questions," Adam says. "He knew we'd find out who released the virus and would try to stop them. The White Outs were the perfect cover."

"We told Vincent too much about the virus and about the future," I say with a sick feeling in my stomach. "We gave him everything he needed to prepare to destroy the world and then set himself up as a leader of it. This is all our fault. And now he has the virus a lot sooner than he did before."

"But why would he want to release a virus that would wipe out most of the population?" Paige asks.

Adam tilts his head and frowns. "Money? Power? Revenge for his son's death?"

"Maybe all of the above," I mutter.

"We need to get the virus," Zahra says. "And then dispose of it somehow."

"I can get us into the other lab," Ken says. "It should be empty now since it's after midnight."

I'm already heading for the door. "Let's go."

Paige sighs. "Guess we didn't over-prepare after all."

FRIDAY

The building Ken takes us to is generic, with white walls, tinted windows, and no signs except the street number. If you were driving by, you'd never think twice about it—which I'm sure is the point.

Ken uses a security badge to get inside the building. Two guards are waiting behind a desk inside the lobby. One of them stands as we walk in.

"Hey, Ken," he says. His voice is warm, but he eyes us suspiciously. "Working late tonight?"

Ken flashes a casual smile. "Yep. Brought some other scientists to help me."

The guard nods slowly. "They'll have to sign in."

"No problem." Adam steps forward, but instead of reaching for a pen to sign in with, he tosses one of the smoke bombs he made with Ken. It hits the ground, and thick plumes of smoke immediately begin to hiss out of it, filling the lobby with a terrible stench.

The guards shout, but I'm already on the nearest one, jamming the chloroform against his mouth. Using her old gymnastic skills, Paige launches over the desk and lands on the guard behind it, then attacks him with her own chloroform.

As soon as the guards are down, Zahra takes care of the security system on their computer. I check the guards quickly, but they don't have any guns on them. Dammit. Even though Ken insists this place isn't heavily guarded, I want to be prepared for anything.

Ken swipes his badge to let us into the elevator. "This way."

We follow him down a long, bland corridor until he comes to a door in the back, which his badge opens with a soft beep. Inside, we find a lab strangely similar to Adam's with computers and equipment, except there's a lot more of it. Low fluorescent lights buzz over us, but none of the computers are on. Rats scurry in cages along one wall. A door is open on the other side of the room.

"The canisters with the virus are in there," Ken says, taking a step toward the door. "But it should be locked..."

Beyond the door is an antechamber with thick, see-through walls covered with biohazard signs and other warnings. Behind that is a room with half a dozen large stainless-steel refrigerators. Vincent, Nina, and Harrison stand in the middle of them, like they were in the middle of a discussion before we walked in.

Any doubts about Vincent being involved in the pandemic vanish at the sight of the three of them together. Especially when I see what they're holding—the canisters full of the virus.

Ken rushes forward toward. "What are you doing here?"

Vincent turns toward us and raises his eyebrows. "This is my building. The better question is, what are you all doing here? Except I'm pretty sure I already know." He jerks his chin at Nina, who points a gun at us.

"Move," she says.

I glare at her, but without a gun of my own, there's not much I can do. She shifts the five of us back into the main room of the lab, and Vincent and Harrison follow behind her. We're forced to stand off to the side, while Nina trains the gun on all of us, her face expression-less. I debate whether I can get it away from her before she can shoot one of us, but it's too risky. We'll have to find another way out of this.

Adam steps forward, raising his hands. "Vincent, the virus is dangerous. Having it here in the present is too risky. We need to destroy it."

"Oh, Adam. Always trying to save the world." Vincent shakes his head. "I can't let you destroy the virus. I have big plans for it."

Dread settles in my stomach. "You're the one behind the pandemic in the future, aren't you?"

He gives me one of his charming smiles, like he's pleased we finally figured it out. "I don't know for certain, of course, but it's in line with things I've been planning for months now."

"But...why?" Paige asks. "Why would you do something like that? All those lives lost..."

"For profit, of course." That charming smile turns sick, twisted, and downright evil. "The goal was to develop a virus along with the cure for it. We'd secretly release the virus when we were ready, and after a few weeks of it wiping out hundreds of thousands of people, the world would be desperate for a cure. We'd be saviors. And a whole lot richer."

My God. Rage courses through my body, and I'm tempted to leap forward and attack him, but the gun in my face holds me back. "I knew you were a jerk, but I had no idea you'd ever stoop to something so evil."

Vincent laughs. "Elena, you were always my favorite. And I'm so grateful to you for telling me about what you saw in the future. It's because of you that I realized I didn't have to develop a virus from scratch, or even modify Adam's cancer cure. I could simply have Ken steal it from the future for me."

"But there's no cure," Ken says, his voice miserable. "I told you I didn't think it was possible to make one."

"No, there isn't. Such a pity."

"Is that why you destroyed my lab? Why you had me shot?" Adam asks. "So I couldn't try to create a cure?"

"No, I had nothing to do with any of that. Although I did sabotage the accelerator to make sure none of you could go to the future again to try to stop me. Or rather, Nina did." He flashes her a proud smile. "Like Elena said, she looks a lot like the woman in black who returned from the future with you."

I knew it was her. But if she wasn't responsible for the rest of it, who was?

"But without a cure, your plan won't work," Zahra says. "What do you stand to gain from the virus wiping everyone out?"

Vincent gazes at the canister in his hand. "Do you know why I started Aether Corporation originally? I was young and idealistic back then, like all of you. I truly wanted to make the world a better place. And many of the things Aether invented did exactly that. I founded Aceso Pharmaceuticals for a similar reason—to try to make diabetes easier to live with. Even when I started Project Chronos and had Dr. Walters create the accelerator, I had good intentions. Sure, profit was a large part of it, but I really did think that by bringing technology and information back from the future we could improve people's lives." His fingers tighten around the canister, and his eyes grow hard. "All of that changed when I watched my only son die."

My hands clench into fists. "He tried to kill you!"

"We had a difficult relationship. I won't deny that. But you were the one who murdered him."

"I had to!"

His eyes narrow. "Did you? Or could you have stopped him some other way? I suppose we'll never know."

Guilt flickers through me. Did I have to kill Jeremy? If I could go back and redo that moment, would I make the same choice? I honestly don't know.

Vincent closes his eyes, his face filled with grief. "Even with the power of time travel in my hands, I can't do anything to save my family, the only people who ever meant anything to me." His eyes snap open. "And after losing both my wife and my son, I realized I didn't care about making the world better anymore. Now I just want to watch it fall."

"And set yourself up to benefit from it in the future," Zahra says, her voice disgusted.

"A bonus, for sure. Don't tell me you were never tempted to do the same thing. I know you all looked into your own fates multiple times. You made changes to the timeline to make your lives better. I just did the same thing. On a larger scale."

"That's different," I say. "We wanted to make sure we had a future. You want to destroy it."

"Ah, but from what you told me it, it won't be destroyed, not completely. Just reduced to a more manageable size. And I certainly like the sound of president." He raises the canister. "So no, I don't need a cure anymore. And now that Ken's brought me these canisters, I don't need to wait ten years to develop the virus either."

Ken takes a step forward. "I won't let you do this."

"You don't have much of a choice." Vincent gestures at Nina. "Kill them all." His eyes rest on me one more time before he walks out of the room with Harrison on his heels.

Nina raises her gun, pointing it at Paige. "Sorry, nothing personal."

Ken charges forward with a roar, and Nina jerks her gun toward him. It goes off right as he tackles her. They go down together, and the gun clatters to the floor.

"No!" Paige cries.

Nina flings Ken off her, right as Paige grabs the gun. She fires without hesitation, her aim perfect, killing Nina instantly with a bullet between the eyes. Then Paige falls to her knees beside Ken with a wail. It all happens so quickly that the rest of us barely have time to react.

Ken reaches up and touches Paige's face, his arm weak. "Paige."

"Stay with me." She kisses him softly on the lips, tears streaming from her eyes. "Please, Ken."

Adam kneels beside Paige to inspect the wound, which is bleeding all over the floor. "We need to get him to a hospital."

His eyes close. "I'm sorry. I'm sorry for all of this."

Overwhelming grief cripples me. I should be going after Vincent, but I can't seem to move. I stare at Ken, but I can't tell if he's breathing anymore. My throat tightens. "Is he…?"

"Not yet," Adam says, but the look on his face tells me it won't be long now.

"I've called an ambulance," Zahra says. While the rest of us were in shock, she was on her phone, somehow managing to stay calm. "They'll be here in five minutes."

Adam rips off his jacket and uses it to try to staunch the flow of blood. "That might not be soon enough. It'll take them five minutes just to get into this room."

I quickly scan the lab and find a long metal cart, then rush over to it. The wheels squeak loudly as I drag it over to Ken's side. "We'll put him on this and get him outside. That'll give him a chance, at least."

Working quickly, the four of us lift Ken, trying to jostle his body as little as possible. Blood soaks through Adam's jacket from the bullet wound, and Ken moans as his back hits the cool metal tray. Adam and Paige begin wheeling him out, both of them speaking softly to him and telling him to hold on. Zahra and I follow behind them as they race down the long hallway. At the elevator, I dig through Ken's pocket until I find his security badge, and then we crowd inside around the cart.

The elevator quickly gets us back to the lobby, where the security guards are still passed out. Adam and Paige push the cart out through the tinted glass doors, but Zahra pauses behind the security desk.

"Elena, wait," she says as she stares at the computer screen.

I turn back and look over her shoulder. "What is it?"

On the screen, black-and-white camera images show Harrison and Vincent in a parking garage below the building. "They're still here," Zahra says.

I glance out the windows at Ken lying on the tray, covered in blood, with Paige and Adam beside him, and then back at the screen. There's nothing I can do for Ken, and I don't have time to worry about him. Vincent is getting away with the virus, and we have to stop him. This might be our last chance.

"We can't let them get away," I say. "I'm going to the garage, but I might not make it in time. In case I can't stop them, get the car so you can follow them."

"I will." Zahra rests a hand on my arm briefly. "Good luck."

"You too."

I race back into the building until I find the stairs, then dash down them toward the parking garage. I don't have a clue where Vincent might be taking the virus or what he's planning to do with it, but it can't be good.

As I bang through the door into the garage, Harrison is already getting into a black car, while Vincent approaches another. I run toward them, my shoes slapping hard against the concrete, but I'm not going to make it. As Harrison's car peels out of the garage, I pray Zahra can follow him.

I make it to Vincent right as he's opening his car door. I grab his shirt and spin him around, but he raises something to my face. One of the canisters.

A fine mist sprays over me. I slam my eyes shut and cough, backing away from him. "Oh my God. What have you done?"

"Looks like you're patient zero," Vincent says. "Fitting, really."

Oh God, oh God, oh God. I scrub my face with my hands, trying to wipe off the clear liquid, but it's no use. "You idiot! You've infected both of us!"

"I haven't, actually. When we tested the virus, we discovered certain people were immune. I'm one of them. Unfortunately, you're not as lucky." Vincent smirks, then shoves the inhaler in his pocket and gets in the car. "Good-bye, Elena."

I'm powerless to stop him as he drives away. For a heartbeat, all I can do is stand there, staring at my hands. I *can't* be infected. It's not possible. I have so much more I need to do. Maybe the spray didn't work. Maybe I'm immune too somehow. Maybe, maybe, maybe…

I draw in a shaky breath. But what if I am?

Oh God. I could be contagious right now. I have to go somewhere where I can't infect anyone else. But where?

The lab. The room where they stored the virus should be safe. If I can make it there, I'll wait out the rest of my time locked inside. No one else will die because of me.

I make it back to the lab, step through the antechamber, and then enter the room with the transparent walls. Inside, there's a button to lock the door in the case of contamination, and I take a deep breath and hit it. Lights flash and the door locks with a puff of air, sealing me inside, protecting the outside world from the virus now slowly destroying my body.

I slump against the thick, see-through wall. It's done. Now all I can do is wait.

* * *

Ten minutes later, Adam steps into the lab. His eyes widen when he sees me inside the contamination room, and he rushes into the antechamber. "Elena? What's going on?"

I glance up at him, and my heart twists. I don't know how to tell him that I'm dying and there's nothing he can do about it. "What happened to Ken?"

"The ambulance took him to the hospital. Paige is with him. I came back to make sure you're okay." He tugs on the door, but it won't open. Thank God. "How did you get locked in there? Hang on. I can get you out."

"No, don't!" My chest tightens. "You can't come in here."

"Why not?"

"Vincent infected me with the virus."

"What?" His hands slam against the transparent barrier. "No! How? Are you sure?"

"I followed Vincent into the parking garage, and he sprayed me with one of the canisters. He said he was immune, and then he took off. Harrison left in a separate car, but hopefully Zahra is tailing him now." I drop my head. "I couldn't stop them. I'm sorry."

Adam bangs on the wall. "No, no, no. I refuse to believe it."

"I'm sorry. Locking myself in here was the only way to keep you safe."

Despair fills his eyes as he stares at me. "Elena…"

I press my hand against the wall on the opposite side from his. The closest we'll get to touching for the rest of my life. "Go, Adam. You need to stop Vincent. He's going to release the virus."

"No, I won't leave you," he says, his voice desperate. "I'll find a way to save you. I just need some time. There has to be a way!"

"You're the only one who can stop Vincent now. You need to go. Please."

"I can't." The sadness on his face breaks my heart a thousand times. "I don't want a future if it isn't with you. With Ava."

Our daughter. My throat tightens, and a hand involuntarily goes to my stomach. I'll never have her now. Never get to watch her grow up to become that eighteen-year-old girl Adam and I met once. She'll never be born now, all because of Vincent.

My hand drops to my side. I'm going to die. I always imagined I'd go out in a more violent way. A knife or a bullet or a beating. Never of old age. Never of cancer or anything like that. And certainly not like this.

"There's nothing you can do for me now," I whisper. "Please go. Stop Vincent. Then I can die knowing you've saved the future for everyone else."

Adam presses his forehead against the wall, his hands in fists, his face anguished. "I won't lose you, Elena. I can't."

He turns around and heads back into the lab, looking around like he's searching for something. But there's nothing he can do. There's no cure for what's flowing through my veins, and even if it were possible, there's no way he could make a cure in time.

"There must be something here, something I can do…" he mutters as he goes through things on the countertops, throwing papers aside. A beaker smashes to the floor and shatters as he shoves things out of the way in a frantic search.

"Adam, please." My voice catches. I'll never touch Adam again. Never kiss him again. Never hold him again. A tear escapes my eye and slides down my cheek.

"It should be me in there, not you," Adam says, as he tears apart the lab, still searching for something impossible. "This is all my fault. If I hadn't gone to the future, if I hadn't rushed the cure, if—"

I bang on the wall with my fists. "Stop! It's not your fault. And you're going to get through this. You're going to make sure the pandemic never happens. And then you're going to finish genicote and save millions of lives."

He shakes his head. "Even if I could stop the virus and go on without you, I can't make genicote now. Someone is always going to use it as a weapon, and anyone who doesn't have cancer will be at risk." At those words he freezes, and something clicks in his eyes. "Unless…"

I straighten up. "What is it?"

"Vincent said he was immune to the virus, right?"

"Yes. And Paige was immune to the Infected's bites in the future too."

"Of course she was. I can't believe I didn't see it before." His eyes are determined as he returns to the antechamber. "I have an idea, but I need to get some things. I don't know how long it will take. Just…hang in there. Okay?" He presses his palm to the wall between us. "I love you."

I rest my hand in the same spot. "I love you too."

He turns away and dashes out of the room. I slump to the floor, wondering if I'll ever see him again. Fatigue settles over me, but it's not from the virus. It's from knowing the end is coming for me, and there's nothing I can do to stop it.

I wait for what seems like an eternity, drifting in and out of restless sleep, until my body becomes sore from lying on the hard floor.

I get up, exhaustion making my limbs slow, and something tickles my nose. When I rub at it, my fingers come away bloody.

The first symptom of the virus.

I check my watch. It's 5:08 a.m. That makes it about four hours since I was infected. Exactly as Dr. Campbell said. I won't have another symptom for twenty-six hours, but there's no way I can deny it now. I really am infected, and I'm going to die a slow, painful death over the next few days. If I'm lucky, I'll die of thirst or starvation first. Damn, I should have brought Nina's gun inside with me and made it quick. Too late now.

I pull out the plastic bag that held our chloroform-soaked rags, which has one left. I have no idea how long it will knock me out, but I don't care. Anything is better than this slow march to death.

I lie down, cover my mouth and nose with the rag, and take a deep breath. A pungent, sweet smell fills my nose, and my fingers and toes begin to tingle. My vision darkens, and the electrical buzz from the computers and lights fades away.

I close my eyes and succumb to the inevitable.

* * *

"Elena."

Adam's voice coaxes me back into the world. My eyes feel like they're glued shut, but I force them open. A sound comes out of me like a croak. My limbs are stiff and heavy, as if they haven't moved in hours. Everything aches, and every breath sends fire through my sinuses.

I blink until my vision adjusts to the light. I'm still on the floor of the contamination room, but Adam's beside me. He helps me sit up and hands me a plastic cup full of water. I take it and swallow gratefully, but the room keeps spinning.

I'm alive. For now anyway.

Adam slowly strokes my head while I drink. "It's okay," he says. "You're okay now."

It all comes back to me, and I jerk away from him. "What are you doing? You can't be in here!"

"It's fine. You're not carrying the virus anymore."

My mouth falls open. "You mean…you did it? You made a cure?"

"Not exactly." A tiny smile touches his lips. "I gave you cancer."

"You…what?"

"I injected you with live cancer cells. Like I did with mice in the lab in order to test genicote on them."

My forehead throbs, and I press my palm to it. "I don't understand."

"Genicote kept being used as a weapon in the future because it's deadly to anyone who doesn't have cancer. Since the Black Friday Virus was derived from genicote, I thought it might work the same way. That's why Paige and Vincent are immune. I checked, and they both had cancer when they were younger." He helps me to my feet as he talks. "I searched this building and found another lab that was also doing cancer research. After I injected you, the cancer cells and the virus attacked each other, effectively canceling each other out—and when they were done, they left you with nothing more severe than a cold."

I take his face in my hands, my chest bursting with pride and relief. "You did it. You found the way to stop the virus and keep the cure safe at the same time."

He nods, his eyes bright. "All this time I was searching for a way to make the cure safe, but in retrospect it was so obvious. I can't believe I didn't think of it sooner. I'll have to work on it some more, of course, and find a way to modify genicote with this new information, but now I know it can be done. It can be made safe… and we can stop the virus too."

Tears prick my eyes, and emotion clogs my throat. I'm so glad he didn't give up on me or on the cure. "You saved my life. And our daughter's life too."

He pulls me into his arms. "I told you I wasn't going to lose you."

I never thought he would be able to make genicote safe, but he did—and by doing so, he may have prevented the end of the world. "I never should have doubted you."

"You had plenty of reason to doubt me. I haven't been the best boyfriend these past few months. I got too wrapped up in work, and I forgot why I was doing all of this. I made a lot of mistakes, and I lost sight of what was important—our future together."

For the past few days, I've kept Adam at a distance, unsure if I could forgive him after what he did or how I'd ever be able to trust him again. Going to the near future and seeing that we weren't married made me question everything between us, and wonder if we weren't meant to be together after all. But Paige was right—Adam made a mistake, but I've made similar ones. If I'd been in his shoes, I would have done the same thing. And I'm tired of worrying about the future of us. If my near-death experience has taught me anything, it's that I want to be with Adam, now and forever.

I draw in a long breath. "Adam, I forgive you. For all of it."

His eyebrows dart up. "You do?"

I nod. "From the very first time we met, every mistake we've made was because we didn't trust each other or weren't completely honest with each other. I'm just as guilty of that as you are. But from now on, I promise to be honest with you." I tighten my arms around him, gazing up at his face. "Our future is worth fighting for. I'm not going to give up on it. And I know you won't either."

"I won't. I'll never keep secrets from you again. I swear it." His fingers run through my hair as he stares into my eyes. "The only future I want is with you. I love you, Elena."

"I love you too."

Our mouths meet in a slow kiss, full of grief and forgiveness and hope. And, above all else, love. Love for each other. For our friends. For our daughter. And for the promise of tomorrow, which we'll fight for until our dying breaths.

* * *

I pick up Nina's gun on the way out of the lab. I hope I won't need it, but Vincent is still out there, and he has to be stopped. He used one canister of the virus on me, but he and Harrison could have up to four others on them. We've got to track them down before it's too late.

When we get down to the lobby, the sun is bright outside, and the security guards are gone without a trace. I stare at my watch, trying to make sense of the numbers there. It's 6:12 p.m., more than thirteen hours since I got my nosebleed. Was I really out that long?

"Where is everyone?" I ask.

Adam holds open the door for me. "I don't know. I suspect Vincent had the guards clear out after Ken was shot. The entire building's been empty all day, which was good for me at least."

I nod slowly as I step outside. "How's Ken?"

Adam's face darkens. "Last I heard he was in surgery. Paige is with him. She said they're not sure if he's going to make it."

My heart sinks. Ken is responsible for the virus being in Vincent's hands now, but he's still one of us. I don't want to lose him too. "And the others?"

"Zahra's been keeping an eye on Harrison. No one knows where Vincent went. I know he's out there somewhere with the virus, but I was so focused on saving you that I couldn't think about anything else."

I try to come up with a plan as we walk across the parking lot, but the heat rising off the asphalt makes my head spin. I probably need more time to recover from the virus or whatever Adam did to me, but that isn't an option right now. "We can check his house first. If he's not there, we might find some clues as to where he's gone. Of course, he might already be on the way to Napa for all we know."

Adam is about to reply when someone steps out of the shadows in front of the car. A woman, dressed entirely in black, with a hood pulled low enough to cover her face. We jerk to a halt, and I raise the gun, but it feels especially heavy in my hand and my movements are sluggish.

"Stay back!" I tell the woman, aiming the gun at her chest. I hope she can't see how my hand shakes ever so slightly.

Her hands come up, like she's surrendering, showing us she is unarmed. Then she pulls back the hood, revealing her face.

My face.

"Elena?" Adam asks, although I'm not sure if he's talking to me or to her.

I gasp and nearly drop the gun. No, it can't be. Michael told me my future self had been dead for many years. But the truth is staring me in the eye right now. *I'm* the one who came back from the future with us. *I'm* the one who shot Adam. *I'm* the one who burned down the lab. And *I'm* the one who killed Chris.

Her dark hair hangs limp around her face, the way mine gets when I haven't washed it in a few days. Her tattoos are identical to mine, although they've faded, and she's wearing the same origami unicorn necklace as me. She's much thinner than I am, and her brown eyes are shadowed with tight, fine lines. I can't tell her age. I met my forty-eight-year-old self in another timeline, and in some ways that version of me seemed both older and younger than this one.

"Why?" I manage to get out. "How?"

"I'm here to kill Adam," she says, glancing over at him. But she doesn't reach for a weapon or make a move.

The words are too impossible for me to comprehend. *Me, kill Adam? Never.* My fingers tighten around the gun. "Why?"

"To stop the virus and save the world."

"But you…you killed Chris." I can barely get the words out. A memory of the light leaving his eyes as he bled out on the ground flashes through my mind. How could I have done that to him?

Her face is grim, but her tone's not apologetic. "That was an accident. I never meant for him to get hurt."

"And the lab?" Adam asks. He's surprisingly calm, considering she plans to kill him. Maybe he doesn't believe she will do it, but I'm not so sure. I barely recognize myself in this future version of me.

"It had to be destroyed as a precaution, along with everything in it," she says. "The backups too. If genicote is never finished, then the Black Friday Virus will never happen."

Adam sighs. "You're too late. Vincent's already stolen the virus."

"I know." Her voice is so dry that it's barely recognizable as my own. "The timeline changed because I came back to stop you. But I still have time to fix it."

This is *her* fault. She's been two steps ahead of us because she's lived through all of this already, but after she shot Adam, Ken went to the future with me instead of him. By returning to this time period, her actions changed the future, but only made things worse. If it weren't for her, Vincent wouldn't have the cure now, and we'd still have years to stop him—instead of hours.

"We tried to stop the virus." She gazes off into the distance, her eyes weary. "We did everything we could. And when we failed, I tried to dig up information on the White Outs. I found that photo of the man in the Beverly Center and gave it to Michael. But I knew it wouldn't be enough. There was only one way for me to stop the virus from happening—by coming back and killing Adam myself."

"How?" Adam asks. "Time travel to the past is supposed to be impossible."

"It is, but I found a loophole. I time traveled to the future—and then came back with you to the past."

Something clicks in my memory and my eyes widen. "You're me from fifteen years from now. Michael said you died near Aether while fighting the Infected so he could escape."

She nods. "That's what I wanted him to think. Instead I used the accelerator to send myself to the future, to a few minutes before you were supposed to return to the present."

"But how did you avoid a paradox?" Adam asks. "You were both in the future at the exact same time."

Paradoxes are caused when a person time travels to the same moment in the future more than once and meets their other time-traveling self. Dr. Walters explained that when two versions of a person are out of sync with time, it causes instability in the timeline that could reset it or destroy it completely. Because of that, we've always made sure to never time travel to the same moment we did before—except when we returned to the future to rescue Chris and Ken. I almost caused a paradox then when I saw my other time-traveling self, and it felt like I was being torn apart. I barely made it out of there—and that was just from looking at her. If we'd actually interacted, who knows what would have happened.

The other Elena brushes hair back from her face. "I made sure to time it so we had as little overlap as possible, then hid in that basement and avoided looking at that Elena until the aperture opened. After you both disappeared, I waited a few seconds and then followed you into the aperture. I wasn't sure if it would actually send me back with you, but it did."

I understand how she did it, and it proves that time travel to the past is possible under certain circumstances, but I still can't fathom the reason for it. "But…why?" I ask. "How could you possibly think you could kill Adam? Don't you still love him?"

"Of course I love him." Her voice trembles as her eyes fall on him. "That's why I'm doing it. Why it has to be me. He made me promise him I'd be the one to end his life."

Adam's mouth falls open. "I told you to come back and kill me?"

"You did. After Ava died, you were the one who fixed the accelerator. You told me to go back in time and kill your younger self. At first, I refused. I couldn't bear to lose you too." A single tear slides down her cheek, but her face remains hard. "As soon as the accelerator was ready, you killed yourself. You didn't want to give me any reason to stay." She draws a gun from inside her jacket. "And now it's time to fulfill my promise."

"No!" I move in front of Adam, protecting him with my body, leveling the gun at her. She won't kill me. If she does, she might erase herself from existence or cause a paradox or who knows what.

Adam moves beside me, meeting my future self's steady gaze. "Killing me won't change anything now. I know I asked you to do that, but that was before. I've found a way to make genicote safe and stop the virus. The future you lived through isn't going to happen anymore."

She turns the gun on Adam again. "You don't know that. Even if you stop Vincent now, it will only delay the inevitable. Someone will eventually use genicote as a weapon and wipe out the world with it. I've lived through that. I did everything I could to stop it, and I failed. Killing you is the only way to make sure genicote is never created. As long as you're alive, the entire world is at risk."

"Vincent's the one with the virus now, not us," I say, trying to reason with her. "We're wasting time when we should be out trying to find him. You could help us. If we work together, we can stop him. Please."

"Don't worry I plan to take care of Vincent next," she says. "I'll make sure every trace of the virus is destroyed."

"What about Ava?" I ask, my heart racing. "If you kill Adam now, she'll never be born!"

"That might be for the best." The other Elena draws in a ragged breath. "You have no idea what it's like to lose a child. To watch her die in your arms, knowing you're the reason for it, and that no matter what you did, you weren't able to save her... No, I wouldn't wish that on anyone."

I step forward, clutching my gun. "If you shoot Adam now, you'll be killing Ava before she's even born. What if we can change the future and save everyone? Even if there's only a one percent chance of us being successful, wouldn't that be enough?"

She stares at Adam for a long time, and the gun twitches in her hand. I'm certain she's going to lower it, but then she shakes her head. "No. If you'd seen what I've seen, if you'd stood helpless as the entire world fell into ruins, knowing you were the cause of it and that everyone you loved would die because of your failures, you'd understand why I have to do this. If it takes the sacrifice of Adam and Ava to ensure that the rest of the world lives on, so be it."

My fingers tighten on my gun. "I won't let you do this."

Her eyes narrow. "If I have to kill you, I will. I always knew this trip would result in my death, one way or another."

"Sorry, but I'm not ready to die just yet." I pull the trigger.

Her mouth falls open right before the bullet pierces her skull. My older self staggers back, and then her knees give out. She collapses to the cement, her gun skidding away, and she doesn't move again.

Oh God. I just killed my future self.

I drop the gun and sink to the ground, my knees suddenly weak. Adam's beside me instantly, calling my name, but his voice sounds far away. I glance at my other self again, and bile rises to my throat at the sight of the blood leaving her lifeless body. She was *me*. An older me, a different me, one who had memories I'll never have of Adam and Ava and all our friends and a life I can't imagine. Now they're gone forever because I killed her.

Adam's arms slide around me, and I bury my face in his shoulder. He's shaking too, as much as I am, and we cling to each other and try to ride out the shock and pain.

"You had to do it," Adam says.

"I know." In that split second before I pulled the trigger, I knew with utmost certainty that she was about to do the same thing. I knew it because she was me, and I was her. And I couldn't let that happen. "But that doesn't make it any easier."

"No, it doesn't." He sighs. "We need to get going."

I nod. Someone might have heard the gunshot. Anyone could drive by and see the body. And Vincent is still out there with the virus. But I can't move. It's too much. The weight of everything that happened over the last couple days pushes me down, making my limbs heavy.

Adam slides his arm around my waist and drags me to my feet. "Come on. We can't give up now."

He's right, of course, but it all seems so pointless. "No matter what we do to try to prevent the future we saw, we only seem to make it worse. How are we supposed to keep fighting?"

"We keep fighting because the only other option is to do nothing. Neither one of us has ever been good at that."

"But what if Future-Vincent and that other Elena are right, and the end of the world is inevitable? Maybe we should be grab some supplies and find a bunker to hide in so we can ride it out."

He turns toward me with an arched eyebrow. "Hey, I didn't spend all night saving your life so you can sit on your butt while the apocalypse happens. Besides, does that really sound like you?"

I let out a choked laugh. "No, I guess not."

He cups my face in his hands. "We're going to stop Vincent. I know how to cure the virus now. We're going to prevent the future we saw from ever happening. But first, we need to get out of here."

I draw in a deep breath and nod, getting control of myself. This isn't over yet.

* * *

We shove the other Elena's body in the back of our trunk, not knowing what else to do. If we leave her there in the lab's parking lot, someone will find her and then the cops will have a lot of questions for me. Questions I won't be able to answer. We'll figure out what to do with her later, after we find Vincent.

Adam drives toward Vincent's house. My hands are shaking badly, so I clutch them in my lap while the memory of my older self hitting the cement replays in my head. Now that the initial shock has passed, I don't regret killing her, not at all. But even so, that doesn't mean it wasn't a hell of a messed-up thing I just did, and something that will haunt me for the rest of my life.

He glances over at me. "Are you okay?"

I ball my hands into fists to make them stop shaking. "Yeah. Or at least, I will be."

That future version of me lived through terrible things and made choices I can't even imagine. Her life was shaped by death and heartbreak and survival. Once, I would have assumed that becoming her was inevitable. But after changing the future so many times, I know better.

Nobody gets to decide our fate except ourselves.

I grab my phone and call Zahra. She answers on the first ring. "Elena?"

My shoulders relax at the sound of her voice. "It's me."

"Are you okay?" she asks, sounding frantic. "Adam told me what Vincent did to you. I've been so worried."

"I'm fine. Adam managed to cure me."

"He found a cure?" A relieved sigh escapes her. "That's the best news I've heard all day. Any chance he has more of the cure around?"

"I don't know. I can ask. Why?"

"We're going to need more of it soon. A lot more."

My stomach drops out from under me. "What happened?"

"I lost Harrison for a few hours, but I hacked into the police's plate scanner technology, added his license plate, and a hit popped up eventually leading me to LAX."

"He went to the airport?" I ask.

"He did," she says, her voice grim. "And by the time I got there, he'd already started releasing the virus. I couldn't stop him. Then he disappeared, maybe onto a flight somewhere. I'm not sure."

I swear my heart stops at the sound of those words. "Jesus. We're too late."

"We weren't prepared for this. We thought he'd hit a mall, not the airport." Zahra sounds more shaken than I've ever heard her. "There's no way to know how far it's spread already. Hundreds of people could be infected on airplanes right now, flying across the country or to other parts of the world. And I still can't find Vincent. For all we know, he's releasing the virus in other places too."

Adam pulls the car to the side of the road and watches me with worried eyes. "What is it?"

I switch on the speakerphone so Zahra can hear us. "Can you cure more people with those live cancer cells?" I ask him.

"Eventually, yes," Adam says. "But I don't have any more right now. I used everything that lab had to save you, and all of mine were destroyed."

"Dammit. How soon can you get some?"

His brow furrows. "I don't know. It's not exactly something you can buy at the store. We'd need to find the right kind of supplier, and then it would have to be slowly administered over the course of a few hours to each person who was infected."

"It'll be too late by then," Zahra says.

I draw in a long breath. "It's better than nothing. Zahra, you can help us find whatever Adam needs to cure people. I'll look for Vincent. We'll make it work somehow. We have to."

Adam nods. "I'll head to Zahra's place so we can go over everything."

"No!" Zahra says. "You can't come here."

"Why not?" I ask.

"Because I've been infected too."

I close my eyes as despair washes over me. "Zahra, no. Are you sure?"

"It's fine," she says, but her voice breaks. "I'm going to hole up in my apartment and do whatever I can here to monitor everything. For as long as I can anyway."

Emotion forms a knot in my throat. "We'll find a way to save you. I promise."

"I don't know if there's anything you can do at this point. Vincent's probably used his canisters too in some other location. But I'll let you know if I find anything."

"You can contact the CDC," Adam says. He briefly explains to Zahra about the live cancer cells and how they work. "They might not believe you, but maybe it will help."

"I'll call them," Zahra says. "Or better yet, I'll make sure all their computers get an internal notice about the virus and how to stop it. After that, I'll go to the news. I'll make sure everyone knows who started this virus too. Vincent won't get away with it this time."

"Good," I say, but it won't be enough. By the time the authorities and media act on this news, it'll be too late. Thousands will die over the next few days, including Zahra. The virus will spread across the world within a week. By the end of the month, civilization as we know it will be over. And this time none of us had a chance to prepare for it.

By trying to prevent the future we saw, we ended up accelerating it. We thought we had ten years, but in the end, we had less than ten days.

If only my future self hadn't come back with us, we might have been able to fix all of this. But by traveling back in time, she set off a course of events that doomed us all.

I sit up with a jolt. Traveling back in time. That's it.

I turn to Adam. "Call Dr. Walters and ask him to get the other accelerator ready tonight. I know how we can undo all of this."

"How?" he asks.

"By time traveling to the moment we arrived in the future for the very first time. If we return through their aperture, it will take us back to a little over a year ago." My heart picks up speed as I realize what this idea means. "We can return to the past and save everyone. Not just Chris and Ken and Zahra, but Trent and Zoe too. We can stop all of this from ever happening."

Adam adjusts his glasses as he considers. "That might work, except it might also cause a paradox. Remember what happened to you the last time you almost met another time-traveling version of yourself. Your future self could only come back here because she managed to avoid you."

Of course I remembered. I hadn't even gotten that close to my other self, and I'd nearly blacked out and suffered strange flash-backs and symptoms. "Okay, so it won't be one of us. We'll get Paige to go back, since she wasn't with us on that first trip to the future. She's immune to the virus, so she won't accidentally bring it back with her either. She can tell our younger selves everything."

"Except it'll probably be a one-way trip for her."

"Unless she simply goes to the future, talks to our younger selves, and then comes back here."

He taps his fingers on the steering wheel. "Hmm. That might work. But what happens when she returns here? Will the future she arrives to be different? Will we remember any of this? Or will her actions cause a new timeline to split off from this one?"

My head spins from everything he's saying. "I don't know. It's a risk we'll have to take. And even if nothing changes in this time-line, at least we'll know that somewhere out there, other versions of us are going to be okay."

He sighs. "I guess that's better than nothing."

Adam calls Dr. Walters to tell him to get the other accelerator ready, while I text Paige and ask her to meet us. She's hesitant to leave Ken's side, but agrees when I tell her it's urgent. We arrange to meet outside Zahra's apartment so that Paige can quickly grab a change of clothes.

When we pull up outside the building, Paige runs down to the car and hops into the backseat. Her eyes are all red and puffy from crying, but she looks ready for anything.

I turn toward her. "How's Ken?"

"He's in a coma," she says, her voice strained. "They did everything they could, but…" She stops and squeezes her eyes shut. "They don't think he'll make it through the night."

"God," Adam says, resting his forehead on the steering wheel. "Not Ken too."

"I'm so sorry," I say. "But we think we have a way to undo all of this…and maybe even save Ken, Zahra, and Chris. But we need your help, and we don't have much time."

Her eyes pop open. "Whatever it is, I'm in."

Above us, Zahra stands at her window. She gives us a sad wave as we drive away, and I quietly pray that we can save her.

* * *

Our headlights illuminate a place out in the desert that I never thought I'd visit again. Six months ago, Adam and I blew up the original accelerator and the building it stood inside here. The place should have been a pile of rubble and little else, but it's clear Vincent's been busy.

Instead of a five-story office building, it's now only one floor and about the size of a small house. A chain link fence surrounds the property, with No Trespassing signs all over it and barbed wire along the top. There's nothing else around for miles, except the freeway in the distance.

The gate is open already, and two cars are parked inside the fence. Neither one is the car Vincent drove off in, but I'm still wary. Our tires kick up dust as we drive inside.

As Adam parks the car, two figures move outside the house. One is Dr. Walters, wearing his usual white lab coat. The other is Dr. Campbell. The last time I saw her was in the future, leading the Miracle Mile refuge. I'm surprised to see her here, since she helped us destroy the previous accelerator.

The three of us step out of the car into the crisp night air and look around. "It's hard to believe Vincent got all of this built so quickly," Paige says.

Dr. Campbell greets each of us with a quick hug. "It's good to see you all again, even if I never thought I'd be back here."

"Neither did we," Adam says.

"What are you doing here?" I ask her.

"I asked Dr. Campbell to help me, since we're in a bit of a time crunch," Dr. Walters says. "The accelerator is just about ready to go."

"Thank you." Adam glances back and forth between the two of them. "We couldn't do this without your help, and I know you're both risking a lot by coming here."

"When Dr. Walters told me what was going on, there was no way I could refuse," Dr. Campbell says.

The two scientists lead us inside the building. I'm hesitant to enter it again after everything that happened on this spot, but this facility looks nothing like the other one did. Instead of the fancy lobby the other one had, this one has unremarkable gray floors, white walls, and nothing that indicates it's owned by Aether. It's also completely empty.

"The place seems to have been abandoned," Dr. Walters says as he hits the button for the elevator. "I've been coming here over the last few days, ever since we talked, and I've never seen anyone else inside. Vincent must have shut the project down."

"He's got other things on his mind," I mutter.

"Is it true he's got some kind of biological weapon and is planning to use it?" Dr. Campbell asks.

"Pretty much," I say. "And he could arrive at any minute to try to stop us."

She tilts her head. "I knew Vincent had questionable morals, but I never imagined he'd do something like this."

"What have you been doing the last six months?" Adam asks her, as the elevator heads down, below the ground.

"I've been teaching physics at a local community college. It's much less stressful than working for Aether, although not nearly as interesting. I confess, I got excited when Dr. Walters called me and said he needed my help. I don't like Aether's methods or motives, but it felt good to be working on something big again."

"We appreciate your help," Adam says.

The elevator opens to a large subterranean room, as massive as the previous one was. The accelerator is exactly where the old one stood, which I'm sure isn't a coincidence, although this one is a lot smaller. It's about the size of a small shower or closet, clearly meant for one person only.

"We'll need a few minutes to finish getting ready," Dr. Walters says.

Adam touches Dr. Walters's arm lightly and says in a low voice, "I'm sorry I couldn't get you the cure for Armando. I promise I'll retrieve whatever I have left when this is all over."

Dr. Walters pats his hand. "I understand. And if we're not successful today, then it won't matter anyway." He and Dr. Campbell turn toward a row of computers near the accelerator, leaving us alone to wait.

Paige looks at the small accelerator and takes a deep breath. "Remind me again what I'm supposed to tell your younger selves once I'm there?"

"Maybe we should write everything down," Adam suggests.

I find a yellow notepad and start writing. With Adam's help, I warn the original team not to trust Lynne and instruct them on what she's going to do and how to get out alive. We tell them about Team Echo, to make sure they meet Zahra, Paige, and Ken. We write about Jeremy and his betrayal. And then we tell them about Vincent's plan, about the future we saw, and about how genicote is always going to be used as a weapon by someone or other. Then Adam instructs himself on how to make it safe.

By the time we're done, our letter to ourselves is five pages long. I fold it up, put it in a plain white envelope, and seal it before handing it to Paige. "That should cover it all."

"The accelerator is ready," Dr. Walters says. Behind him, the machine hums with an electrical buzz and glows with low blue lights.

"You sure you're okay with this?" Adam asks.

Paige nods, her eyes gleaming with unshed tears. "Yes. Even if I can't make it back, the sacrifice will be worth it to save all of my friends."

She hugs me tight, and I hold her for way too long, unwilling to let her go. This might be the last time we ever see her. Or maybe she'll make it back, but none of us will remember her bravery today. Even if she succeeds at saving the world, we might erase our friendship in the process.

When I finally step back, Adam grabs her in a hug next. As Paige steps away, tears slide down her cheeks, but her eyes are determined. "I'm ready," she says.

We move to the side as she heads for the machine, with our letter tucked into her pocket. She's almost to the accelerator when the elevator jerks to life. The five of us turn toward it as the doors slowly open.

Vincent stands inside. With a gun in his hand.

Paige pauses for a split second and then bolts toward the accelerator door, but she's not fast enough. A shot rings out. A second later she stumbles, then crashes against the wall of the accelerator before sliding to the floor.

She's dead by the time she hits the floor.

"No!" I yell, but there's nothing I can do. I start to rush forward anyway, but Adam grabs my arm and yanks me back so I don't get shot too.

We duck behind office equipment as Vincent stalks forward, gun in hand. I'm shocked he killed Paige, but he's clearly familiar with guns, and not hesitant to use them. Then again, if he's willing to wipe out the world with a biological weapon, shooting someone is probably easy for him.

"Going somewhere?" Vincent asks with dark amusement in his voice.

From behind a cubicle, I yell, "Put your gun down. You're outnumbered."

"Elena, good to hear you're still alive. I thought you'd be worse off by now, but you always were a survivor." He grabs Dr. Campbell from behind a desk and presses the gun to her temple. She lets out a quick cry, then goes silent. "Surrender, or I'll kill her next."

I hesitate. I have no weapons on me. I left Nina's gun behind earlier after I killed my future self. While Vincent may be outnumbered, I'm the only one who can take him on, but not when he has a gun trained at my friend's head.

My future self was willing to end one life to save the world. But am I?

Vincent drags Dr. Campbell toward the accelerator. "Come on. We know how this is going to end. You're all going to die, whether it's here now or from the virus in a few days. As for me? I'll be at my vineyard in Napa, which I've spent the last few days preparing, thanks to your warnings. I'm ready to start the next phase of the world. It's a pity none of you will be there to see it."

I creep around along the desks, until I'm moving up behind him. He always loved giving speeches and hearing himself talk. I was counting on that to hide my approach.

"What happened to you?" Dr. Walters asks from behind a cubicle. "You used to be a good man."

"Was I? Or did I just do a good job of pretending?" Vincent presses the gun harder against Dr. Campbell's forehead, and she whimpers. "Time's up. Give up now, or she's dead."

I rush him from behind, but he hears me coming. He shoves Dr. Campbell aside and fires his gun at me, but the shot goes wide. I aim a jab at his face, but my movements are slow, still impaired from the virus, and I miss. He slams the gun against my head, making me stagger back. As pain crashes through my skull, I level a kick at his hand, knocking the gun wide. Then I hit the floor, hard.

He's on me in an instant, his large hands going around my throat. His eyes are wild as he tightens his fingers, squeezing the life out of me. I struggle, but it's like my brain and my body aren't connected anymore, and I can't get my limbs to do what I want. A slow smile spreads across his face when I try to fight him off and fail.

"Good-bye, Elena," he says, as the world begins to go black.

Adam yanks Vincent off me, and I suck in a huge gasp of air, my fingers going to my throat. Vincent starts to get up, but Adam rams the gun into the older man's chest. Without hesitation, he fires. One, two, three times.

Vincent's face is a perfect mask of surprise that mirrors my own, before all the life leaves his eyes. Adam's never killed anyone before. The closest he came was shooting the Infected in the future. I guess he weighed the same choice I did, and ultimately decided it was worth killing one person to save everyone else.

Adam stands over Vincent until he's sure the man is dead, then drops the gun like he's disgusted and rushes over to me. "Elena! Are you okay?"

I cough, trying to get air into my lungs. It's like no matter how much I wheeze, I can't get enough oxygen. "I'm alive," I finally manage to say. "Thanks to you."

He examines my neck, making sure I'm okay, then brushes the sweaty hair away from my face. "I had to stop him. He was going to kill you."

Adam helps me to my feet, and I stare down at Vincent's lifeless body. It's over. This man brought us together, but he also used us for his own purposes. Our lives never meant anything to him, but he can never hurt us again.

While Dr. Walters checks on Dr. Campbell, Adam and I kneel beside Paige, but she's already gone. A single tear slides down my cheek as I realize I'll never get another of her hugs or see her bright smile again. Another one of our friends is dead because of Vincent.

And now we have no one who can go to the future without causing a paradox.

Adam removes the letter from Paige's hand, which is clenched tightly around it. He stares at it with an empty look in his eyes. "What do we do now?"

I glance at the envelope in his hand. "One of us will have to go to the future."

He shakes his head. "That will cause a paradox. No. It's too risky."

"It might, but what other choice do we have?"

"We'll have to find someone else. We need to…" He trails off when a tiny trickle of blood drips from his nose. He wipes it away, then stares at the blood on his sleeve.

A choked cry escapes me. "Oh God, you've been infected."

"It seems that way," he says quietly.

I grab his arm, staring at the blood on it, refusing to believe it. Adam can't be infected. He just can't be. "How?"

"It doesn't matter."

I cup his face in my hands. "We can cure you though, right?"

He grabs my hands and presses a kiss to my knuckles. "No, we can't."

"But why?" I ask, my voice rising. "You know how to do it now. We'll get the cancer cells from somewhere. Zahra will figure it out. We can save you!"

"There's no time. Even if we could find the supplies we need, it'll be too late for me."

I feel so powerless, so completely helpless to save the man I love. Fat tears begin to slide down my face. I've lost everyone I care about in the entire world. All my family. All of my friends. I can't stand to lose Adam too.

No. There's one way I can save him.

"It has to be me," I tell him. "I have to go to the future."

"No," Adam whispers. "What if you can't come back? What if you cause a paradox?"

"It's the only way to save everyone. To save *you*. I have to do it, no matter the risk."

He shakes his head, but he doesn't say anything because he knows it's true. Dr. Campbell and Dr. Walters are both too old to time travel without suffering from future shock. Even if they did go, they could be infected right now too. We can't risk bringing the virus to the past.

That only leaves me.

Dr. Walters clears his throat. "Causing a paradox might actually work in your favor this time. It could reset the timeline, wiping out the last year as though it never happened."

"Or it could kill her," Dr. Campbell adds. "Or destroy the timeline completely."

Dr. Walters nods. "True. It's impossible to know for sure."

Resetting the timeline sounds like a good idea—until I realize what it would mean for me and Adam. If we reset the timeline, this past year will never have happened. We might never get together. We might never fall in love. We might never get married and have a daughter.

What if, by resetting the timeline, we prevent our life together from ever happening?

One look at his face tells me he's come to the same conclusion.

"We can't," I whisper. "There has to be some other way."

Adam wraps his arms around me. "No, you were right. This is the only way. You have to go to the future and reset the timeline. It's the only way to save the world."

"But what about us?" I ask.

"We'll find our way back together somehow. No matter what happens, our fates are intertwined." He touches the origami unicorn necklace around my neck. "In every future, every timeline, every lifetime, it will always be me and you."

"The accelerator is ready," Dr. Campbell says softly.

I nod, but I'm not ready to pull away from Adam just yet. I wipe at my eyes, drying my tears on his shirt. I don't know how to say good-bye to him, or to everything we've built together.

I don't know what will happen after I walk through the accelerator. I might never return. I might fail and return to a dying Adam and a world in ruin. Or I might reset the timeline and erase everything we've had together—possibly wiping it from my memory forever.

There's no other way. To save the world, I have to sacrifice my own life.

I dig my fingers into his shirt. "I love you, Adam."

"I love you too." He slants his mouth across mine, giving me a long, deep kiss that's almost enough to keep me here with him, no matter what happens to the rest of the world. But I taste the sadness on his lips and I know it's not just from losing me, but because of everything we've already lost and still stand to lose. If I have even the smallest chance of undoing all of that, I have to take it.

Pulling away from him is the hardest thing I've ever done. I touch his face one last time, memorizing every inch of him, and pray I never forget what it feels like to be loved by the kindest, smartest, and bravest person I've ever met.

He tucks the letter into my hand, and I force myself to turn away from him while I still can. Dr. Campbell and Dr. Walters both give me a quick hug each and wish me luck before I slowly step into the accelerator. My last glimpse of Adam is when he shuts the door, locking me in. My pulse races and my breathing comes fast and heavy, but I'm doing this. I'm really doing it.

The countdown begins as the accelerator powers up. The voice is so familiar it's like an old friend now, welcoming me home.

"Five."

I remember the first time I kissed Adam in the rain.

"Four."

I remember the first time he told me he loved me, when I was too scared to say it back.

"Three."

I remember the first time we met Ava and saw both of ourselves in her.

"Two."

I remember a hundred other moments, both small and large, that made up our relationship.

"One."

I close my eyes and let the memories go.

00:00

It's pitch-black, except for a tiny lighter flame that flickers in front of me. I can barely make out five figures behind it, but I hear voices. Familiar voices.

"What the hell was that?" Chris asks. His voice sends a rush of relief through me. I never thought I'd hear it again.

The lighter raises up, illuminating Trent. I haven't seen him in over a year, since I found him dead in a dumpster. My throat tightens, and I want to laugh with joy. He's alive. Zoe is too, huddling near Adam with her blue hair and black nails. Afraid of the dark, but still so very alive. My gaze rests on Adam, who looks so much younger than when I last saw him, even though it's only been a year.

Our plan worked. The accelerator sent me thirty years into the future, and our past selves are here for the very first time. This is the beginning of their original twenty-four-hour period in the future. I remember the moment perfectly. The shock of realizing we'd actually time traveled. The suspicion I felt about the people on my team. The uncertainty of standing in this cold, pitch-black room and wondering what was going on.

"Is someone else here?" the other Elena asks.

I move forward, into the flickering light, holding up my hands. "It's okay. It's me."

Adam gasps, Chris swears loudly, and my younger self takes a step back. I try not to look at her, but I can already feel a sharp pain growing inside my skull. The paradox.

I lived through it once before, but it never gets any easier. The universe can't seem to handle two instances of people out of sync with their own time period. It won't be long now before it corrects itself somehow.

"Elena?" Adam turns to look at the other version of me. "How?"

I clutch the letter in my hand. "I don't have time to explain. I'm here to warn you."

I take another step toward the other Elena and pain lances through my brain, so piercing it makes my vision go dark. I bend over, pressing my hands to my temple, trying to fight it off. I hear the younger me let out a loud cry, while the others shout. I'm powerless to do anything as my body feels like it's being ripped apart from the inside out.

Memories flash through me, flickering back and forth between mine and hers. Seeing Adam for the first time and the last. Stepping into the accelerator over and over and over. Watching our friends die again and again.

Yet somehow, through the agony, I know this is the right path. Warning them won't be enough. They'll still make similar mistakes, no matter what I tell them. I'm the only one who's seen it all. Every future, every death, every choice we've made that led to this point.

Adam yells my name and breaks through the darkness, pulling me back to the world. Our eyes meet, and I see the same love in his eyes as I saw in his older self before we said good-bye. He's my other half. My best friend. My soul mate. I was scared to lose him, scared that by coming here and changing things we'd never be to-gether—but not anymore. No matter what happens, we'll find our way back together.

I know what to do.

I turn away from Adam and step toward the other Elena. This time, I don't fight the storm churning inside me, even though every movement is pure agony. No, this time I embrace it.

There's a high-pitched whine in my ears, and my knees feel like they'll give out at any second as I reach my hand out to my younger self. She hesitates, but then she raises her own hand toward me.

The second our fingers connect, we both gasp. Searing pain shoots through us, like a lightning bolt jolting through our bodies, connecting us with crackling energy. I see through her eyes, and she sees through mine. Memories flash so quickly I can't focus on any of them. My body is torn apart and put back together again. And in the last second, before it all goes black, I wrap my fingers around the origami unicorn pendant Adam gave me.

The world splinters into a million tiny pieces of glass. Darkness envelops me, and I'm floating. Time and space mean nothing any-more. I simply am.

And then reality snaps taut again.

I'm standing in the basement underneath the building in the desert, wearing the heavy jacket and black clothes Aether gave to us for our first trip to the future. The letter in my hand is gone, but Adam's necklace is still around my neck.

Zoe's kneeling on the cement floor, with Adam crouching be-side her. Chris glances around like he's not sure what the hell is going on, but he's ready to punch his way through it. Trent's eyes are wide as he holds up his lighter, providing the only illumination.

The flame goes out. "Where are we?" Trent asks. "*When* are we?"

I'm reliving the moment when we got to the future for the very first time, when we discovered the building was empty and abandoned. The moment I interrupted when I arrived from the other timeline and caused the paradox. But now there's only one version of me standing here.

The paradox wiped out everything from the last year of my life. All the other trips to the future. All the changes we made to the timeline, for better or worse. All the deaths we couldn't stop.

I'm the older Elena and the younger one. And I remember everything.

This time, I know what I have to do.

WEDNESDAY

At 7:02 p.m. I check the table for the tenth time, making sure everything is in its place. Chips and guacamole. Plates. Silverware. It's the second time I've hosted this anniversary party—for me, anyway—but I'm still just as nervous somehow.

It's been one year since I caused the paradox. Today is the anniversary of our first—and only—trip to the future. Except this time, we're definitely celebrating and not mourning.

The doorbell rings while I'm adjusting the napkins. Max barks and wags his tail while I open the door for Chris.

He grabs me in a quick, loose hug. "Hey, Elena. Am I the first one here?"

"Yep. Where's Shawnda?" I ask, even though I know the answer.

"She wanted to make it, but Michael is sick so she's home with him. She sent these brownies along though."

"Thanks."

Adam steps out of the kitchen. "Hey, man." He and Chris clasp each other on the back. "Glad you could make it."

I smile at Adam. This night is already different from the one in my memory because he's here this time, not working in his lab. He still has the lab, of course, but he's not obsessed with making the cure like he was. I know he'll make genicote eventually and be the hero he's supposed to be, but this time he won't rush it. And now I know the secret to making it safe.

The doorbell rings again, and I open it to see Trent and Zoe waiting outside. Trent's hair is shorter and neatly trimmed, while Zoe's is now pink. My heart warms at the sight of them. I don't know if I'll ever get over the relief of seeing them alive.

From what I can figure, the paradox merged me with my other self when it reset the timeline, but for some reason I kept my memories even though no one else did. Maybe because of my eidetic memory or maybe because I was the one who caused the paradox. I'm not sure.

This time, during our twenty-four hours in the future, I knew Lynne Marshall, the project manager for Project Chronos, was the real murderer. I convinced Adam and the others that trusting one another was the only way to stop her and save our lives. Adam told everyone about his true purpose in going to the future—to bring back the cancer cure for his mom and Lynne's daughter—and we formed a new plan.

When we got back from the future, we pretended to have future shock, just as we did before. Then Adam made sure Lynne's daughter got the cure, giving Lynne no reason to hunt us down this time. We prevented her from becoming a murderer and saved all of our lives in the process.

Then we began to work on our next part of the plan: taking Aether down for good.

The other time travelers from Team Echo arrive over the next few minutes and begin to fill the apartment. Even though our team pretended to have future shock, Vincent still sent the others to the future anyway. After they returned from their first trip, Adam and I made contact with them. We convinced them to help us stop Vincent, and along the way we became friends. Just as I knew we would.

Everyone grabs food and begins to settle around the TV. I watch from the doorway with a small smile on my face as they all chat with one another.

"Scoot over," Trent says to Zahra as he wedges himself beside her on the couch.

"There are plenty of other places to sit," she snaps at him, although she doesn't move away.

"This spot has the best view of the TV." He gives her a sly grin and offers her some guacamole and chips from his plate.

She rolls her eyes at him and takes a chip off his plate. The two of them have this cute love-hate thing going that I never could have predicted, but that somehow totally works. They're both still in the denial stage, but it's obvious they're going to get together sooner or later.

"How's art school going?" Paige asks Zoe as they pass by me to grab a soda.

"It's pretty good," she says, giving Paige a warm smile. She's still shy and quiet, but Paige's friendly exuberance easily won her over.

"And your sister? Is she okay?"

Zoe nods and her eyes light up. "She's at home watching a movie with my girlfriend tonight. I still can't believe I got custody of her after all these years."

Paige throws her arms around Zoe. "I'm so happy for you."

They rejoin the rest of the group, and Paige finds a seat beside Ken, who gives her a quick kiss. On the other side of them, Chris and Adam chat with the final member of our group of former time travelers: Jeremy.

I debated for a long time about what to do with Jeremy, but in the end I decided I couldn't punish him for something he might do, or something he did in another life. Instead, I have to help him try to make different choices. Better choices.

"Here we go," Zahra says, turning up the volume on the TV.

Everyone goes quiet as the news report plays across the screen. A woman's voice says, "Vincent Sharp of Aether Corporation was indicted today for illegally running experiments on minors, among other charges."

As we watch, Vincent scowls as he's led out of the downtown office building in handcuffs, along with Dr. Kapur and Lynne. There's no sign of Dr. Walters or Dr. Campbell—we convinced them to leave Aether months ago.

As Vincent is roughly shoved into the back of a police car, we all cheer. We've been working to bring down Vincent and end the time-travel program for the past year, and it's finally over. Now we can move on with our lives.

Zahra rewinds the clip so we can watch it again, but Jeremy gets up to grab more food. I head into the kitchen with him and set down my plate.

"You okay?" I ask.

"Yeah." He draws in a shaky breath. "My dad's done some terrible things. I'm glad he's going to pay for them."

I rest my hand on his shoulder. "You're a better man than he is."

"Thanks, Elena." He flashes me a smile and rejoins the others in the living room. Hopefully now, with his father out of the picture, Jeremy will never become the person I saw in the other timeline. He doesn't have a reason to form Pharmateka or try to beat his father in some twisted game.

I'm still going to keep an eye on him though, just in case.

With Vincent heading to jail and Aether crumbling, it feels like my whole life is ahead of me. I know what I want, though. I saw it in one of the futures I visited. A life with Adam, where we try to make the world a better place.

In a few years, after we both finish school, we're going to start Future Visions with Chris. I plan to invite the others to join us too, if they're interested. Sure, their skills might be bit on the shady side, but I trust them more than anyone else. They're my friends. My family. My future.

Adam leans against the doorway, crossing his arms. "What are you thinking about?"

I turn to smile at him. "Nothing."

He pushes off the wall and approaches me. His dark hair is perfectly messy, his glasses askew, his blue eyes full of intelligence, strength, and love. His hand moves to my face, his knuckles sliding down my neck before circling the origami unicorn pendant I always wear. "You have that look on your face like you're somewhere else. In another timeline." He tilts his head. "Remembering another life."

Adam's the only one who knows what I've been through, or some of it anyway. I told him as much as I could so that he'd understand how I knew certain things. He still asks me about our future sometimes, but I refuse to tell him anything else. I don't like keeping secrets from him, but sometimes it's better not to know your own fate.

I keep the knowledge of our future daughter inside me like a warm light. Someday we'll see her again. I'll make sure of it.

"The only life I want is here with you, now." I slide my arms around his neck and pull him close for a kiss.

For once, I don't know what the future will hold. But I know we'll face it together.

ACKNOWLEDGMENTS

Completing a trilogy has been one of the most rewarding and challenging experiences of my life. I started writing *Future Shock* in 2012, and I'm deeply grateful to everyone who has joined me on the journey from the first spark of an idea to the publication of this final book. I couldn't have done it without your support.

To Gary, for being the best husband ever. I wouldn't be an author today if not for your unwavering faith in me.

To my parents, Gaylene and Peter, along with the rest of the Adams and Briggs families, for all the encouragement over the years.

To my agent, Kate Testerman, and everyone else at KT Literary, for all their hard work getting this series out into the world.

To the entire team at Albert Whitman for everything they do behind the scenes. In particular, my editors, Wendy McClure, Eliza Swift, and Alexandra Messina-Schultheis, who make each book shine; my awesome marketing and publicity team, Annette Hobbs Magier, Laurel Symonds, and Tracie Schneider, for everything they do to promote my books; and Jordan Kost and Paul Stinson, who made my covers so awesome.

To all the author friends who have shared this journey with

Diane Baldwin

ELIZABETH BRIGGS

is the *New York Times* bestselling author of the award-winning Future Shock trilogy and the Chasing the Dream series. She graduated from UCLA with a degree in sociology and has worked for an international law firm, mentored teens in writing, and volunteered with dog rescue groups. Now she's a full-time geek who lives in Los Angeles with her husband and a pack of fluffy dogs. Find her online at www.elizabethbriggs.net.

me through the years, with extra special thanks to Rachel Searles, Kathryn Rose, Jessica Love, Audrey Coulthurst, Sybil Bartel, Stephanie Garber, and Riley Edgewood.

To the lovely authors who were kind enough to blurb *Future Shock*: Karen Akins, Melissa Landers, and Amy Tintera.

And finally, to the friends, readers, bloggers, teachers, librarians, parents, and booksellers who have read the series or shared it with others—thank you, thank you, thank you.